USA TODAY BESTSE

DALE M

Offed in the Orchids

Lovely Lethal Gardens 15

OFFED IN THE ORCHIDS: LOVELY LETHAL GARDENS, BOOK 15
Dale Mayer
Valley Publishing

ISBN-13: 978-1-773363-71-4
Print Edition

Books in This Series

Arsenic in the Azaleas, Book 1

Bones in the Begonias, Book 2

Corpse in the Carnations, Book 3

Daggers in the Dahlias, Book 4

Evidence in the Echinacea, Book 5

Footprints in the Ferns, Book 6

Gun in the Gardenias, Book 7

Handcuffs in the Heather, Book 8

Ice Pick in the Ivy, Book 9

Jewels in the Juniper, Book 10

Killer in the Kiwis, Book 11

Lifeless in the Lilies, Book 12

Murder in the Marigolds, Book 13

Nabbed in the Nasturtiums, Book 14

Offed in the Orchids, Book 15

Poison in the Pansies, Book 16

Lovely Lethal Gardens, Books 1–2

Lovely Lethal Gardens, Books 3–4

Lovely Lethal Gardens, Books 5–6

Lovely Lethal Gardens, Books 7–8

Lovely Lethal Gardens, Books 9–10

About This Book

A new cozy mystery series from *USA Today* best-selling author Dale Mayer. Follow gardener and amateur sleuth Doreen Montgomery—and her amusing and mostly lovable cat, dog, and parrot—as they catch murderers and solve crimes in lovely Kelowna, British Columbia.

Riches to rags … Finally it's calm … At least for the moment … If she's lucky …

Needing a break from all the murder and mayhem, Doreen and Mack plan an outing to see the local orchid show. Some of the displays are in the community center, but the more prized specimens of this genus require a visit to some of the gardeners' homes, a rare opportunity not afforded to everyone.

This trip, not quite a date, affords Doreen a chance to enjoy not only the company of Mack but to get to know a few more of the colorful locals. But, when one of these locals ends up dead just after their visit, the dark underbelly of orchid growing is exposed and, with it, an old murder, … not to mention another new one.

Doreen and Mack just can't catch a break. But can they catch a killer before he kills again?

Sign up to be notified of all Dale's releases here!

http://smarturl.it/dmnewsletter

Chapter 1

Saturday, Mid-July; Kelowna, BC

CORPORAL MACK MOREAU, a local RCMP detective, had become Doreen Montgomery's close friend. Mack was right, this outing was a perfect idea.

Doreen could feel a budding excitement at the thought of going out, not only with Mack at her side, but to the orchid festival. She'd never had any experience with growing them herself, although they were plants that her husband had deemed appropriate for her to oversee and had his gardeners keep several in the greenhouse. But she had never really tried to do anything with them. They appealed, but they also almost repulsed her because they had such a strong connection to her soon-to-be ex.

But this was the first time to potentially enjoy them without his presence, and she would see some really rare ones today. As a gardening enthusiast, she knew just enough to get herself in trouble, so deemed it necessary to not get into any conversations about orchids, outside of asking questions regarding the long-held fascination she'd had over the unique plants. Many people did really well with orchids, and others found them incredibly difficult to grow. They were so special and had captivated people for centuries.

Doreen waited on her front porch with her three animals. She had even coerced a leash onto Goliath, a Maine coon, who didn't seem to be arguing too much about his leash today. Her huge beautiful blue-gray parrot, Thaddeus, sat on her shoulder, and she heard Mack's truck rumbling toward her.

"Alright, guys, here he is," she said to her critters. Mugs, her pedigreed basset hound, was on a leash too and barked excitedly, his tail wagging in great joy as the truck pulled up into the driveway. Goliath lay on the top porch step and looked about with disdain. As the truck rolled to a stop, Mack opened his door. "Do you need help to get in the truck?"

She shook her head and walked down the last few steps and onto the sidewalk toward him. "No, we're ready to go." She walked around to the far side, opened up the passenger door to his truck, and urged Mugs up onto the seat. He was beside himself with excitement, so getting him into the footwell of the truck was one thing. But he was bound and determined to get onto the seat, where he could completely lick Mack's face.

Mack was laughing, as he tried to calm down the excited dog.

Thaddeus, on the other hand, appeared to be happily nestled against her neck and just content to be going with the flow. Goliath hopped up onto the dash and sprawled out in front of them. Then Doreen climbed in and sat down comfortably, closing the door. "We're ready."

"I guess you don't go anywhere without the animals, do you?"

"Not if I can help it," she said. "It's nice to have them.

And they love these outings."

"And this one is outside, so animals are allowed." He backed out of the driveway and went around the cul-de-sac.

"Exactly," she said happily. "I can't express how much I'm looking forward to this. I hadn't realized how depressed I was and in need of something fun and different in my life."

He glanced at her in concern.

"I'm fine." She shrugged. "It's just—well, this was a good idea, and I'm really looking forward to it." Something was almost lame in her response, but she wouldn't go into it too much.

"Depressed?" he asked.

"I should have known you'd lock onto that."

"That's because it's so unlike you."

"And it's not typically me," she said. "I don't know. It's just been kind of a downer the last few days."

"That last case was rough. I know."

"It was," she said. "Seeing that side of humanity wasn't an easy thing. Dealing with Denise and her mind games, it was a bit much."

He agreed. "You know that it's likely to be really busy at this outing."

"And that's good too." She rubbed her hands together. "I haven't seen very many people lately, and I'm ready."

He laughed. "Good enough. I thought you would ask Nan to come too."

"She's going already," she said. "The retirement home already booked one of their buses full of people, but they'll go before the general public."

He rolled his eyes at that. "That sounds like a good idea." He sighed. "Your grandmother can create all kinds of chaos."

"She sure can, but she can also calm it down," Doreen said. "So she's an asset to have, when the rest of them get going."

He chuckled. "I haven't seen too much of that aspect of her. Ever."

"No, but you will over time."

"Did she help smooth things over with your ex?"

She glared at him. "We're not talking about him." His eyebrows popped up, and she winced. "A little too forceful, huh?"

After a few seconds of silence, he continued. "Is that part of the depression?"

"I have no wish to see him, and I wish he'd stop calling me." At that, Mack stared at her in surprise. She shrugged. "Sorry, I haven't been telling you about it. You've had your hands full already, and I didn't want to bother you."

"You need to tell me about things like that." His tone was serious. "I can't have Mathew getting out of line."

"He *lives* out of line," she muttered. "And don't worry. I have told Nick every time."

"Maybe I need to find out what my brother is doing about it."

"Maybe." Doreen gave him a tiny shrug. "It seems like absolutely nothing's happening. Mathew refuses to sign the document Nick drew up."

"Ah, I'm sure we can trust Nick to deal with that."

"I just wonder if he's asking for so much money that my ex will never agree."

"He's not asking for more than what anybody else would ask for."

"I don't need all his money."

"And you aren't getting all of it," Mack said. "I think

Nick's asked for 50 percent, plus something to make up for all the stress Mathew's caused you since the separation."

"Well, that I approve of." She laughed at the idea. It sounded good but would never happen. It was a nice dream. If she could get something until Nan's houseful of antiques sold, she'd be golden. "It's been brutal."

He chuckled. "It has been, but you have done very well for yourself."

"Maybe, but I think that has more to do with Nan's generosity."

"Your bank balance is not the point," he said. "It's all about how you emotionally and responsibly handle things, and you've done really well with that."

She smiled, appreciating the kind words, and she appreciated him. They had such a nice relationship, and she hadn't realized where this closeness came from, but somehow those warm feelings were there, and she didn't even know what to do with them. Yet she refused to act on anything with him, not until she settled up with her ex. The thought of getting into another relationship and dealing with those issues made her wince. It wasn't her style at all. But then again people rarely waited, and she knew that she was being old-fashioned about it. But still, she had to do what felt right for her.

Mack pulled up beside another truck in a parking lot in front of an empty building next to a field.

She glanced around. "Are we allowed to park here?"

"The market space is full of the orchids," he said, "and this building and property are no longer being used. It's the old school district building. So you can park here for the market, and nobody minds."

"Well, you're the cop." Laughing, Doreen opened the

door, and Goliath hopped down, and so did Mugs. She struggled to get out with the leashes still on the animals, as they were not willing to wait. She called out to Mugs. "Hey, wait up, buddy." But he danced around on the grass, too excited to sit still. She looked back at Mack. "It's not just us who are looking forward to this outing," she said. "Look at these animals."

Even Goliath's tail twitched back and forth in assumed disdain, but his eyes were bright and clear, and his nose was in the air, sniffing everything.

"Do you think they'll be a problem?" Mack asked.

"I don't know why they would be," she said. "They've been really easy to deal with all the time."

"Maybe." But Mack looked at her a little doubtfully.

"I won't leave them in the truck." She shook her head. "So either we're all going, or we're staying."

"Nope, we're going." He walked around to her side of the truck. "Do you want me to take one of them?"

She handed him the leash for Mugs, who was happy with the handoff. "Sure, here," Together—her walking with Goliath and Mack with Mugs, plus Thaddeus sitting on her shoulder between them—they headed toward the display. When she saw how many people were here, she stopped and stared. "Gosh, I wasn't expecting this many."

"Why not?"

"Because I've never seen anything in Kelowna with this many people. There must be hundreds or even thousands of people." The whole area, which was a normal marketplace every Wednesday and Saturday, was completely full of booths similar to the usual market setup, but everything displayed now was orchids.

"It's a beautiful sunny day," she whispered, "but orchids

are still beyond temperamental."

"Which is why only some of the display is here," he said. "The rest is on a tour at everybody's personal greenhouse."

She nodded. "That part is fascinating. I mean, I've seen them get ready for commercial sales," she said, "so I wasn't really expecting that there would be this many here."

"It's a very popular hobby apparently."

She nodded. "I've heard that. Mathew thought they were *the thing* too."

"He grew orchids?"

"Mathew had his gardeners grow orchids," she corrected. "I'm not sure that's the same thing at all."

"I don't think it is." Mack snorted. "I tend to think of a hobby as being something you do yourself, not something you direct your employees to do."

She nodded, as they walked up to the first booth. She smiled at an older gentleman, sitting with a blanket wrapped around his shoulders. "Are you cold?" she asked, frowning. "It'll be almost 100 degrees today."

He looked up at her and glared. "My orchids should be at home."

"Oh dear," she said. "Could you not keep yours in the greenhouse? I'm not sure how that works."

"Only so many could do the home tour." He shrugged. "And I could pop mine and move them, so I did." He glanced down. "But still, some of my more special ones are at home."

She nodded. "I can see that. I'm sure that a lot of people don't bring out their best specimens just for that reason."

"Well, we have an amateur section." He pointed. "And we have the professionals. The professionals got to keep theirs in their greenhouses. I just missed the professional designation by this much." He held up two gnarly fingers pinched together.

"I'm sorry," she said. "I don't know that I would have brought mine out either."

He nodded. "At least you understand something." He huffed as he looked around. "I'll stay here for a few minutes, but that's it."

She smiled, then nodded and moved on, watching as another group of curious people stepped into the void that she had left behind. "I wonder if his attitude is the same for everyone," she muttered.

"I don't know," Mack said, "but, when you think about it, anything that'll be in a limited supply will cause some trouble. This is the first year of the event, and there are definitely different levels of growers."

"Oh, yes," she said, "and some of the professionals or the more advanced hobbyists will have quite the conflict with bringing them in here with the others."

"Which is why those are on the home tour," he added.

She nodded. "That in itself has got to be stressful for the owners and the orchids."

"I imagine it is," he said. "We'll do that tour after we walk around here."

"These are lovely." She stopped, staring. "His were pretty. I mean, I loved the pinks and purples he had. But these? Wow!" Ahead of her was a series of orchids more of a silvered-blue color. The whole table was just in that one shade. She smiled at the woman sitting on the other side. "These are truly beautiful."

The woman nodded quietly and didn't say anything, but it was obvious she had been pleased by the comment. Doreen didn't even know what else to say. She was just stunned at the glorious displays, as she moved from booth to booth to booth.

They finally got down to the far end of this section. Mack asked, "Do you want a coffee? They're offering refreshments too."

She looked up at him. "For free?"

"Of course not." He laughed at that. "They have to make money for next year's display as well." He pointed off to the side, where Doreen saw a short line before several trailers that appeared to have coffee and snacks.

"I'd love one." She was inordinately pleased at the idea of wandering around with a fresh coffee.

He led her off to the side into the shortest line. With the animals tucked up close to keep them out of the way, they waited until it was their turn, and he ordered two coffees for them. When he picked up two huge cookies and added it to their tray, her heart warmed.

"Now that," she said, "was a really good idea."

He grinned, as he handed her a cookie. "Can you handle all of this and Goliath?"

"I can if Goliath behaves himself," she said, "but I'm not sure how much walking around I'll do if he'll give me trouble. I'd need a free hand for that, though you can't be much help if you've got Mugs."

"Well, that's your fault for having so many animals." He laughed.

She smiled, knowing he didn't mean any of it, and they stepped off to the side, while she ate the cookie. With that down, the coffee was barely cool enough to have her first sip. "I'm really happy to see so many people here." She took in her surroundings. "I wasn't thinking about it being much different than the contest with the local produce or the kiwis." She shook her head in remembrance of that case. "But it's really something to see how many people come together in a setting like this."

"It's all done in good fun," he said, "and anything that's good fun is good for a community."

She nodded. "I just don't have much exposure to that," she murmured. "So this has been an excellent opportunity to see how the community pulls together."

"You saw some of it," he murmured, "when it came to doing your deck."

"That is very true." She smiled. "And I love my deck."

"Good, because a lot of people came together to make that happen in a very short time frame."

"Very true," she muttered, then thought she recognized somebody from her deck crew. She pointed off to the far side. "Isn't that one of the guys who did the cement work?"

Mack looked over and nodded. "Yeah, good eye. I'm not surprised to see him here. He's a gardener. Lots of people in town are gardeners."

"Well, there are gardeners," she said, "and then there are orchidists."

He laughed. "Yeah, I'm not sure I know the difference."

"And I don't really either, in the sense that I've never tried to grow orchids myself," she murmured.

"I'm surprised. I would have thought this was definitely your kind of thing."

"I think because they were my husband's thing and because he thought that it was something that we should do since it was a high-class, well-respected hobby, I never got into it. Anything that he thought was a good idea, I tended to avoid."

"Passive resistance, I like it."

She smiled. "Is that what I was doing?" she asked. "I think I was just trying to avoid trouble. No way I ever could do it to suit him."

"And sometimes you do whatever you must in order to make things work," he said. "Don't judge yourself for that."

"That's something I seem to always do," she murmured.

"But not today." He tucked his arm into hers. "Let's check the other booths."

And together they wandered through until they came up to the far side. She stopped and stared because she recognized several other people ahead of her. "I don't know," she said, "but I think I spoke to some of these people downtown."

"Why not?" he asked. "It's a small town."

"It really is, isn't it?" She relaxed.

He smiled. "And you've done just enough investigative work that has taken you to multiple corners of the town," he said, "so I'm not at all surprised if you recognize people."

"As long as they don't mind me being here," she whispered. He stopped and turned to look at her. She shrugged. "Some of the conversations weren't all that easy."

"Yep." He chuckled. "That's what happens when you think what you're doing is the best thing. But you forget that you impact other people, and, when you do, it's not always something that they remember well. Like the ones who end up in jail. But let's not worry about it today." And he led her down another aisle.

When she came to the end of that last aisle, she was stunned at how many people were growing orchids. Some of them were doing it easily and obviously were full of quiet joy at what they had accomplished. Others were more competitive and were asking people to rate them, so they could put it on their table. Some even had ribbons to be handed out. But Doreen wanted to see the ones in the private greenhouses. "I guess people really had to open up their doors to make something like that home tour happen. I bet there was some resistance to that."

"Less than you think," he said quietly. "Everybody likes to be recognized for doing a job well done."

She thought about it and nodded. "I guess that's human nature, isn't it?"

"Absolutely, and, in this case, it's a good thing. I mean, look at how much the community has come together over this."

She smiled when she looked around and saw just what he meant. "No, you're right," she said. "Must be hundreds of people here. And probably hundreds more doing the home tours."

"And we'll get there too," he said, "but just think how much joy something like this has brought to so many people. How much it's brought them together and got them out of their houses and made it a great day. Then think about all the people here who are taking part and how much the recognition is helping them."

"No, you've convinced me." She laughed. "This is a great thing. I agree."

"It is." He nodded. "And, if you ever want to get involved in something local, you could always volunteer for some of these events. They always need organizers."

At that, she thought about the women in the kiwi competitions and winced.

"And it doesn't have to be a bad experience," he reminded her.

Still withholding judgment on that point, she just nodded quietly, as they walked back to the truck. "I think one of the biggest things that I noticed," she said, "is that sense of joy, how everybody seems to be so happy just to be out and about."

"Well, it's been a long summer," he said. "There have been a lot of headaches, a lot of hassles, as you know. I can't imagine that people were all that eager to stay at home and to not do something fun. Today was a perfect day for it. The weather is gorgeous, and you can see everybody out here is enjoying themselves."

"Including us."

"Including us." As they got in the truck, he grabbed the printed tour map. "Now we're supposed to find all these other places."

"And these orchids are what again?"

"The ones grown by all the professional growers or the professional hobbyists. I'm not sure exactly what the criteria was to get into this level," he said, "but there were requirements. And it was cut off at twenty private showings."

"So everybody else back there didn't make the cut, which had to be like what? Three hundred of them?"

He looked at the back of the pamphlet they'd picked up. "There were 412."

"Wow, that's a lot of people."

"It was," he said, "and now we have these twenty different homes to go to."

"So these are the ones being judged?"

"Yes." He nodded. "So the people visiting these homes to see these special orchids are not just us and the general public but the judges too."

"And do you think the growers know when the actual judges come, versus members of the public who come through?"

"I would hope so," he said, "but maybe that's part of it. Maybe just being an observer of it all is what the judges want."

"Maybe, but I suspect they'll come with some authority that will make everybody nervous."

He laughed at that. "Maybe so, but then we're used to that. We tend to make people nervous ourselves."

"You do," she said, with spirit. "Me? I try to make everybody feel at home."

Chapter 2

MACK DROVE DOREEN and her animals to the first four of the twenty houses. The fifth had so many people parked outside that they skipped it and went on to the sixth. By the time they hit the ninth house on the orchid tour, Doreen was wearing thin.

"Are you still up for going to all the rest?" he asked.

"Well, I feel like I have to, since we started this."

He chuckled. "We can also end it."

"Maybe, but these people have put so much effort into it that I don't really want to let them all down. Plus these orchids are even more spectacular than those at the market show."

"That's the spirit." He carried on to the next house. And she was good for a couple more because these orchids were gorgeous. When they walked into the sixteenth house, it had a different atmosphere.

She sniffed the air and winced. "It smells like he's growing something else in here as well."

He chuckled. "And we can't make a comment about it."

"Says you," she replied. "I know it's supposed to be legal here, but I'm still not all that thrilled about having it everywhere."

"We're in their house, and they're allowed to do as they will."

"I got it." She held up a hand. Goliath didn't appear too happy to be getting out of the vehicle again. She was more concerned about how the animals were handling all this getting in and out than herself. As they wandered through the garden, she was struck by the absolute beauty of the place. "This house," she said on a gasp.

He nodded. "This is where you get to see how other people live."

"But it's …" And she was nonplussed for words. "It's absolutely stunning," she murmured.

"And some people live like this all the time," he said. "Even you, who had so much money at one time, didn't have a house like this."

"Because this is more than a house." She stared at it. "This is very much a home."

Behind her, a woman spoke, in a soft tremulous voice. "Thank you for that."

Doreen spun to see an older woman, leaning against the doorjamb. She wore capri jeans, with flip-flops on her bare feet and a button-up shirt that hung over the top of her belt. With her shirtsleeves rolled up to her elbow, she didn't look in the least like she had money. Doreen smiled. "This place is stunning. Something is so very special about the atmosphere."

The woman nodded. "We've lived here for hundreds of years," she said. "My family was one of the first to settle in the area, so an awful lot of history is here. A lot of family, a lot of births, a lot of deaths."

Doreen said quietly, "But also a lot of laughter and joy."

The woman beamed. "How very lovely of you to say so." She looked over at Mack. "Hey, Mack. How are you?"

He walked forward and gave the older woman a gentle hug. "Hi, Edna. It's been a long time."

"And here I figured you disappeared or were overrun with work." Edna turned toward Doreen with interest. "So that means you must be Doreen then."

"Why must I be Doreen?" She tilted her head to the side, looking from Mack to Edna.

"The animals," Edna explained.

"Ah, yes, they are a dead giveaway, aren't they?"

They all chuckled, as Edna pulled back Doreen's hair to see Thaddeus sitting there. "And you must be Thaddeus."

Thaddeus immediately rose to his full height, fluffed out his feathers. "Thaddeus is here."

"You are indeed, big guy," she said, "and, my, you're doing so well." Doreen was confused, until Edna explained. "I'm the one who had this guy brought in for your grandmother."

She stared. "Really?"

"Yes, I had three at one time, and this guy took a shine to your grandmother, so I let her keep him."

"Oh," Doreen said suddenly, "you're not looking to get him back, are you?"

Edna looked at her in shock and then started to laugh. "No, my dear, not at all," she said. "Besides, these animals have lives, thoughts, and heartbeats of their own. He wouldn't take kindly to me upending him."

"No, I don't think so," Mack said. "He's definitely happy where he is."

"Getting into lots of trouble, from what I hear," Edna murmured, with a knowing grin.

Doreen wasn't exactly sure who this person was, but obviously she knew Nan and had a lot of history in town and, like her grandmother, probably knew everyone. "Thaddeus has been such a godsend to me," she said warmly. "I love having him in my life."

"And that, my dear, is all that matters," Edna said gently. "And it shows. He obviously looks very happy on your shoulder. He never would ride on mine. His brother that I had wouldn't either."

"Well, he and I definitely take a lot of long walks and look after each other," Doreen said, smiling broadly.

"That's good," Edna said. "I suppose you're here for the orchids, aren't you?"

Mack nodded. "May we see them?"

She laughed. "Like you even care," she said affectionately.

"Hey," he protested, "maybe I do."

She shook her head at him. "No, but I appreciate that you're here. So let's go take a look at them."

As they walked farther into the house, Doreen glanced at Mack, and he had a small smile playing at the corner of his mouth.

"She's an icon in town," he said. "Everybody knows her."

"Except me." Doreen rolled her eyes.

"You haven't been here long enough to know everyone yet," Edna called back, obviously having heard the conversation.

Doreen flushed because the one thing she knew was manners, and talking about somebody, particularly in their own home, was definitely not on the list of good manners. "I'm so sorry," she said. "Please forgive my lack of manners."

"Ah, *posh*, don't worry about it." Edna waved it off. She led them into a different hallway.

"Oh my," Doreen said, "did we come in the wrong way?"

"You sure did," Edna said, "but I watched you and realized it was Mack. I figured he was just coming in the way that he knew. You weren't looking for the home tour signs."

"Oh, sorry," Mack apologized. "You're right. I've been here several times, and I just automatically came in."

"That's all right," she said. "There isn't always a right or a wrong way to do something. It's what you know."

Definitely some undercurrents were going on around Edna, but they didn't appear to be harmful or negative, so Doreen followed along. As they entered the orchid area, she gasped. "Oh my." The greenhouse was massive. The double panes of windows were at least fifteen feet high. "This is more of a solarium."

"That's exactly what it is. My grandfather built it for my grandmother many years ago. At one point in time it was all heated by wood, but now we have geothermal in here."

Stunned, Doreen looked at the wonderful room and the beautiful plants and knew she must look like a fool because Mack came up beside her. "Your jaw needs to close at some point in time."

She shook her head, turned impulsively to Edna. "You are blessed to have this."

Edna gave her a beaming smile. "You're right. I am, and the good part is that I'm lucky enough to know it." She said, "Come on now. Let's go down this aisle to my special orchids over here."

"What makes these special?" Mack asked.

"Well, they're very rare," she said, "and nobody's allowed into this area without a guard."

"A guard?" Doreen raised both eyebrows.

"Absolutely," Edna said. "You have no idea how vicious the world is when it comes to stealing orchids."

Doreen didn't even know what to say. "Really? I hadn't considered it to be that cutthroat." She frowned. "But I should have, I suppose, because it is something my husband was always into."

"Right, the husband. Another reason everybody keeps wondering what the deal is with you."

"Me?" Doreen looked at her in surprise.

Edna nodded. "Just like you're very busy, off solving all these cases with Mack here, the world is trying to figure out what makes you tick and what brought you here in the first place."

"A pending divorce and my grandmother," Doreen said. "It's very simple."

"Most things in life are." Edna smiled. "But they're all waiting to see what you do with your life now."

"I'm pretty much just getting in Mack's way apparently." Doreen laughed. "And thankfully he has enough patience to not get too angry about it."

"Well, you've done an awful lot of good for the community," Edna said, "so I wouldn't worry about it too much." She motioned them around the corner. "Here we go." As she stepped forward, she gasped and stopped.

"What's the matter?" Doreen asked, bumping up behind her.

There on the floor was a woman with a very puffy face, who appeared to not be breathing. They all raced forward.

"It's Miriam," Edna cried out, and she reached down, with two fingers at her throat. She looked back at Mack in panic. "Get help, please!"

Mack already had his phone out and was calling for assistance, but then he dropped down beside Edna and looked over Miriam. "She's not breathing."

"No, no, no." Edna frantically tried to lift the much heavier but younger woman into a supine position. "No, no, she'll be fine. She's got to be fine."

Mack put his hand on Edna's shoulder. "She's not fine, Edna. Put her down now, so we can help her." He looked back at Doreen and shook his head.

She stared at him. "What happened?" she whispered.

He shrugged. "Let's start CPR." He checked Edna, who was staring down at Miriam, both hands holding the woman's head close to her chest.

"Edna, lay her flat, please. Doreen, help me count." He started chest compressions. "Edna, when did you see her last? Edna!"

Pulling her gaze from the woman on the floor, she whispered, "Not that long ago—a couple hours at the most. We were doing all the preparations for the show."

"And Miriam, what was she doing?" he asked.

Edna's gaze widened. "She was guarding the orchids," she whispered. And she bolted to her feet, then looked around and cried out, "Please don't let this be about the orchids."

She raced off to the side wall, while Mack could only watch, as he tended Miriam. And, sure enough, Edna stopped in front of a raised planter, as Doreen raced along behind with the animals, getting caught up in the leashes.

"What is it?" Doreen asked.

"It's gone. My rare, my incredibly rare, Miosa. I've always called it *my heart*." Her hand instinctively rested on her chest.

"An orchid?" Doreen gently reached out to Edna.

"Yes." She stood in front of the bare spot on the raised planter. "I cultivated it with Miriam. She is my best friend, the woman of my heart and soul." She looked back at Doreen. "So many people judge us for it, but we really love each other."

And Doreen understood. "Nobody has the right to judge you for being happy," she said gently. "And, if she brings you happiness, I'm so grateful that you've had those years with her."

Edna looked back to where her friend was. "She told me that she would be here and would keep an eye on this one particular orchid," she whispered.

"She looks like she had an allergic reaction."

"Yes, and that's quite possible. She's an asthmatic. And sometimes she's had some really terrible reactions. She's also allergic to bees," she said bitterly. "She kept stuff with her all the time, so I'm not sure what happened." She frowned. "Obviously something went wrong. So very wrong."

"I'll tell Mack." Doreen hurried back to Mack, still carefully watching the rise and fall of Miriam's chest. "Miriam has asthma, and she's had some bad allergic reactions apparently."

"Check for a pulse, would you?" Mack said.

Doreen bent closer to Miriam. "Oh, it's there, very faint, but definitely there. And her lips aren't so blue."

Just then the paramedics arrived. Doreen hurried to pull the animals out of the way, as Mack stood and passed on the information they had.

Chapter 3

AS THE PARAMEDICS worked on Miriam, Doreen tried to stay out of the way with her animals and looked around a bit. Mack spoke to Edna briefly, then walked over to Doreen. So far, nobody else had come to this far side of the solarium. "I'm not certain that she told you yet, but it's missing."

"What's missing?" he asked quietly.

"The orchid she was talking about." She nodded toward a spot where there was a label, but the actual place where the plant should be was empty.

He stared at her. "Are you saying that somebody stole it?"

"I don't know," she said. "Maybe Miriam moved it for some reason. Or maybe—" And then she stopped and shook her head. "I'm not going there."

Mack narrowed his gaze at her. "You better not."

And just then Mugs decided that he'd had more than enough of calm and quiet, and he started barking and barking, pulling at his leash, which Doreen held. "I'd better take the animals outside."

He nodded. "That's a good idea." Goliath took that

moment to jump up onto one of the tables full of pots and potting soil, and the whole thing started to teeter, and a few things fell. Mack reached out, stabilized it. "Yeah, I definitely think you better get them out of here. I'll straighten this up."

She nodded and hurriedly pulled Goliath off the table, scolding him. "Come on, Goliath. Come on. Let's go outside. Mugs, stop it, please!" Exasperated, she tried to retrace her steps out of the greenhouse solarium area, but the layout was confusing and this house was huge. By the time she got to a door, she was back in the actual house and not outside where she was supposed to be.

She looked back at Mack, saw that the paramedics had brought in a gurney, and Mack stood with a hand on Edna's shoulder, trying to give the first responders room to work. Her heart sank for the older woman and for Miriam, who obviously stayed here because of the friendship and the relationship she had with Edna, even though Miriam was obviously deathly allergic to something here. Doreen sincerely hoped that the relationship hadn't finally killed her.

Miriam herself looked to be in her seventies, and who knows? Maybe the fact that she'd had some adverse reaction to something was just the final straw. All Doreen knew was that Miriam looked to be in very critical condition, and, for that, Doreen was sad. But the animals were not interested in being calm, and Doreen didn't know what was going on with them. "Mugs, calm down," she scolded him. But he kept barking and barking.

Finally, pushed to her limit, she managed to find a way back outside and ended up in a small side garden. Mugs immediately raced to the fence and barked. "Are you chasing something?" Doreen was confused, but nothing was out here to tempt Mugs. "It's just us."

But then she heard a weird howl and turned to find a cat, looking at them with glittering eyes. "Oh, I'm so sorry," she whispered. She pulled on Goliath's leash, who even now was stalking the same cat. "Whoa, whoa, whoa, no cat fights." This was a scenario she hadn't come across yet. So far, everybody avoided them when they were out, but this cat had been cornered on his own turf. And her animals were causing the problem.

She looked down at Goliath. "Behave yourself," she warned him. Then she tugged him backward, trying to get him out of the way, so the other animal didn't feel so threatened. But Goliath wouldn't give an inch, and finally the other cat jumped onto the fence and disappeared. Doreen glared at her critters. "That's no way to behave," she cried out. "That cat didn't do anything to you."

Looking around for a gate, she had no idea how to get out and back to where Mack had parked. Even to the driveway would be preferable, and so she kept wandering, yet not wanting to interfere into the personal life of this woman, who was obviously suffering two blows today. However, it was hard for Doreen to find her way through the maze.

Finally Doreen found a door to a nearby building, and she poked her head inside. It led through to a garage. With relief, she raced into the garage, only all kinds of plants, pots, trees, and gardening supplies were in here. She groaned. It may have been built as a garage, but that didn't mean it was a functioning garage. Just another space where Edna kept a lot of her gardening surplus. Another door was on the far end, and Doreen raced down with the animals, more than ready to get out of here before she was discovered and before somebody thought she was trespassing.

She opened the door and stepped into what appeared to

be yet another side garden. She cried out. "Where am I?"

At that, a man spoke behind her. "What are you doing here is a better question?"

She turned ever-so-slowly, not liking the tone of his voice, and cried out softly when she saw a huge man standing in front of her. "Oh, I'm so sorry," she apologized, stepping back. "I was in the solarium, but then I was supposed to take the animals out, and I got turned around." She knew she was babbling, but she didn't know how to stop.

"Turned around and confused, huh?" he said. "Are you here to steal things?"

Her gaze widened. "No, no. Not at all. That's not what I'm here for at all."

"Really?" he sneered. "It seems like everybody is after something. And everybody always wants something from Edna."

"I don't," she said immediately.

"Really?" He obviously didn't believe her.

And she couldn't blame him. She was someplace she shouldn't be, but she didn't know how to get out of here. "If you could show me how to get out of here," she said, "I'd be happy to take my animals and go."

Immediately his gaze dropped to the dog and the cat. "Well, now I know why Mona was howling."

She winced. "Yes, my cat didn't want to give way to his dominance. I'm so sorry. It's clearly Mona's home and obviously she should be allowed to be in her home."

The man stared at her, almost in fascination, and she realized that, once again, her tongue was out of control. She took a long slow deep breath. "I'm sorry," she said. "Could you please show me how to get out of the house?"

He pointed to another door she hadn't seen. "Take that to a long hallway and, when you come out the other side, you'll see the main garage just around the corner, with the driveway."

She hastened to the doorway. "Thank you," she called out, then disappeared through the door, hurrying as fast as she could with her animals. When she got down to the other end of the hallway, she turned to look back, and, sure enough, the man stood there, staring at her. She didn't even bother saying anything and just bolted out the next door. As soon as she got outside, she felt the sunshine and the fresh air on her face. She took several deep, calming breaths.

"Wow." She looked down at her animals. "Talk about bad behavior."

Mugs gave her a disdainful look, and she realized that he wasn't any more to blame than Goliath was—or Doreen—but, at the same time, they were to blame. They'd been caught in somebody else's house, where they shouldn't have been, and she was just as much to blame.

With a groan, she walked forward a few steps, looking for Mack, but, of course, he was still busy helping, at least she presumed so. She would really like to go home now. She'd had more than enough of the orchid tour. The terrible accident here, at the same time as the possible theft of a prized orchid, just made it that much harder. But she kept walking and soon found the huge driveway, and thankfully there was Mack's truck.

With relief she raced over, opened up the passenger side, thrilled to find it unlocked. Piling all the animals inside, she jumped up herself, then slammed the door shut and just sat here, quivering in place. What started out as a fun and adventurous day with a good friend had ended up being a crazy unsettling moment, where she and her animals had definitely not shown their best sides. She could only hope Mack was having better luck.

With a heavy sigh, she looked down at Mugs. "What on earth got into you anyway?"

Goliath too, although telling off Goliath was akin to helping him completely ignore her, like he always did. Even Thaddeus hadn't been terribly happy with the whole scenario. She slumped back into the truck seat, quite content to wait for Mack to return.

Chapter 4

WHEN MACK OPENED the driver's side door, Doreen bolted upright. "Easy, easy, it's okay."

She sighed and sagged back into the big front seat. "Sorry." She rubbed her forehead. "I must have zoned out while I was waiting for you."

"I did phone you a couple times." He motioned at her pocket.

She fished out her phone, then checked it and winced. "So many people were around at the market," she said, "so I just turned it off."

"That's fine." He nodded understandingly. "I was worried when I couldn't find you. But, at least, you found your way back to the truck."

"I did eventually, but it wasn't as easy as it should have been." She told him about getting lost and then caught wandering around by the man who had pointed her way outside.

"I'm sorry," Mack said. "I shouldn't have asked you to take them outside, when you didn't know how to get there."

"But who knew it would be that hard to get outside of a house?" she muttered. She looked at him. "What about

Edna?"

"Well, she's called someone to be with her at the hospital, and she'll head out with Miriam in the ambulance," he said. "They've had several close calls with Miriam before, but this was completely unexpected."

"It must be tough to have a relationship with somebody whose hobby is something that will always give you health problems."

"Maybe," he said, "but they've been together for a long time, and we're not exactly sure what's happening."

Doreen looked at him in surprise. "It wasn't an allergic reaction, exacerbated by the asthma?"

"I have no idea," he said. "Obviously she looked pretty swollen, and that seemed to be what Edna thought too, but hopefully they'll sort it out at the hospital. I did find something interesting though. Well, Goliath did actually."

"What are you talking about?"

"Remember when he jumped on that table and all that stuff started falling?"

"How could I forget. I was mortified."

"As I was picking things up, I found this on the floor underneath." Mack pulled something from his shirt pocket.

"What is it?"

"An EpiPen, what someone with serious allergies and airway problems would carry to save their lives in the midst of a negative reaction. I'm wondering if she was trying to use it and dropped it, then couldn't find it or something."

"What if someone stole the orchid, and Miriam had an attack, and the thief knocked the EpiPen out of her hand? Can stress cause a reaction like that? Or maybe stress can set up the whole allergy scenario to hide a more sinister plot? Or maybe—"

"Hold it. We don't know any of that and don't need to speculate. The main thing is, we found her and got her headed to help. She's in pretty rough shape and not out of the woods by any means."

Doreen nodded. "No, you're right," she said. "It's just very sad. I feel heartbroken for Edna. It's obvious that they care for each other very much."

"Yes, they've been best friends and partners for a long time," he said, "long before it was accepted as a norm."

She nodded. "And, for that, I'm sorry because we should be allowed to have the relationship that makes us happy, as long as we're not hurting anybody else."

"That is a nice liberal attitude," he said, "but you and I both know the world doesn't operate so easily."

"No," she whispered.

He looked at her. "It's not the end of the outing I had hoped for."

"No, but it was good until then," she said.

"We didn't get to all the other orchids either."

"I know." She winced at that. "What about the missing orchid? Did you find out anything more?"

Mack shook his head. "We'll have to wait to ask Miriam."

Doreen nodded. "I feel bad for everybody who doesn't make it here on the tour."

"They can visit the homes on the tour in any random sequence. If they end up here, the police will send them away."

"Let's hope everybody else had a good showing then," she said. "I can't imagine how the last person would feel if nobody showed up."

He stopped, looked at her. "You want to keep going?"

"I don't think the tour's still on, is it?"

He nodded. "Oh, sure, still another four hours, I think, where you're allowed to go and view the orchids." She hesitated, and he said, "I think you may be on to something. Let's go take a look at the rest of the orchid tour. That'll get our minds off of Edna and Miriam for a while."

She smiled. "That would be a good idea to have something different to think about."

He turned on the truck and looked at the animals. "If they'll behave?"

"I'm still not sure why they weren't behaving anyway in the greenhouse," she said quietly. "It's not like them to be difficult."

"But they were on a leash for a long time, and it was hot in there," he reminded her. "We have to keep that in perspective too."

"I wasn't even thinking of that," she said, "but you're right. It was hot. Greenhouses may be ideal for orchids but not for animals."

"Exactly, but why don't we try another one and see how that works?" And, with that, he headed off.

"Did you know it was Edna's place before we got there?" she asked.

"Oh, yes," he said. "The same as I know the next one is Smudge's."

"Smudge?"

He laughed. "Yes. He used to run a business here with compost. He'd collect all kinds of green and brown matter and then build these huge compost piles that he would keep turning, adding to, churning out absolutely beautiful black gold. All the gardeners used it all the time."

"When you say *used* to, does that mean he doesn't do it

anymore?" she asked. "Compost is always welcome."

"Not only welcome, it's wanted," he said. "But then the city took over the big operation of most of it, and he dealt in some specialized compost, but he ended up ill with diabetes. He struggled controlling it and, when his son moved to the coast, Smudge decided his place would be too much work for him to keep up all on his own."

"I think that one of the hardest things is when the kids end up leaving town, even though you've done all you could to get them to stay."

"I think so too." He nodded. "When you think about it, I mean, in a lot of cases, these are some of the founding families, who expect their traditions to carry on. But this time, there just wasn't any industry for his son to carry on with. Sure, they could make compost, but it was hard to make enough money on something like that to support the additional family."

"I guess," she said, "though it's still sad."

He looked over, smiled. "That's because you're a romantic at heart."

She didn't know how to take that, but Thaddeus lifted his head. "Romantic, she's romantic."

"No, that's not what he meant," she argued, as Thaddeus started cackling.

But Mack laughed and laughed. "He does pick up a selective set of words, doesn't he?"

"And not all the time," she said in exasperation. "He picks up certain things, and you think he won't remember something bad, yet he does. Then he picks up something completely unrelated that has nothing to do with anything, and he just won't let it go."

At that, Thaddeus stretched, crowed, and then started

his little laugh again, which always made her wonder if he knew what it did to her.

"See that laugh he has? That's just creepy."

Mack laughed. "It is a little creepy. But then he's a little creepy."

She nodded. "He's also very, very beautiful, and he knows it."

"Thaddeus is beautiful," he said in a soft preening voice.

She groaned. "See what I mean? He's never silent when it comes to getting attention."

"Can you blame him?" Mack had a huge grin on his face. He turned the corner. "Now we're heading up here to Smudge's place."

She leaned forward to see a large area, maybe a couple acres. "Everybody has land here," she said enviously.

"That's one of the requirements to grow things, isn't it? You need to have enough room to put in a garden."

"And I never thought about having a big garden," she said, "but I've only recently realized just how hard it is to get land of your own, to keep it up, and to hang on to it."

"Well, having it is one thing. Keeping it is entirely different," he said. "Then, when you do have it and do keep it," he murmured, "who do you pass it on to? And that's where the trouble lies for some."

"I hadn't even considered that," she said. "It sounds so sad to think that nobody inherits some of the grand places." He pulled up and parked off to the side, while she looked around. "At least it's not as crowded here."

"No, and half these vehicles are probably Smudge's anyway." He chuckled.

She hopped out, and this time Mugs immediately bounded around the truck wheels. He lifted a leg, while

Goliath looked at him in disdain.

"That cat only has only one look on his face," Mack announced. "Complete disdain for the world around him."

"I think it's more a case of thinking he's just above it all."

"That's the same thing," he said, "and then he does something that completely surprises you."

"He's very humanlike," she murmured. "And he never really lets me forget it. But, every once in a while, I start to think that he's straight animal or straight cat, and then he does something so very relatable."

At that, Goliath walked closer and stood up on his back legs and put his front paws on her thigh.

"What does he want?" Mack asked.

"This." She bent down, lifted him into her arms. Goliath's paws immediately hit her shoulder and stayed there.

"Wow, nice trick. A cat that asks to be lifted and carried."

"He likes it when he gets tired," she murmured. She buried her face in his soft fur for a long moment.

"Do you think we need to go home then?" Mack asked in worry.

"No, they'll be fine for a little bit," she said, "but I may ask you to take Mugs again, if you don't mind."

He immediately held out his hand, and she passed the dog's leash over to him. "And this time let's see if we can keep Mugs in control."

She chuckled. "I don't even know what he was going after back there in the greenhouse. It could have been anything from a mouse to a cat. Once we were outside, we did find another cat called Mona that Mugs and Goliath were not very happy to see," she murmured. "We haven't seen too many other cats in their own space, and I just realized how much training I need to do to get them to understand that they can only be jerks in their own home."

"They should never be jerks."

"No, that's quite true."

"What will you do when they act up in the next home on this tour?"

Doreen nodded. "Come on. Let's take a quick look, and then we can go to the next place."

"That depends if you stop and visit with Smudge." Mack tossed her a big grin. "But it's all good. He's a good man."

"The world needs a few good men," she said.

A man with a raspy hoarse voice said, "You're looking at one of the best men around. What's taking you so long?"

She stopped in her tracks, as she looked at a grizzled old guy, who appeared to have two strands of dark hair sticking out of the top of his head and yet a thick beard on his chin.

"Hi." She felt a little awkward. "I'm Doreen."

"Yeah, I know who you are," he said. "The animals told me that."

She stared at him. "The animals told you?"

He started to belly laugh. "Oh, she's a live one." He snorted at Mack.

"That she is."

She wasn't exactly sure why they were laughing, but, hey, it was better than everything else that had happened so far today. "Are you part of the orchid show?" she asked quietly.

"I am, indeed," he said. "Come on in, and let me show you."

She looked around. "Are other visitors here too?"

He nodded. "Yeah, they're inside, wandering around on

their own."

"And you didn't give them a tour?"

"Nope," he said. "Why would I want to do that? Now you, on the other hand, are a different story."

"Why?" she asked in confusion.

He chuckled. "You're very interesting, so I'm happy to talk to you some more. Make sure you keep the animals in line though."

She immediately tightened her arms on Goliath. "I will," she promised, hoping that she could deliver. As they walked in, she looked around to see none of the high-end open cedar, stone, and glasswork of Edna's house nor a huge solarium either. But, as they headed to the back, she saw an open area, where a wood stove was set up for winter. In here were fruit trees—citrus, grapefruit, and lemons. She stared at them in surprise.

He laughed. "Yeah, I do like my fruits."

"I think most people do," she said in amazement, "but they don't set aside a whole part of their house to grow them."

"You've got to make priorities in life," he said, "and, once I got out of the compost business, at least commercially, I had to do something that made me happy, so this is it."

"And I understand that too," she said, "because, wow, this is beautiful."

"Thank you," he said, with quiet pride.

She looked around, more confused than ever at exactly what he'd done, but it worked, and, if she didn't look at the structural problems that he possibly created by opening up all this, then it looked even better. "I presume you had to get permits for all this, huh?" There was silence, and she turned, and he just glared at her. She held up her hand. "Sorry, just curious. Forget I asked," she said. "I don't work for the city. I just heard it's hard to get them. I don't care myself, and I figure that, if you did this work all yourself, you probably did a better job than anybody."

He looked at her and looked at Mack.

Mack nodded. "She's being real."

Smudge let out a big sigh. "Well, missy, you better learn not to open your mouth when it comes to these topics because nobody wants to hear that. Everybody keeps the city and all the city officials as far away as they can."

"I get it," she said, "and I'm sorry."

He nodded. "I'll trust you because of Mack. But, boy oh boy, if some of the other old-timers around here heard you talk like that, you'd be in some trouble."

She winced and whispered to Mack, "Sorry."

He just shrugged, and they kept on moving, as Smudge led her to where all the plants were.

"Wow," she said, "this is so lush."

"It's the compost," he said, "my own secret blend."

She nodded. "It's doing the job in a beautiful way." She shook her head in amazement. "I can't imagine how hard it was to get that orchid so colorful. I mean, just look at how green and how vibrant everything is."

"Well, it took a bit."

Such obvious pride was in his tone that she knew she was slowly getting back on track with him. She smiled. "You've done a wonderful job. I've never seen anything like this." There was just so much life to everything that it really stunned her. But, at the same time, she could also see that he'd spent a lot of his lifetime working on how to make this the best orchid that it could be, and the good news was, he had made it something special, and he deserved to be proud.

And she couldn't imagine any other way to be. She looked over at him. "You've really done something phenomenal here."

He looked at her, grinned, and, in a country-boy imitation, said, "Aw, shucks, thank you, ma'am."

Chapter 5

AFTER SEEING SMUDGE'S gardens, Mack and Doreen finally said their goodbyes, but it was with a touch of sadness because she'd found some real people here on the tour. As they walked out to Mack's truck again, he looked over at her. "Well?"

"I really enjoyed Smudge," she admitted. She helped Mugs back up into the truck. "He's quite a character."

Mack chuckled. "That he is. Old Smudge has been terrorizing this town for a long time."

She could just imagine. And even Mack obviously didn't mind it because only joy was in his voice. "I think we're missing people like that," she murmured. "People who act from the heart, even if they do walk that fine line between legal or not."

"We try not to worry about it too much," he murmured. "There's enough in this world that we need to keep close track of already, without looking for more trouble."

She nodded. "And you know what? That makes a lot of sense. It's just so sad that so much of the stuff going on around here would have people tattling on them."

"I don't know if anybody tattled on them, per se," he

said. "We just like to keep track of the plainly illegal stuff, without worrying about nitpicking at bits and pieces of stuff that's just at the edge and not hurting anybody. What did you think of his orchids?"

"Stunning. But also more surreal," she said, "because of the setting."

He looked at her, as he started up the engine. "How?"

"If you think about it, Edna's place was stunning too, but the whole solarium just gave it a very elevated look. It's not like people are being judged for their orchids alone here on the tour. In my opinion, it's the whole setting. Whether that's intended or not, I don't see how you can avoid it."

"So you're saying that people will judge not only the plants themselves but how the house is? That's not fair."

"It might not be fair, but I bet you that it'll happen. I mean, Edna's place was unbelievable. But Smudge's place is equally unbelievable, in a much more rustic *country cabin in the middle of the woods* scene. I mean, it was stunning, really gorgeous. But because it was set up as it was, it added much more emphasis to the surreal beauty of his garden. Plus his were all oranges and golds, which seemed to blend into the surroundings, making it that much more natural looking."

"I hear what you're saying," he said. "We can hope that people wouldn't judge it by that though."

"I don't know. I think we're asking a lot of people to have them separate the two."

"You don't think people can?"

"Well, they probably can," she said, "but it won't be easy. I don't even think they'll be aware of just how much that exterior look really affects the decision-making process."

He nodded and didn't say anything more, as they pulled out and kept on driving.

"He'd be a good source of compost though."

"Not anymore," he said. "He's out of the business."

"He might be out of the business,"—she chuckled—"but, if you were good friends with him, I'm pretty sure he's got a steady supply of the good stuff."

Mack shot her a quick glance, before he pulled into traffic. "You could be right," he said. "But you don't need any, do you?"

"I have to dress the garden somehow, and it's definitely in need of some good loving care, so prime nutrients are where you'd start."

"Ah, well, you might get something from him, but I wouldn't count on it."

"No, I wouldn't either," she said. "I'm sure you have to be part of his inner circle to get something from him."

"I would think so." He laughed. "Besides, in this case, I'm sure trade secrets are a big part of what he doesn't want everybody to know about."

"That's very true." She nodded, then chuckled. "When you think about it, when growing orchids—when competing especially—so much of that entails keeping things secret, so they can have the best and thus be the best."

"And you're not like that?"

"I don't know that I'm competitive," she murmured. "If you think about it, all my life I haven't really had that opportunity, so I don't know if that's something that I am or not."

"It would be interesting to see," he said. "Maybe you should enter one of these contests next year."

She burst out laughing, and Goliath switched his position on her lap, finally curling up in this massive ball, as if ready for a good nap. "It's not so much that I'm not interested," she said, "but I don't have anything to show, and I won't have anything decent to put in for a competition for years. And then, when I think about how *killer* these competitions can be, I'm not sure I'm the right personality for it."

"Just because you've seen some pretty ugly stuff with these contests," he said, "that doesn't mean that you'll come up against it yourself."

"No, maybe not," she said, "but I'd hate to think that anything was as competitive as what I saw before."

"Well, we would hope not."

"And, with the orchids, you don't think they are?" she asked curiously. "I would have thought that whole competitive streak would come out in full force with something like orchids."

"Why orchids versus anything else?"

"Because of the cachet that goes along with the orchids. They're very high-end. They're highly regarded all over the world. Some are extremely rare. I didn't get to see the one of Edna's that was incredibly rare. I hope it's just missing, not stolen. And I would love to see it eventually, even though I don't know that much about them. My ex would have a field day here."

"I hope he doesn't know about the tour then," Mack muttered, frowning.

"Oh, I never even thought of that." She stared at him in surprise.

"Thought about what?"

"If he even knows about it," she said. "I don't know, and I certainly haven't told him."

"Good."

She frowned. "I know you have reason to not like him,

but I don't know that he's *that* bad of a person."

"He physically and verbally abused you. He cheated on you while you were still living there. He tried to cheat you out of the monetary settlement that you deserve," he said. "He had shady business practices that even you began to take notice of. He controlled everything you did, you ate, you wore. All good enough reasons not to like him. Stop making excuses for him."

His tone had turned just brisk enough that she realized it was a subject she wouldn't discuss with him for quite a while. But then, maybe that was okay too. Mathew wasn't exactly somebody she wanted to discuss in her world of genial conversation. And Mack was right; Mathew hadn't treated her well. She should stop making excuses for him. But she also just wasn't a vindictive person, as so many others were, and it bothered her in a way. "Do you think I'm too nice?"

"Absolutely."

"Wow, you didn't take even a moment to think about it."

"Nothing to think about," he said. "I've known a lot of people in my time, and a lot of them would have immediately eviscerated your husband the minute he showed up again."

"Ah. … Well, I don't know how much of that is my inability to see my way out of this or just not wanting to confront him."

"It's probably a whole lot of things." Mack's tone was gentle now. "And I shouldn't harp on it."

"No, you probably shouldn't," she said thoughtfully, "but, at the same time, I guess somebody should tell me to grow a pair."

Startled, he looked at her, and then he laughed hysterically.

She grinned at him. "See? Laughter is good for you."

"I laugh a lot," he said, "especially since you came into my life."

"Is that a good thing?"

"You're the one who told me earlier that I needed to laugh more, so I'll say yes."

She nodded. "I think you should laugh more. I think it's good for everybody."

He pulled onto the main road. "Three more places. Are you up for it?"

"Let's try one," she said. "The animals are looking a bit tired."

"We can do one and see."

"Maybe we should do the last one on the list," she said impulsively. "I feel like people won't make it through the whole thing, and I feel bad for anybody who's waiting for everyone to show up."

He nodded. "That's a good point, happy to go to the last one. But what if everybody else thinks like you did? Now, all of a sudden, the last one gets everybody, and the ones just before the end don't get anybody."

"Oh, wow," she said. "Now you're making me feel guilty." He chuckled, but she could see his point. "Fine, we'll go to all three. Let's just make it fast and not stay long."

"I don't have a problem with that," he said. "You're the one who has the tendency to linger around."

"I do not," she protested. They were still at it when he pulled up to another house. She looked at him. "Well, this doesn't look all that awe-inspiring."

"But remember what we said. It's not supposed to be about the location or the surroundings."

"And, for that reason alone, I'll be curious to see what he is growing and how well he does."

"Do you really think it makes a difference?"

"I don't see how it can't," she said simply. "Whether we like it or not, people are still tuned to what affects them, and I think the whole picture, the whole presentation is what will make for the winner."

As they walked in, they were greeted by an older woman. Her face lit up. "Hello. My aunt will be delighted to see more people."

"Has the crowd eased down?" Doreen asked.

"Oh, yeah," she said. "It was pretty busy for a while, but I think people are getting tired. A lot of greenhouses were on the tour list."

"We were even debating whether we should come or not," Doreen admitted.

"I'm really happy you came. This is her big day, as she would say."

"Has she been growing orchids for long?"

"Many, many years. She has just never opened herself up to something like this before, so she's pretty excited. She doesn't have too much longer to live, so this is making her day."

"Oh." Doreen felt a little odd at hearing that.

The woman immediately noticed. "I don't mean to make that sound bad," she said, "because I know that she's so thrilled that people are here."

Feeling a little better, Doreen walked ahead of Mack, carrying Goliath in her arms, as he had deemed himself too tired to walk.

The woman looked at the cat, shook her head. "I'm surprised you're carrying him. He's huge. He's got to be heavy."

"You wouldn't be so surprised if you knew him," Mack said. "He really does rule the roost."

The other woman laughed. "You know what? My aunt had a cat like that. It was pretty hard to do anything with him that he didn't want to do."

"Exactly," Doreen said, "and this one's definitely a character, but he's mine, and I adore him."

"Of course," the woman agreed. "That's how it should be."

With the fact that they were all animal lovers entrenched in everybody's mind, they headed to the garden to have a look. A simple greenhouse was connected to the home and inside was one single orchid. It was bloodred. "Wow," Doreen said. "What a color."

And, in many ways, because only one orchid was displayed, the sheer simplicity of the location really emphasized the glory of the striking orchid.

"She's been working on it for a long time," she said, "but this is the only one that she's cultivating right now."

"And is this her own unique one?"

"It absolutely is. She wants to register it but is struggling with getting it recognized."

"Of course. I understand there's quite an issue with it."

"They started to get fussy about it all and won't let just anybody register an orchid anymore." She rolled her eyes at that.

"I've heard of that too," Doreen admitted. Mack frowned at her. "My ex had some issues about it. He used to get quite irritated by it all."

"Yes, exactly," the woman said.

"Is your aunt around?"

"She is sitting outside."

"May I talk to her?" Doreen asked curiously, unable to take her eyes off the orchid.

"I'll go see."

As she left them to go the backyard, Mack looked at her. "Why do you want to talk to her?"

"If she has been waiting for this for a long time, she might appreciate hearing that somebody really loves the work she has done."

Mack looked at her, a strange glint in his eye. "Yes, you're too soft," he murmured, as the woman entered and motioned them to walk outside.

"No," Doreen said, "I just think sometimes we forget about the humanness of our lives here."

"Maybe, but you're definitely a softy."

And her heart did melt when she walked forward to see a much older woman, struggling to get out of a chair. Doreen immediately raced forward. "Please don't get up on our account."

The woman stopped, hesitated, then looked behind Doreen and her gaze shot up. "Mack?"

He stepped forward, then leaned over and gave the frail woman a hug. "Hi, Gloria. How you doing?"

Doreen looked at him and back at Gloria. "You two know each other?"

"Not a whole lot of choice in this town." Mack gave her half a smile.

The older woman looked at him, her face softening. "Mack was instrumental in me keeping my sanity at a point in time when I wasn't sure I'd make it."

Something was very interesting in that comment. Doreen looked to Mack for an explanation, but he wasn't giving any.

The older woman said, "My husband was killed in a bad accident a long time ago, and my son, well, he was murdered."

At the word *murder* Doreen stiffened. "I'm so sorry. That's got to be difficult."

"I lost my husband long before Mack here was born. And then, when my only son, Lionel, was murdered, well, I mean, I could really turn to nobody. It's hard to watch your heart break with strangers."

Doreen could understand that.

"But I loved growing orchids. It helped. Then I had my philanthropy too. I kept busy. I made new friends. And eventually met Mack." She looked over at him, then smiled at Doreen. "He's a good guy."

Mack looked uncomfortable, shifting uneasily on his feet.

The other woman walked forward to join them, facing Doreen. "I'm Elle, Gloria's niece." Then she turned to Mack. "I didn't even recognize you," she said. "I'm so sorry."

He looked at her, shaking his head. "Hey, it's fine, I wouldn't even bring it up if Gloria didn't remember me."

Gloria chuckled. "Trust Mack to think anybody won't remember him. Just look at the size of the man."

Doreen nodded. "Hard to ignore, isn't he?"

"An impossible presence too." Gloria smiled, as she motioned at the nearby chair. "Come and visit for a little bit, if you want."

"I just wanted to congratulate you on that absolutely stunning orchid," Doreen said.

"Thank you." Gloria seemed gratified to hear it. "It's the hobby my son and I used to do together," she said, her expression dimming briefly.

"I'm sorry," Doreen whispered. "I didn't mean to bring up any bad memories."

"You didn't, my dear. You didn't. When you get to my age, at least bad memories are still memories," she murmured.

Mack looked at her with the gentlest smile on his face. Doreen really appreciated the fact that he could relate to people so easily. She turned back to the older woman. "Your son would be thrilled to see you here, sharing it with us."

"He was pretty private about it, so he's probably rolling over in his grave, horrified that I would bring it out for the public." She smiled. "But, at some time in your life, you have to stop hiding everything and start giving a little bit more. At this stage, I'm trying to give so much more."

Chapter 6

GLORIA CONTINUED. "I don't have too much longer to live, and I just want to make sure that my conscience is clear and that whatever I have to leave behind is left to the right people."

It was an odd topic, but, for anybody looking at passing on possessions as they went to the other world—whatever that world would bring—maybe this was normal talk. Doreen glanced at the niece to find her biting her lower lip and holding back tears. Shifting Goliath's position, Doreen walked over and gave the woman a gentle hug and whispered, "She's quite something."

The niece smiled through her tears. "She is, indeed."

The two of them stepped off to the side, as Mack and Gloria spoke at length on other subjects. Doreen wasn't terribly interested in overhearing Mack's discussion, as she listened to the niece expound about the pain that Gloria had been through with her husband's car accident and then her son's murder. "I'm so sorry," she murmured again.

The woman nodded. "And that's the trouble. We can all be sorry, but it never helps. It never changes anything."

"No, and not much anybody can do about it."

The woman looked at her. "You're the one who gets involved in cold cases, aren't you?"

"I do, much to poor Mack's chagrin," she said easily. "I'm Doreen."

"I'm Elle." The woman laughed. "I can see that," she said. "I don't imagine he likes anybody interfering in his work at all."

"No, he sure doesn't." Doreen smiled. "But that's okay. We've worked out a way to stay amiable in spite of it all."

"It's obvious that you guys are a great match."

Doreen recoiled ever-so-slightly, thinking about other people gossiping about them. Look at her own nan. Doreen didn't say anything to that.

Then Elle said impulsively, "Well, if you're ever bored …"

At that, Doreen chuckled. "I don't know about *bored*," she said, "but what do you mean?"

"You could always look into my cousin's death."

She stared at her for a long moment. "You mean, it hasn't been solved?"

Elle shook her head. "No, they never found out who killed him."

"Oh, dear." Doreen slid a sideways glance at Mack, who didn't appear to hear this conversation at all. "Was it local?"

"No, he went out of town to a flower show," she said for clarification. "He was in Vancouver and was murdered there."

"Ah," she said. "I don't know if I can get any information on it or not."

"We suspected somebody from here did it at the time," she said.

"Why would you say that?" Doreen asked.

"Because he'd had several fights with somebody local, about orchids of all things." Elle groaned. "I've come to actually hate the damn things."

"I'm sorry to hear that," she said. "They're truly beautiful."

"They are, but, in our family, I don't think they've been good luck at all. Sometimes I think they've been the cause of everything." With that cryptic remark, Elle turned and walked away.

Knowing she wouldn't get any information from Mack, at least not willingly, Doreen followed the woman. "Do you have any details on the case?"

Elle looked at her in surprise. "Mack won't give them to you?"

"Only what he can, but what he can't give me is the insider information."

"I don't really have much," the niece said apologetically. "Don't worry about it. I shouldn't even have asked you."

"If it's something that we can solve before your aunt dies, maybe it would give her some closure and make her passing a little more peaceful."

"I know she would love to have answers."

"But you said Lionel died down on the coast?"

She looked confused for a moment and then shrugged. "I know my uncle was killed down there. No, that was my cousin." She stopped, sighed. "I'm sorry. Everything is confusing me these days. It was my uncle who was killed driving on the way to Vernon. Of course that was even longer ago."

"That's fine," Doreen assured Elle. "It's very easy for these mixed memories to trip us up." And not so unusual in somebody of Elle's age—around seventy, Doreen guessed.

"So easy that you're so sure you know what had happened. Then, the next thing you know, you don't know anything," she murmured.

"And it can happen that way. Indeed, it can."

"If you wouldn't mind looking," she said, "we would appreciate it. But—we don't have any money to pay you."

"Oh, dear me, no," Doreen said. "I can't guarantee you any results, but, at the same time, the price is right. I do this for free." She stopped and shrugged, trying to formulate an answer that would make this woman with the huge eyes more likely to give her the details Doreen needed. "I guess I do this because I feel compelled to help out the families," she said. "I know that the dead are already gone, but, for the families who don't get any answers, it's torture."

"It really is," Elle said. "At the time there was just so much gossip going around, so many questions, so much misinformation."

And, once again, Elle appeared to have drifted off into another world, maybe thinking more along the lines of her uncle, not her cousin. In an effort to clarify what the problem was, Doreen said, "Your uncle's accident must have been terrible."

"It was terrible, just losing him like that …" She shook her head. "I was so young. I don't know that I've ever really recovered. Aunt Gloria would probably say that I haven't."

Doreen frowned. "Do you have any family of your own?"

"You mean, kids? No," she said. "I never went in that direction. I was married for a short time, but that was all." She paused. "I was just happy to be here, and, with cousin Lionel and Aunt Gloria in my life, everything was fine, until he died."

"How did he die?"

"An accident," she said, her tone bitter. "No. That was my uncle. Lionel was mugged, stabbed to death." She shook her head. "Honestly I've been confused a lot lately. I've been getting my uncle and my cousin confused as well, much less their tragic deaths. I think my aunt is in better shape mentally than I ever have been, at least since all the deaths."

"I'm sorry. That makes it even tougher."

"When you can see the signs coming at you, and you don't know how to avoid them or what to do, it makes it really scary," she said. "Sometimes I wish I could go at the same time Aunt Gloria does because I just don't understand what'll happen to me afterward."

Doreen looked at her closely. "If you don't mind me asking, how old is Gloria?"

"My aunt is ninety-eight," Elle said.

She stared at Gloria, then back at her niece. "Seriously?"

"Yes, ninety-eight and she doesn't look it. Me, I'm sixty-five, and I look like I'm her age." She shook her head. "Sometimes life isn't fair."

"No, it isn't," Doreen said, "but sometimes we do what we can to make it a little bit better."

The woman smiled. "You're very nice. I'm happy for Mack. He's done without anybody for a very long time."

"Do you know him well?"

"Well enough," she said cheerfully. "He's so much younger than I am, but I've been in town the same number of years, so our paths have crossed many times."

"He seems like a good man," Doreen said, "and he's always been fair in his dealings with me, when honestly he probably had good reason to yell at me more than a few times."

The woman laughed out loud. "Yes, but he has a lot of patience."

"Very good to know." Doreen chuckled. "I know I've exasperated him a lot."

"It's good for him," she said. "You can't afford to get into a rut."

Doreen looked at her. "Do you have anything to do with the orchids?"

"No, I hate them honestly," she said boldly. "Ever since my cousin died, I've absolutely detested them and would cheerfully have nothing to do with them."

"Ah, that makes it even harder, doesn't it?"

"It sure does," she said, her voice rising. "I just think that they get so fanatical, and everybody goes so over-the-top in terms of their cultivation and the compost that they used and the special techniques, the hours of sun and exposure and whatnot. I mean, you don't understand how nuts these people are."

At that, her aunt rebuked her with a sharp voice. "I am not nuts, thank you," she said. "It's a passion, and I'm sorry you've never understood it."

Elle sighed. "I'm sorry. I'm just thinking about all the years that you guys have spent doing this."

"But years that were happy," she said as a reminder.

"Maybe, but for somebody who doesn't have much to deal with any of it, it's hard to sit back and to watch you all go so nuts."

"And there you go using that term again," her aunt said in exasperation.

"And I don't mean it that way," Elle said. "You know that."

"Maybe, but these people don't. For all you know,

they'll think you're crazy."

"Maybe I am," Elle said quietly. "Maybe I am." And, with that, she turned and left them.

Gloria winced. "I shouldn't have said that. She's definitely having an awful lot of issues lately."

"What issues?" Mack asked.

"Everything affects her—and in the wrong way," she murmured, "like, literally everything. It's so frustrating. And it seems like she's declining faster mentally than I am."

Doreen walked closer. "She definitely seems to be struggling."

"Very much so, and I just don't know what'll happen to her when I'm gone," she whispered. And this time there was a sheen of tears in her eyes.

"Seems you've had a long and glorious life," Doreen said. "I'm sure she'll be fine."

The older woman looked at her sadly. "I'm not so sure," she murmured. "She hasn't been the same since, well, all the tragedy."

"Losing her uncle and her cousin must have been terrible shocks."

The older woman nodded. "And Elle and Lionel were so close. It was heartbreaking to see her afterward. I mean, it was tough on me to be sure, but it was devastating for her." Gloria sighed. "We're all such simple folk, and to think of things like this going on around us is just devastating."

"You never had any idea who killed your son?" Doreen asked.

"No. If I could have pointed Mack here in any direction, I would have."

"You did, many times," Mack said gently. "But we could never find any evidence to support it."

"No, and that's the problem," she said. "The onus of proof always ends up on the victim or the victim's family, and it seems like these guys just get to go scot-free."

"Maybe," he said gently, "but we do pride ourselves on trying to find the truth."

The older woman looked sharply at Doreen. "It's connected to orchids, you know."

Doreen stared. "Are you sure about that?" Turning toward Mack, her mind immediately went to poor Miriam and Edna—and their apparently missing orchid.

"Oh, yes, I'm very sure. It's one of the reasons I put the orchid out for the competition today," she murmured. She looked at Mack. "I know you won't approve, but I guess I was hoping to flush him out."

"And what would having the orchid on display do to flush him out?" Doreen asked curiously.

"Because my son was killed for it. And this orchid is very close to the one stolen from him at the time. It's a little bit different but not by much. Only in that it's generations older. But anybody who sees the two would know they're same plant."

Doreen frowned. "And so, by bringing it out, what does that do?"

"I'm hoping that somebody will see it and will realize they don't have the only one."

Doreen was trying to piece this together. "And the orchid that Lionel was killed for, it was taken at the time, but was it the only one of its kind?"

"Oh yes, it was stolen. It was our rare gem," she said. "And instead I had to start all over again."

"Yet you did?"

"I did. I did for my son's sake because it was so important to him."

"Was that smart?" Mack asked quietly.

"Of course not." She gave a half-broken laugh. "But, when nothing else is left in your life but facing death and knowing that your family is in shambles behind you," she said, "we do the darndest things." And, with that, she slowly stood and grabbed the cane at her side. "I'm sorry, but I must lie down now."

"Of course," Mack said immediately. "Please take care of yourself."

She nodded. "I will. I just hope somebody takes care of my niece, when this is all over with." And she slowly walked back into the house.

Doreen sat here, the animals quietly at her side, as if understanding something odd was going on. "Mack?"

"I'm not sure." He stared where Gloria had gone.

"It doesn't sound terribly healthy."

"No," he said, "but, when you think about it, knowing the destruction that happens to a family when there's a murder, it's not as unexpected as it may seem."

She nodded slowly. "I get it, but this one feels …" Then she didn't know what to say, so she just shrugged.

"Come on," he said, draping his arm on her shoulders. "Let's go look at the last two on the tour."

She sighed. "I guess so, but it just feels very odd, after hearing about this family."

"Maybe, but let's hope we end on a better note, if we continue the tour."

And, with that, they headed out to the vehicle and on to the next greenhouse.

Chapter 7

MACK PULLED UP to a huge waterfront house and a massive greenhouse along Abbott Street. Doreen studied the area, as she got out of the vehicle with her animals. "This is the wealthy area, isn't it?"

"Definitely old money here," Mack said succinctly. "This is *the* address, if you want to live in Kelowna."

She chuckled. "Apparently I can't afford to put that address on anything."

"Nope, me neither." He gave her a big grin. "But for these people, this is quite the house."

Doreen and Mack were escorted through the house and to the greenhouse, as if given a tour, yet they weren't allowed to lollygag. It was a quick visit.

"*Here's the orchid, make a decision, and carry on.*"

They were back outside in ten minutes. She looked at Mack, then at Goliath sleeping in her arms. "Wow. I'm glad it was fast, but, at the same time, I'm hesitant to go to the last one."

"We said we would," he said firmly.

She groaned. "You, sir, are a taskmaster."

"Sometimes I have to be." He grinned. "It's the easiest

way to deal with you."

"Are you doing this so I won't be upset later?"

He shrugged. "That's as good a reason as any, but we might as well finish it now."

"We should probably leave the animals behind this time. They are beat. And so we can't be long there either."

Mack nodded in agreement.

Once they were all settled into the truck, he quickly drove to the other address. It was also on Abbott but downtown, on the other side, almost at the bridge. They hopped out, easily spotting the greenhouse. While this may have been *the* street address to have in Kelowna, the house itself was very old and didn't have any of the pizzazz of the earlier one.

An old man stood at the door, rubbing his hands together. "You coming to look at my orchid?" he asked.

"Yes." Doreen smiled. "Have you had many people?"

"There were lots earlier," he said, "but then it all dwindled down to almost nobody."

"I guess that's to be expected." She frowned. "Twenty people were on the tour list, plus all the public showings of orchids."

He nodded. "I just want people to see mine," he said. "It's beautiful."

"I'm sure it is"—she nodded—"particularly if you've had it in competitions."

"First-time showing for this one," he said. "I almost didn't put it in, but I decided to at the last minute."

"Why is that?" she asked.

"To spite Gloria," he said, with a gleeful laugh.

She stiffened and turned to look at Mack.

"Gloria seems to be doing okay," Mack said, his smile

stilted. "I know she enjoyed quite a lot of company today."

"Of course she has," the man said, "but wait till she hears that I put mine in too."

"Wow, I can't wait to see this." Doreen walked behind him. He opened the door to the run-down greenhouse. Yet, obviously, like Gloria, he came from money, given the residence address. However, this guy didn't seem to have much money left. "Have you lived here long?"

"Since forever. One of the originals. Like Gloria."

"So you've been rivals ever since, have you?" Doreen tried to get the gist of just how deep the rivalry went between this man and Gloria.

"You could say that." He laughed. "I mean, we're friends on the surface, but the competitiveness on the orchids, well, that's pretty hard to be friendly about."

"Okay," she said.

He stepped back. "Voila."

She looked at the orchid and gasped. "Oh, wow." Part of her shock—which she hoped he took as surprise at the beauty of the flower—was an obvious fact before her.

The orchid here matched Gloria's.

Chapter 8

DOREEN SPUN TO look at Mack, who studied the orchid, one eyebrow up, a hard look on his face.

The old man cackled, then rubbed his hands together. "Isn't it a beauty?"

"It definitely is," she agreed. "I never thought to see another one just like the last one."

"Yep, and that's why I'm showing it," he said. "Just to spite her."

"I'm not sure I understand the *spite* part," she said cautiously.

"She stole it from me." His gaze turned hard. "That old witch, she had no right to it in the first place."

"That's a pretty strong statement." Mack's tone was harder than she expected to hear. But then he was friends with Gloria.

"It's the truth." The old guy jutted out his chin.

Doreen could tell the old man was getting all fired up, as if looking forward to a fight.

"So, did you steal it from her, or did she steal it from you?" Doreen asked.

The old man cackled. "*Huh.* Aren't you a smart one. I

didn't steal it at all. And neither did Gloria." Doreen stopped and stared. He nodded. "It was that useless, no-good son of hers."

All the breath whooshed out of her. "The one who's dead?"

He nodded. "He was never any good and couldn't do anything right, from the get-go really," he said. "Talk about a waste of space."

"Wow." She paused. "Considering the fact that he is dead, you might want to be a little nicer."

"I'm not into being two-faced about anything. I am how you see me," he said, "and I call a spade a spade."

"Maybe, but that doesn't mean you have to call a dead spade a spade."

He laughed at that too. "Wow, you're a fun one. I was really hoping that this could get some nice discussion going about exactly what happened."

"What do you mean by that?" Mack asked.

"Lionel stole my orchid from me," he said. "And I want justice for that."

"Justice for what?" she asked quietly. "I mean, he is dead and gone. So what are you expecting?"

"Recognition," he roared. "This is my orchid. One that I genetically grew so very carefully for years and years and years, and then he pops up with his version and says it's his."

"Version?" Mack immediately pounced.

He nodded. "Yeah, his version. Which is identical to mine. I don't know what he told Gloria, but it was all lies."

"But, if you don't know what Lionel told Gloria, you can hardly say it was a lie," Doreen said reasonably.

He glared at her, not liking her logic at all. "Don't get all fancy with me right now," he said. "She lied and so did that stupid punk kid of hers."

She wondered at the age of the *stupid punk kid* but figured he had to have been well on in years, given the current age of his mother—though the woman who called herself his cousin was thirty-three years younger than his mother, so wouldn't have been his contemporary. At least Doreen didn't think so. She wanted to ask for the old man's name but caught Mack's eye and an almost imperceptible shake of his head.

For whatever reason, he didn't want to pursue this. She frowned at him because all kinds of answers could be found here, if they just dug a little bit deeper. And the old man didn't seem to care either way.

"You find out that he did this and then you prove it," he snapped to Mack.

"And why would I do that?" Mack's tone of voice sounded bored.

She almost envied him that. But it's obvious the old man was getting even more upset.

"Because he lied and he stole. And there should be justice for that."

"If he wasn't dead already, what would you like to see for justice?" she asked calmly, trying to keep things on a much more even keel, before it blew up into something much uglier. Mack glared at her for even continuing the conversation, but it was obvious this old guy really felt that he had been wronged.

"I don't know," he said. "He made a lot of money off my orchid."

"In what way? I don't really understand."

"Prizes."

"Well, if that were the case, why didn't you speak up

earlier?"

"Because he destroyed mine." The old man spoke with fury in his voice. "It took years and years to bring it back up to this vibrancy and health and power again."

"So aren't you worried about somebody else stealing it, now that you've brought it back into the public eye again?" She knew that Mack was glaring at her, but it seemed like a reasonable question to ask.

The old man nodded immediately. "Absolutely, I am," he said, "but I'm also dying, and I want to see justice before I go. I want recognition that it was my orchid."

"And would that make you happy? Would that make all this go to rest?" she asked quietly because she could see that, indeed, some pain was involved. She just didn't understand how that came to be, when it was obvious an awful lot of history was here, and who knew what was the right and the wrong of any of it. Just because he said he was right didn't mean that that's the way it was. As she knew from her own work and investigations, it was never that simple.

The old man nodded. "I'd certainly be a lot happier," he said. "People would no longer doubt me and laugh at me."

"Why would they laugh at you now?" she asked because she didn't like the sound of any of that. She knew people could be mean, but often, if they were shown the error of their ways, they immediately corrected themselves.

"Because I've been telling everybody it's been my orchid since the beginning. They all think that I'm the one who copied Lionel."

"Well, that makes sense," she said. "When you think about it, most people would see the evidence in front of them."

"Exactly," he pounced. "But I know the truth."

"And that's not enough, is it?" she asked.

He shook his head. "Nope, it sure isn't."

Mack looked from the orchid to the door and back again. "How many people have you had in here today?"

"Quite a few." He sniffed in disdain. "Not as many as Gloria, I bet."

"That's probably just because of where you were on the list," she murmured.

He shrugged. "I think it's because everybody knows and loves her, whereas I've got a bad name."

"And why do you have a bad name?"

He stopped and stared, then looked at Mack with one eyebrow raised.

Mack shrugged. "I don't really know the history either."

"Of course you do," he said. "You're just ignoring it." He turned to look at Doreen. "Gloria and I have been at it for years."

"But it's never come to any physical confrontation, has it?" she asked doubtfully, as this older man had shrunk down to five foot nothing. He was bent over and didn't look like he could harm a fly at this point. But maybe in his day he'd been a bantam rooster with a lot of firepower, if not just from his mouth by hurting Gloria's feelings but also causing quite a ruckus in public.

"Gloria banged one of my vehicles, so I had to press charges. She got off." He pointed an arthritic finger at Mack. "So much for the law."

"Was it an accident?"

"Well, that's what everybody said, but I know better," he said, with a sniff.

"Were you both into orchids back then?"

"We've both been into orchids since forever," he said.

"And her orchid came from mine."

Doreen stiffened slowly. "Of course you have some proof of that, right?"

The old man stared at her. "What proof could I possibly provide? We've been arguing about this very topic for decades."

"And what's behind that?" she asked.

He shook his head. "I thought you were smart, but maybe not."

"So …" She gave an exaggerated sigh, trying for patience. "When something like this goes on between a man and a woman for a long time, most people would assume that there was some love affair gone wrong."

He stiffened at that and glared at her. "That just goes to show that you don't know anything," he snapped.

But there was no protest like one that went too far one way. She nodded to herself. "In other words, she turned you down and married her son's father."

He snorted. "The guy had lots of money."

"And I'm looking at where you live," she said, "so I presume you did too."

"Sure, I did, but I wouldn't tell her all that I had. Last thing you ever want is to have somebody marry you just for your money."

"So you guys never did get married, or do you even have that level of history?"

"Of course we're not married." He gave an exaggerated shrug.

She looked over at Mack. "Sorry. Apparently I'm missing lots of pieces, being a newcomer to town and all."

The old man stopped and stared. "How long have you been here?" he asked.

"Just a few months," she murmured, looking around. Although this address might say old money, there was definitely a lot of new money needed to bring it up to snuff. It had the smell of something that had been sitting around for a very long time without anybody looking after it. Almost a mustiness. She frowned, as she stared around. "You have a beautiful home here, and the location is gorgeous," she said.

"But the house has fallen down around me," he replied.

At that, she wouldn't argue because that's exactly what it looked like. "You can't fix anything?" She looked at him, trying to keep any pity out of her voice, thinking he would probably annihilate her for even suggesting such a thing.

"Don't want to," he said. "Hate having strangers in my space, hate having anybody around who I don't want around."

"If you hired somebody to fix up your house, wouldn't you want them around?" she asked.

"No. Which is why I don't hire anybody because I don't want anybody around." And then he started to chuckle. "But I might handle having you around," he said. "You at least seem to be somebody who will tell me the truth."

"Yep, if I can."

"Then tell me, which orchid is prettier?"

She looked at him in surprise and realized she'd walked right into that one. Mack had stiffened at her side too. "You know, because they are identical," she said smoothly, "I can't possibly say, can I? They're both exactly the same."

"No, you don't get off that easily."

"Why not? You're the one who already said they were from the same plant."

"Sure, but that doesn't mean that they're identical. Each one'll have its own petals, colors, highlights, the greens, the formation of it," he said. "They won't be identical." He used both hands as he spoke to make fake quotation marks in the air. She studied him, not really liking this guy very much, unsure if she sympathized with him or if he was just a cranky old man trying to make life difficult before he kicked off the planet.

"I still couldn't tell you because to me, my untrained eye, they look identical."

He snorted. "They're not." He looked over at Mack. "You, with the cop's eye, what would you say?"

"Hers is more beautiful," Mack said, with a hard gaze.

Then the old man almost went a little bit crazy. He stomped his feet, shook his head, his fist clenching in the air, as he repeated over and over, "It's not. It's not. Mine is more beautiful. Mine is more beautiful." At the end he was practically shouting at them.

She backed up slightly, so she was up against Mack, and he took a step away, dragging her with him. Slowly they made their way toward the entrance, the old man shaking his fist in their direction. "Go on and get out of here, the lot of you," he said. "You're wrong. You're wrong, and I'll prove it."

And, with that, Mack ushered her out the front door, closing it carefully behind him. She raced to the truck and hopped in. Mugs started barking like crazy. She wrapped her arms around him and just held him close, trying to still his wiggling body. She looked at Goliath, sprawled across the edge of her seat, but he appeared to be completely disinterested. Thaddeus paced across the dash, until Mack got in, and then the bird walked up Mack's arm, bent his head against Mack's cheek. "Thaddeus loves Mack. Thaddeus loves Mack."

She stared at Thaddeus. "He is such a two-timer." Mack burst out laughing. "Hey, I'm glad there's something to laugh about," she said. "That was not exactly a pleasant meeting."

"No, it sure wasn't. I'm not exactly certain where he's getting all this from." Mack shook his head.

"Do you think anybody else will come here?"

"I hope not," he said. "The tour's almost over."

"No, I mean, maybe *almost* isn't quite good enough, is it?"

He shook his head. "I'm not sure, but this guy is definitely something I might warn people about." He sat here for a long moment, strumming the steering wheel with his fingers.

"I think you should say something."

"We'll just sit here and wait until the tour's over," he said. "That way I can keep anybody else from going in."

"But that doesn't mean he won't let people in if they come late," she warned him.

He frowned at that, and she just waited because Mack frequently came around to the same way she was thinking. Finally he hopped from his vehicle, pulled out his phone, and made a phone call. She didn't even bother listening because all she wanted was to make sure that nobody else would walk into that place and get slammed with the same reception they'd gotten.

The old guy was not necessarily off his rocker, but he was obviously very disturbed about the sequence of events. And she wanted to save anybody else from interacting with him while he was so angry.

When Mack hopped back in again, he said, "I spoke to the district, and the show is definitely over."

"What about people who, you know, are laggards in the tour."

"The tour organizers are coming around to all the houses, putting up No Entrance signs, meaning, the flower show is over."

"Okay, good, that might do it."

"Well, it should. If somebody goes in after that, then they go in at their own peril."

"Which still isn't a good answer," she reminded him.

He turned on the engine, shook his head. "No, but only so much I can do."

She frowned. "It would be nice if we could just make sure," she fretted.

He looked over at her. "Do you think he'd really hurt somebody?"

"I don't know." She shook her head. "He was really upset."

"And maybe with good reason, but I don't want to think about that." He raised one eyebrow at her.

"No, because you're good friends with Gloria."

"I don't know about good friends," he said, "but I certainly know her a lot better than I know him."

"I don't even know his name."

"Stranden."

She shrugged. "That name means nothing to me."

"No, he's just another old-timer who's been around here since forever and obviously feels like he has been mistreated."

"And, if he's correct, obviously he would have good reason to be very upset about it," she murmured.

"Sure, but how do you prove something like that? Stranden never filed a report on this. We certainly don't have the manpower to go into a decades-old theft case like that. I mean, to steal an orchid? I don't even know what's involved. I'm not a gardener, like you. Is it just picking up a planter box and walking it to the new house, or is it a case of a cutting or what? I don't understand this at all," he murmured.

"Well, I might be a gardener," she said, "but I don't have any real exposure to how orchids are propagated and certainly not the competitiveness behind it. Sure, my ex was a bit of a fanatic about it all, but I don't have a clue about the rest of it either."

As Mack drove down and out the long driveway, someone pulled up with a sign, one of those sandwich board signs to prop up. It read Flower Show Now Closed.

Mack honked the horn at him and waved as they drove out.

"Okay, I feel better."

He nodded. "Now let's get everybody home," he said. "We're all a little more tired than we expected."

"And we have no food at home." He looked at her in surprise, and she shrugged. "I haven't shopped."

"You were supposed to go out yesterday, weren't you?"

"Maybe, but I didn't have the energy for that."

"You worked at my mom's?"

"Yep, and then I did a lot in my garden," she said. "I felt like I haven't done anything out there, and, now with my beautiful patio and deck, it was something I needed to do."

"Well, we could go out for dinner."

She smiled. "Wow, that would be lovely."

"That's what I thought," he said, "but I'm craving fish-and-chips."

"I don't even know what to say about that."

Chapter 9

"YOU CAN START by telling me if you like fish-and-chips." Mack glanced at her and then focused on the road.

"Yes," she said, "I do. But I have the animals, and no way we can go inside a restaurant with them."

He chuckled. "I've got that covered."

She watched with interest as he pulled off the highway and into the long strip mall. Off to one side was a fish-and-chips place.

He said, "Stay here, and I'll be right back."

She watched as he hopped out and strode into the restaurant. Mugs started barking, as if he knew that food was imminent. Goliath's tail twitched faster and faster, as if completely pissed off that they were delayed getting home. Thaddeus had returned to her shoulder and was curled up, as if he was tired.

"I'm tired too, guys," she murmured. "I wouldn't mind just going straight home. But, if this is something we can pick up and take out, now that's a different story." Because that would mean food as soon as they got home, and they were only about ten minutes away. And yet it was still ten minutes, and, when you were tired, even ten minutes seemed like a heck of a lot.

She watched the traffic around her. It was late on a Saturday but still not late as far as evenings went. People were still out shopping at the local grocery store right beside her. She wasn't familiar with this area because she never really spent any time in this corner of town, but it seemed to get steady traffic and to stay busy. For that, she was grateful. Nobody needed to be out of work in this day and age, and she should know.

It sucked trying to get a job, and, for all her best efforts, she was still not getting very far with that. And that just brought her back to the whole lawyer thing. On a whim, she pulled out her phone and sent Nick a text, asking for an update. She got a response almost immediately, saying he didn't have one. She frowned at that, as she pocketed her phone. Just then Mack came flying out of the restaurant, a big bag in his arms. She looked at him in surprise. "Did you get something already?"

He nodded. "I did."

"Are we taking that home?" she asked hopefully.

He said, "Well, we could. Otherwise we can take it down to the beach."

"Beach," she said immediately.

He chuckled, as he moved the large bag onto her lap, brushing Mugs a bit off to the side. Mugs immediately caught the scent of the food and shoved his nose into the side of the bag, putting a great big dent in it.

She told him to get over. "They're hungry too."

"Well, that would be one vote for going home. Unless you think they might have enough to keep them busy at the beach that they'd be okay for a little while."

"They'll be okay for a bit," she said, "but not too much longer."

"Still, they should be doing what we say, not us doing what they say," he said, with a laugh.

"Yeah, that's the theory," she said. As it was, he drove in the direction of home, then took a couple corners away and down to a spot where he parked. "The beach is right here. It's a private little spot."

Curious, she hopped out because she hadn't seen too many beach access areas on the lake. As a matter of fact, she could really use a few more places she could walk to. Then she stepped out with all the animals gathering around, almost tripping her up.

Mack hurried to her side and snatched the food. He waited for her to untangle herself. "You ready?"

She nodded and then followed him down the path, where the beach opened up suddenly. "Wow," she said. "This is beautiful."

"It's not too far from you," he said. "I thought you would enjoy it."

"Absolutely," she said.

Several big logs were off to one side, so he moved to that area. "Are you okay if we sit here, or do you want to sit on the beach itself?"

She looked blissfully at the water. "I'm really hungry, and I would love to walk in the water, but after we eat." She sat down on the log, straddling it, as he did the same, placing the bag on the log between them. "I'm surprised you could get it so fast."

"They do an awful lot of takeout there," he said, "and they're used to people running in and picking up stuff."

"Well, that was running in and picking up all right," she

murmured.

"You looked like you were too tired to deal with the thought of figuring out food or sitting in a restaurant."

"I am," she said. "Something was just so very wrong about Stranden."

"It's definitely a curiosity," he murmured.

"I'm not sure that's the right word. He seemed pretty adamant that Gloria's son had stolen the orchid from him."

"And yet I've known Gloria for many years," he said. "I can't imagine it."

"Maybe it wasn't Gloria. Maybe Stranden was right, and it was the son," she said. "Did you know him?"

He shook his head. "No, I didn't. But I do know her, and I can't imagine that the son would be any different."

"I can," she said immediately. "We've seen it time and time again, where some people are strong upstanding citizens, who wouldn't do anything wrong and who would bend over backward to help somebody. But then you get somebody else in the family, often a child who's been enabled a bit too much," she said gently. "They turn around and make everything bad and ugly for the family because they have a very different perception of what they should get in life. Especially without having to work for it."

"Well, we can't find out anything right now," he said. "So let's eat." He opened up this huge bundle wrapped in newspaper, filled with pieces of fish and another one full of fries.

She immediately snatched up a fry and popped it into her mouth. "Oh, they're still hot."

He nodded. "Another reason why I wanted to go somewhere close, so we could eat a hot meal."

She picked up a ketchup packet and raised an eyebrow

in question. When he nodded, she immediately ripped it open and dumped ketchup on one corner and then repeated it with several other packets. And, while she busily doctored the fries, he split up the fish. But even with four pieces on her side, a pile was still left.

"Wow," she marveled. "How much did you get?"

"Enough that we don't have to worry about being hungry." He smiled. "It's reasonably cheap."

When he told her how much it was, she stared. "For all of this?" He nodded. "Wow," she repeated, looking down at it. "If there was a way to warm it up, I mean, just one of these meals would give me food for several days."

"I hadn't thought of it that way," he said, "but you're right. An air fryer would do the job nicely. We'll have to keep an eye out for a cheap used one for you."

She was quite amazed that, even after she had her four pieces, and he had several more, still more fish was left over. "I'm impressed," she said, finally full. "That is a really good value for the money."

"It certainly is, even for takeout. If you go into the restaurant, it's an all-you-can-eat deal."

"I always wonder about those," she said, "because, when I'm really hungry, I could probably eat more. But, if this is what you get on a normal serving, it's of no advantage because I can't eat more than this anyway."

"And this way you get to take it home," he reminded her.

She beamed. "And I have become a huge fan of leftovers."

"Only because then you don't have to cook for yourself."

She chuckled. "That's very true, but now I can do eggs and pasta and the odd other dish," she said. "Although I haven't been doing too much cooking of late."

"Yes, we have to get back at it," he said, with a serious nod. "I was thinking about something like roast chicken because, if you did that, you would have several meals."

"You mean, from the one chicken?"

"Absolutely," he said, "should be quite a bit of food for you."

She nodded, but thoughts of Stranden wouldn't leave her alone. "I know you don't really want to talk about it, but, if he was the owner of the original orchid, and it was stolen, can anything be done about it?"

He shrugged, shaking his head. "Not unless they're pressing charges, and, in that case, it would probably go through the court system," he said. "I really don't know. I've never come up against something like this."

She didn't want to just put it off to the side and ignore it. "Still, it's hard to minimize how strongly he felt about it."

"I know," he said, "and that—" He paused. "I'll have to talk to Gloria about it."

"Are you sure you don't want to do it now?"

He shook his head. "No, I really don't," he said. "I just want to put all this away and forget about it for now."

She chuckled. "Let me know how that works for you."

He just grinned.

As soon as they were done eating, she gave some of the leftover fish to both Goliath and to Mugs, while Thaddeus pecked away disdainfully at a fry. She got up. "I'll just walk down the beach really quick."

He nodded. "I'll clean this up."

And she left him to it.

She was just tired enough that she didn't feel guilty about it either. As soon as she got to the water's edge, she kicked off her shoes and socks and waded alongside the water's edge. It was just too beautiful. And, with the sun setting, it had been an unbelievable gorgeous day. When Mack finally joined her, she looked up and smiled. "Thank you for bringing me here."

"Not a problem," he said. "It helps to have a few new locations to go to."

"And this one is a beauty." Just then, his phone rang. She looked up. "You're off duty, aren't you?"

He nodded. "Yeah, but it's Dispatch calling."

"Uh-oh." She waited while he took the call, but he stepped away so she couldn't hear. When he returned, his expression was grim. "Now what?"

"I have to go back to work."

She stared at him, frowning. "I thought you just said it was your night off."

"It was."

She heard the finality in his tone. She nodded and headed back to the beach, where her shoes and socks were. "Can you tell me what's wrong?"

"I might as well," he said. "You'll find out soon enough."

"Oh, what's the matter?"

"Gloria," he said.

She looked at him in shock. "What about her?"

"She's dead."

Chapter 10

MACK DROPPED OFF Doreen and her animals at her house. With confusion, wonder, and horrific thoughts rapidly swirling around inside her head, Doreen watched Mack drive away. He hadn't given her any information or details. She knew that Gloria was dead, but he hadn't said it was a murder. The fact that the police had been called in surely would indicate that, but Doreen couldn't be sure of it. She snatched up her phone and quickly texted him. **Was she murdered?**

There was no answer for the longest time, and she figured he was driving. Finally she got his terse response.

I have no idea.

And then nothing.

She stormed around the house, pacing back and forth, wondering, because she wanted to know just so many things, and she knew she wouldn't get answers anytime soon. Finally she made herself a cup of tea, put away the leftovers, and then, sitting outside on her deck with a notepad, her mind working furiously, she wrote down all the things crossing in and out of her consciousness. Gloria could have been murdered. She could have had an accident. She could have died of old age. Gloria had made some serious inroads on longevity, after all.

When Doreen finally calmed down enough, she just sat and relaxed, watching the river flow, as she drank a cup of herbal tea. When her phone rang, and she saw it was Mack, she snatched it up with relief. "And?" she asked impatiently.

After a moment of silence, he said, "Good evening, Doreen. How are you?"

He spoke in such a drawling and sarcastic tone, she winced. "I've been waiting since you left in such a rush," she wailed.

"We don't know anything," he said. "It looks like it could be a natural death."

At that, everything inside her stilled, and she sagged into her deck chair with relief. "Thank the good Lord for that," she whispered.

"I guess you thought she was murdered, huh?"

"Well, you are a cop."

"We are called to unattended deaths too," he reminded her. "And, in this case, I wasn't called as a cop. Her niece asked them to call me."

"Oh." She gave a half laugh. "It would have helped if you'd told me that."

"It wouldn't have helped anything," he said. "You still would have gone in a million different directions and not necessarily come up with the right answer."

"It's a little hard to come up with answers," she said, "when I don't have any details."

"Exactly. I'm on my way home now. The police are here and, because of my connection, I'm not involved in the initial phases."

"Right, that makes sense, I guess. But I didn't think you

knew her that well."

"I don't necessarily, but I was brought in, so I'll be part of the team working on it, but it's better if the forensics team handles everything."

"But why forensics?" she asked sharply. "You said it was a natural death."

He stopped and then more carefully said, "Yes, I did, but we don't know for sure."

She frowned at that. "But you must be thinking there is a possibility that it wasn't. Otherwise no need for forensic evidence."

He groaned. "I forget how fast you pick up on nuances."

"I think I've been involved in enough cases now," she said, "to automatically assume the worst. And that's what you're doing."

"I'm not assuming anything. I'm just being careful."

"Because of that old man Stranden? Or Miriam?"

"Miriam?"

"It seems that this orchid propagation is serious business. Two suspicious medical catastrophes and—"

"Well, Stranden was definitely a bit concerning, wasn't he?" Mack asked.

"There was certainly hatred, anger, frustration, and loss in his voice," she said quietly.

"*Loss*?" he asked.

"Yes, I definitely got a sense of loss. As if Stranden and Gloria had had a relationship a long time ago, and he wasn't the one who ended it."

"I didn't get that at all."

"I did, and remember how he reacted when I asked him about it," she said. "And they're both of an age."

"I think Gloria was quite a bit older."

"How can you tell? Stranden doesn't look to have aged as well as Gloria did. Or can you guess the ages of seniors now?" she asked, with a humorous note. "Plus, I don't think Nan puts an age restriction on any of her friendships."

At that, Mack burst out laughing. "I don't even want to think about that. Yet I'm not sure Nan would turn down anyone who was willing, as long as she was interested."

"No, I'm not so sure about that either." Doreen stared off at her flower garden, absentmindedly noting that the dahlias were in full bloom. "I think it's more of an occasional thing, as long as they're warm and willing and at least have salt-and-pepper hair."

He chuckled. "Your nan is amazing."

"I wonder how she'll take the news," she murmured.

"Did she know Gloria?"

Doreen stopped and frowned. "You know what? I'm not sure. But given her age and Gloria's, you would think so."

"And yet maybe not," he said.

"Right. Who is to say? But I should at least ask her."

"Or not," he said, his tone sharp. "I will."

She sniffed at that. "How will that look?"

"What if I need to ask Nan some formal questions?" he asked.

"Yes, I understand that," she said, "but you know she'll want to talk to me."

"She can talk to you when I'm done."

"Fine," she said, "if you want to be that black-and-white about it."

"I do."

"You're hedging." She shrugged, yet knowing he couldn't see her over the phone. "So, any details?"

"No."

"You said it was natural causes, so I don't understand why you can't tell me something."

"Her niece found her in her chair, sitting, as she'd taken her last breath."

"Oh, wow. So it definitely sounds like natural causes."

"Exactly," he said in exasperation. "Why do you always doubt me?"

"I don't doubt you at all," she said. "I'm basically just confirming your findings. Now what about Miriam?"

"As it turns out, Miriam will be just fine. And she told Edna that she had moved their prized orchid, just as an extra precaution, until someone was in the room with it, which led to her asthma attack. Her EpiPen must have popped out of her pocket when she fell. I haven't spoken to her as yet, but—"

"Oh. Mack, that's wonderful news. Edna will be so relieved. Things were looking so grim, I was afraid we'd found her too late. Have you given any thought to connections, beyond the obvious, of course?"

"Getting a little ahead of yourself, aren't you?" he asked.

"Oh no, I'm just looking at the big picture."

He snorted at that. "Sometimes the little pictures are exactly what they seem—completely innocent."

She chuckled. "Honestly, I'm not trying to get in your way."

"Yet somehow, without even trying, you always manage to."

"I'm just talented that way," she said, chuckling.

"If you say so." He sighed. "Anyway you should be heading off to bed."

"Yep," she said, "and now that I've heard from you, I will."

"What? Were you waiting up for me?"

Just enough curiosity was in his voice that she wondered if she should give him the truth. Then, thinking of what Nan's advice would be, she said, "Of course." She added, with a smirk, "You took off on a case, so, of course, I'd wait up for you."

His heartfelt groan came through the phone, and she laughed. "Besides, I wanted to thank you for such a wonderful day and dinner."

His voice warmed up considerably and made her realize just how much she wished he was here beside her, so she could thank him personally. It really was so much colder over the phone.

"You're welcome," he said. "It was a lot of fun, mostly, wasn't it?"

"It sure was," she said, "even if it had a rough middle and a rough ending."

"Some days have rough endings," he said sadly.

"And, in Gloria's case, well, I don't know about rough, but I know that she lived a long and hopefully mostly happy life. Therefore, we should be happy each day too, shouldn't we?"

"Absolutely. If Gloria hadn't died today, there was a good chance it would have been tomorrow."

"I'll keep that thought in mind," she said. "Not that it's a terribly pleasant one."

"No, but the first guarantee of birth is death," he reminded her.

She winced. "Now that's a cynical attitude."

"It's reality," he said. "It's a matter of making the best of the life that you have, while you're here."

"That sounds like a lecture."

He burst out laughing. "However you want to take it—but I bet Gloria would agree."

"I would imagine you are right on that. Anyway, I'm heading to bed. Good night, Mack, sweet dreams."

She didn't hear his answer as she hung up, but she was still smiling. It really was nice to have that man in her life. And, of course, thinking about that just brought up the fact that she still had one man to get *out* of her life. She frowned at that and sent Nick yet another text, asking for an update. Her phone rang almost immediately.

"For somebody who wanted nothing to do with this," Nick started, "you're awfully pushy."

She winced. "Sorry." She asked hesitantly if there was any news.

"No," he said, "and I'm happy to see you being this active. I'm just a little surprised. You made it sound like you didn't want any communication about him at all."

"I do and I don't," she said. "He drives me to distraction, and I fear what he'll do, and I don't want anything to do with him. Yet I know I'm so much better off to have him gone from my life. But then I realize he isn't gone from my life, and I need to do whatever I must do to get him gone—if that makes any sense."

It was a bit convoluted, but she hoped he understood. And, when he said something a few minutes later, she realized he really did get it. "And thank you for understanding," she murmured.

"Oh, I get it," he said. "It's just fascinating, that's all."

"What's fascinating?"

"Being anxious to have it done. I just wondered if there was a reason."

And now that hint of humor was in his voice, and she

realized where he was going with this. "Not particularly." She tried for a cool, sophisticated tone. Where the heck was all that breeding that had been forced into her all those years about hitting the right tone? "I'm just enjoying life right now, and I don't want him to come around and ruin it all again."

"I get it." He was still chuckling. "I'll let you know as soon as I know anything." And, with that, he rang off.

She winced, staring down at the phone. "I didn't handle that well, did I?"

But nothing to be done about it. Nick thought she was sweet on Mack, and she thought she was sweet on Mack too. She was just a long way from being in any position to do anything about it. Mostly because she didn't dare start something she couldn't finish, and, while she still had her husband hanging around, it felt like that was exactly what she was doing.

"And then again," she muttered to Mugs—who didn't seem to notice, as he was still stretched out at her feet, exhausted from the day's outing—"it sounds more like I'm just making excuses."

And what was she supposed to do with that? She got up, wandered down to the creek at the back of her yard, stood at the river's edge, and studied the water that flowed calmly downstream.

"Look at the stones now, Mugs," she called out. "We can walk out here easily." She wasn't even sure when the water level had gotten this low, but now the rocks on either side were showing up. Even the rocks in the middle now gave her some sort of a divider line along it. Mugs suddenly stood at her side and barked, as if realizing that she hadn't gone to bed and instead was down at the water. She bent down and cuddled him slightly, only to see Goliath sitting on one of the big rocks along the edge of the river.

"Goliath, don't do it," she warned. He just looked at her, then reached out one paw and tapped the edge of the water. She stared at him in shock. "You don't like water," she cried out, stepping toward him. He got up on his haunches and it looked like he would fall for a moment. She stopped in shock. "Goliath, don't get wet," she said. "I don't know how hard the water flow is now, but it would be hard to get you out."

She knew, for sure, she'd end up soaking wet. On a nice hot sunny day, she might be okay with that, but, in the evening, when it was cool, she really didn't want to go for a swim. She realized he was taunting her. "Goliath, don't you dare." She tried to make her voice stern.

But he continued to look at her and tapped the water ever-so-slightly with his claws extended.

She realized just his claws dragged through the water, not actually his paw getting wet. She stopped, standing still, and stared at him. "You're worse than a two-year-old," she announced. And, at that, his nose went up, and he twisted, sending one of his back legs sky-high, and he proceeded to clean his butt.

She stared. "And you're in the most precarious position I've ever seen you in," she cried out. "Why the devil can't you come over to the shore and do that?"

Almost immediately she heard a flutter of wings, and Thaddeus headed toward the cat. "No, no, Thaddeus, don't!" But, sure enough, he tried to land on the rock beside the big cat, but, instead he hit Goliath on the shoulder. Goliath howled and spun, landing on the rock, looking for a moment as if he would be fine; then he slid right into the river. She cried out, racing toward him, completely flabbergasted to see his claws hanging on to the rock, as he slowly pulled himself back up on top. He glared at Thaddeus, who moved off to the side and made some muttered comment that she swore sounded like an apology.

Goliath launched himself from the rock onto shore, where he shook out his fur, and afterward raced up to the house. Stunned, she stared at Thaddeus, who now paraded back and forth on the same rock, as if he were the king of the castle.

"Did you do that on purpose?" Thaddeus spun around, then pinned his beady-eyed gaze on her and started to cackle. She shook her head. "I don't want to believe you just did that." And he cackled louder. "Thaddeus," she said, in a stern and scolding tone.

But he completely ignored her and turned, with his wings out, and then hunched them around his head. "*He-he-he.*"

She was completely flummoxed. But, at the same time, coincidence was something Mack wasn't a fan of, and she was starting to believe that here. But did that apply to birds? Particularly one as crazy as Thaddeus?

Sunday Morning

THE NEXT MORNING, she found herself eyeing Thaddeus with a wary look, as she made coffee in the kitchen, plating up some cheese and crackers for her breakfast. As she opened the rear kitchen door, he fluttered out ahead of her, and she muttered, "I'm still not sure if you didn't do that on purpose." He completely ignored her, which is what she would have expected all the time. But she watched as Goliath came out and gave the bird a wide berth as well.

"Good choice, Goliath. We don't want to take any chances, do we?" Goliath shot her a look, and, with every step he took, his tail twitched and curled in the air. He had long since gotten dry, but she knew it would be a long time before he made that mistake again. Or maybe not. At least she hadn't had to go for a swim to save him. And, while Mugs would have been more than happy to jump into the fray, it had all happened so fast that he had basically missed the entire scenario.

And that just brought up more laughter in her mind. She knew that retelling this story to Nan and Mack would give her lots of mileage and laughter. As she sat down outside on her deck at her table and chairs, with her first cup of coffee, nibbling on her cheese and crackers, she checked her watch, wincing at the time. It was already eight, and she hadn't even gotten halfway through her cup of coffee when her phone rang.

When she saw it was Nan, she immediately snatched it up. "Hey," she said. "How are you doing?" She heard sniffles on the other end, and Doreen knew Nan had heard about Gloria. "I'm sorry," she said. "I gather you heard the news."

"Mack called me," she said. "How dare you not tell me?"

Doreen winced. "He told me that I wasn't allowed to."

"So," Nan said, "since when would you allow that to stop you? I'm your grandmother, and you should have told me."

"Would it have made you sleep any better?"

"Of course not," she said. "I wouldn't have slept at all."

"Exactly. And you could do nothing for her, so finding out this morning was not the worst idea."

At that, Nan sounded a little mollified. "Fine," she said, "but it would have been better if the news had come from you."

"I figured you would have heard the news already from somebody at the center."

"Nobody heard."

"Ah, so you're the first to hand out the news then, correct?"

Nan gasped. "Oh my."

Almost as if Doreen could hear the wheels turning in her grandmother's head, she warned, "Just no betting on it, right?"

"What's to bet on?" Nan snapped. "Gloria was my friend."

"How long did you know her?" she asked quietly.

"Decades," she said. "Absolutely decades. She was a lovely woman." And genuine warmth filled Nan's voice.

Now standing at her creek again, Doreen stared across at the water, still shaking her head when she caught images in her mind of what had happened last night. "I'm sorry, Nan," she said. "You're losing lots of friends."

"This one was a real friend," she said. "Lots of the others were just people I knew."

And, of course, there was a distinction, one that Nan did make fairly clear when it came to various people in her life. "I'm sorry," she said. "It's still tough."

"Very, and her niece? I already talked to her. I'll help her with funeral arrangements."

"That's nice of you," she said warmly. "I'm sure she could use the help."

"You could offer too, you know."

"I think there'll probably be lots of people around here

to help, without a stranger butting in."

"Maybe, … but, when you think about it, a stranger butting in is only a stranger until you butt in," she said. "Then you become either a pain in the butt or a friend."

"Or you become somebody who just butted in where they weren't wanted," Doreen snapped back.

"Which means you're the pain in the butt."

"Which I don't intend to become," she said. "I don't know these people, and I didn't get a sense that I was terribly welcome."

"Oh dear," she said, "it's always hard being the one on the outside, isn't it?"

"It is what it is," Doreen said. "Personally I'm quite happy to skip making funeral arrangements." It seemed like there'd been a lot of death in her world lately. And, as long as she could keep out of the more miserable side of the arrangements, the better, as far as she was concerned. "So I guess you'll be busy all day with her then?"

"No, I don't think so," she said. "Elle will take some time and figure out what she wants to do."

"A celebration of life sounds like a good idea to me."

A moment of pause came on the other side. "See? You are better at this than I am."

"No, it's just what I've heard a lot of people are doing lately," she murmured, "which sounds a whole lot better than a funeral to me."

"No, you're quite right there," she said. "Besides, funerals are stuffy, and that's not Gloria at all."

"What was she like?"

"Did you meet her at all?"

"I did last night, over the orchids," she said.

"Oh, those dreaded orchids," Nan said.

"What about them?" Doreen asked.

"They became her life, after her son passed away. They were a hobby before, but, once he passed away, they became an obsession," she murmured. "I told her often that it wasn't healthy, but she told me the last time to mind my own business." Nan went off in peals of reminiscent laughter. "Gloria was good that way. She was good to me and good for me."

"But still quite an age difference, wasn't there?"

"Oh, decades," Nan said.

Doreen frowned because she didn't think that many years were between them. One decade maybe. Nan had to be eighty-something. But Doreen wondered if Nan was taking license with the fact that Doreen didn't know exactly how old her nan was—or how old Gloria was. "She sounded like she was quite lovely. I did meet her with the orchid tour, but last night she did look very tired."

"It's all just way too much for her," Nan said. "I told her to calm down and to relax about it all, but she was determined that her orchid win best in show."

"Why is that?" Doreen pondered.

"Because of her son of course. It was his orchid that she was so intent on getting perfect."

"*Hmm*," Doreen murmured. "Maybe she'll win."

"If I could bribe anybody to make it happen, I would."

"I don't think it matters at this point in time," Doreen said gently.

"Of course it matters," Nan said.

"Well, Gloria won't know," she said.

There was a moment of silence. "You don't know that." And, with a sniff, Nan hung up on her.

Doreen stared down at the phone. "Did I say something

wrong?" she asked Mugs, who sat attentively at her side, staring at her plate of cheese, and now at the few crackers. She glared at the dog. "Oh no, you don't. I need to eat something."

But she also had leftover fish-and-chips. She thought about that for breakfast and wondered if Mack intended to claim some of it. She hoped not because she really could use it herself. But that would be the height of selfishness, since he had paid for it. She picked up the cheese and crackers and started munching. "It's not much of a breakfast, but it's what I've got."

Mugs barked, jumped up on his back legs, and placed his front paws on her thigh. She sighed, picked up a piece of cheese, and offered it to him. It disappeared so fast she wasn't even sure if he got it or not. She shook her head at him. "I did feed you already, you know."

As if he were working to get more food out of her, he gave her the most woeful look out of those huge chocolate-colored eyes. She reached down, scrubbed those ears gently, and gave him a big hug. "You are definitely my best friend." And, with that, Goliath, as big as he was, landed with the softest of jumps on the patio table beside her. She looked at him and chuckled. "And there's no cheese left for you either."

He looked at her suspiciously, sniffed all around the plate, and then walked over and batted her shoulder with his head. She immediately cradled his huge head with both hands. She loved the little tufts of hair coming off his ears. She kissed him gently and gave him a hug and a cuddle. "Feeling a little bit lost after your swim?"

His diesel engine kicked in, and he just rubbed against her, melting her heart. Mugs was still standing up on his back legs, so with one hand on each of the animals, she spent the next few minutes petting them. When finally Mugs jumped down, she picked up her coffee and had the rest of it in a big sip. She pushed her chair back, then stood. "Just wait right there. I'll go get more coffee and more cheese."

She walked back into the kitchen with her empty plate, sliced up a bit more cheese, and added a few crackers. Quickly filling her coffee cup, she headed back outside again. As she sat down, a stranger walked along the river at the back of her yard. He lifted a hand in greeting, and she immediately called out, "Good morning."

Mugs started barking incessantly, racing toward the river. "Mugs, come back here," she yelled, wincing, because he'd never done that before. It was not like they got very many people coming along the creek, but Mugs was definitely getting more territorial, and, of course, since she had taken down her fence, there was nothing to stop Mugs from racing up and down the river's edge, chasing people. She ran to the edge to see Mugs standing there, at the edge of the property, barking and barking and barking.

"*Woof, woof, woof.*"

She grabbed him by the collar and scolded him. "That's enough of that." She saw no sign of the man who had lifted a hand to her. But then Mugs may have chased him away at a flat-out run. She wondered briefly who it was, but it could have been anybody—or nobody. With Mugs under control, she brought him back to the deck, then quickly realized that her cheese was missing.

Goliath sat there, just looking at her, as he licked his paw.

"Seriously?" she asked, shocked. "Since when did you start eating cheese?"

Of course he didn't answer. She wasn't sure what she expected, but it certainly wasn't to lose some of her breakfast. She picked up a bare cracker and munched away, glaring at the cat. And then she studied Thaddeus, sitting on the chair across from her, with a piece of cheese in his mouth.

"You?" she cried out.

Thaddeus flapped his wings in the air and cried back, "You?"

"Oh no you don't," she snapped. "We're not doing this imitation stuff. No way." He cackled once, then hopped up onto the table. Immediately Goliath jumped down and took off. She snorted.

"Yeah, I don't blame you, Goliath. He also got you in trouble over the cheese. I thought it was you, and I'm so sorry." Goliath stalked off, stiff-legged, his tail in the air. She glared at Thaddeus. "What the devil is going on with you right now?" She glared at him. And there were really no answers that she could get from him, but it made her happier just to yell at him. Then she relented. "I guess you must have been hungry."

He gave her a gentle look, then crawled his way over toward her, leaned in close, and whispered, "Thaddeus loves Doreen."

Once again, her heart melted. She scooped him up into her arms, hugged him ever-so-gently, and buried her face in the softest feathers she'd ever been close to in her life, just cuddling him. "You might love me," she said, "but you do drive me to distraction."

He snuggled in deeper. He really didn't care what distraction he caused her or what trouble he was; he was all about Thaddeus. But then, all animals were. She was just blessed that they agreed to spend some time with her as it was.

At that, she chuckled because most nonanimal lovers would think she was nuts. But she could only hope that animal lovers could relate totally. Especially about the cat part. Something about Goliath always made her feel like she should be grateful that he managed to spend even a few moments with her. Mugs was just delighted to be with her; absolutely nothing was devious or egocentric about him.

But Thaddeus? She wasn't quite so sure because the jury was still out on that recent behavior of his. And it's not like she was well versed in animal language anyway. She was learning as she went. Sometimes she did pretty well, and other times they just completely mystified her.

As she finished the last cup of coffee in the pot and sat here mulling over what to do with the day ahead of her, a scream ripped through the neighborhood.

Chapter 11

DOREEN BOLTED TO her feet and raced up the river path toward the sound. As she got up several houses past her cul-de-sac, she then followed the screams across the street. She came across a woman, standing on her backyard deck, shrieking at the top of her lungs. Racing toward her, Doreen immediately noted that she didn't appear to be injured—no blood, no visible wounds. Doreen patted the woman's shoulder, asking, "What's the matter? What's the matter?"

The woman seemed to be somewhere in her sixties or seventies. But, heck, what did Doreen know? This woman could have been eighty or ninety, after seeing Gloria.

The woman finally stopped screaming, and she stared at her, but she visibly trembled. "Somebody's in my house," she cried out. "Somebody's in my house."

Doreen highly doubted anybody was in the house at this point in time. That shrieking should have been enough to bring multiple neighbors outside—and the intruder to leave the premises—but, as Doreen looked around, she was the only one here. "I'll go inside and take a look."

She stepped toward the house but the older woman

grabbed her arm. "No, no, don't. He'll be in there still."

"Why is that?" she asked. The woman didn't have an answer for her. "But you're scared that he still is, right?"

She nodded carefully.

"What did you see?"

"I came down the stairs, and he was in the living room, opening up the cabinet under the TV," she said, "my husband's cabinet."

Such a bewildered look was in the woman's gaze that Doreen wondered if shock had hit her yet. "Do you think he was looking for something?"

The woman just stared at her blankly.

"When you started screaming, what did he do?"

"When I was screaming, I raced for the kitchen," she said, "to come out here."

"So you didn't see where he went, right?"

The older woman shook her head. "No, I think he's still in there. I think he was looking for something."

"What was inside that cabinet?"

The woman shrugged. "My husband's stuff—the VCR and his tapes. He's got some of those old recording machines. I don't know." She waved her hand. "We need to call the police."

Doreen privately agreed, but she was also itching to get inside the house and see who the stranger was. She pulled out her phone and called Mack. "There's been a break-in at my neighbor's house," she said. "I heard the screaming and came over, and we're standing on the back deck. She found a man in her living room, going through the cabinet under the TV."

"How many houses away from you? What's her address?" She turned to the woman who recited it carefully.

"Okay, I'll be there in a minute."

Doreen ended the call, put her cell back into her pocket, and smiled at the woman. "A detective is on his way." Relief washed over the older woman's face, but her body still shook. "Is there somebody I can call for you?" Doreen asked in concern. "Do you have any siblings or any children here?"

The woman took a moment to pull herself together, and she nodded. "My son is in town. Maybe I should call him." But she hesitated. "I know he's at work, and he gets in trouble if he gets personal phone calls."

"Ah," she said, "I'm sure Mack will contact him anyway, when he gets here. What about your husband? A friend? Do you have anybody you can call to come stay with you?"

The woman shook her head. "No, I'll be fine." She looked nervously at the house.

"We won't go in there until Mack is here, and we'll get him to check over the place. Did you lock up?"

She nodded. "I always keep it locked. … Ever since my husband passed away, I've kept it locked. Oh dear," she said, "I don't even know that I want to stay here anymore."

"Was it ever a question?"

"My son doesn't want me to stay here. He wants me to go to that *home*," she said, with disgust in her voice as she got the words out.

"You mean, Rosemoor?"

The woman recoiled, as if that were the worst name possible. "Yes."

"My nan is down there," she said, "and she loves it."

At that, the woman stopped and stared. "Isn't she locked to her bed overnight? Don't they keep her inside and force medications down her throat to keep her quiet?"

Doreen stared at her openmouthed. "What? Oh, heavens, no," she said. "She has a nice little patio and a small kitchenette. I go see her all the time. If you ever want to see for yourself," she said, "I can take you and give you a tour. I know Richie. I know many of the people down there now."

The woman looked like she didn't believe any word of it.

"Where did you hear those awful rumors?"

"Everybody knows it's a home, and they all know what happens when you're in a home. You get locked up and force-fed medication until you die."

"Wow." Doreen didn't know what to say to that. She stared at the woman. "Well, it might be time to figure out the truth of that," she said, "because I guarantee you that's not how it is at Rosemoor."

The woman sniffed. "I've heard of people who live there," she said. "You can't convince me otherwise."

Not at all sure what to say to this woman, who seemed to have such strong feelings about the matter, Doreen was relieved to hear Mack's vehicle coming up the drive. "The police are here," she said calmly.

The woman looked at her in surprise. "I don't hear sirens."

"No, it sounds like Mack came in his own truck." As the woman looked at her suspiciously, Doreen shrugged, pulled out her phone, and texted him. **We're on the back deck.**

But when he walked through the kitchen door, the woman in front of her shrieked. "It's the intruder."

"No, it's not." Doreen grabbed the older woman's hands firmly. "This is Mack." Doreen looked at him. "You came through the front door?"

"It was unlocked," he said, "and this guy was standing on the front step, waiting for me."

Doreen looked down to see Mugs, his tail wagging furiously, as he wove between Mack's legs.

"Of course he was." She shook her head. And then she turned to look at the woman. "What's your name?"

She looked over at the big man fearfully. "Amie, *I-E*," she said. "Amie, *I, E*."

At that, Doreen frowned. "*IE* is your last name?"

The woman looked at her as if she were completely bonkers. "No. Amie, with an *I* and an *E*, not a *Y*," she clarified. Then she looked at Mack. "I need to see some identification."

He nodded. "Absolutely." He pulled his badge from his pocket and handed it over. The woman looked at it, pulled out her own phone, and punched a couple buttons, calling what Doreen presumed was speed-dial for her son.

"Jonathan, I have a policeman here. At least I think it's a policeman. How do I tell?"

Doreen heard a sound of exasperation on the other end of the phone, but Amie read the badge number off to him. "Do you think it's real?" she said. "It could be fake. Maybe he bought it at a Halloween store or something."

Doreen barely managed to keep a straight face, as she looked over at Mack. He shook his head ever-so-slightly, and she realized it probably wasn't the first time he'd come up against this. But, for Doreen, this was hilarious. Finally the woman hung up her phone, looked over at Mack suspiciously, and returned the badge. "He says you're okay."

"I'm glad to hear that," he said gently. "Now, do you want to tell me what happened?"

"Not much to tell." But she gave Mack the same story that she had told Doreen.

Mack nodded. "So you didn't get a good look at him."

"Well, I certainly didn't ask for his name," Amie said in exasperation. "I came straight outside. That's what my son and my husband always told me to do."

"And it's a good call," he said. "Did you see anything about him?"

"Only that he was bending over my husband's cabinet." She looked toward the living room. "I should check to see if he stole anything."

"Would you know?" Doreen asked suddenly.

The woman looked at her and then slowly shook her head. "It was my husband's stuff," she said. "It was just lots of boxes of things."

"Boxes?"

"You know, like, VCRs and DVDs and things like that. Black boxes, all different sizes."

She watched Mack's lips twitch ever-so-slightly and realized that dealing with this woman was something that he had seen before, and he was doing a very good job at being respectful. On the other hand, Doreen was full of curiosity.

"Interesting," she murmured. "So I guess it's back to that same question. If he did steal something, who would know?"

"I don't know." Then she brightened. "My son would know."

"Does he know all the stuff that your husband was involved in?"

The woman looked at her askance. "What do you mean?"

"I just mean the stuff that he would have kept in that cupboard, the VCR and DVD stuff or whatever?" she said, confusing herself even further.

The woman looked at her, then at Mack. "I don't know.

I didn't have anything to do with that."

"Right," she said, "which is why I was wondering if your son would know."

"He knows everything." She gave a firm nod.

"Ah, well, that's good then." Doreen frowned, mentally shaking her head. "Maybe we should call him."

"Oh no, I told you that he doesn't like to be disturbed at work."

Doreen looked at her, puzzled. "But you just called him."

The woman seemed confused for a moment, looked down at her phone. "Did I?"

Mack gently said, "I'll need his name and phone number."

"Oh no, you can't call him at work," she said. "He gets angry."

"You just talked to him, and he didn't get angry. I am the police, and I will be calling him,"

The woman frowned. "I'm not allowed to give out phone numbers and names either."

Mack just studied her for a moment.

"Even to the police?" Doreen asked.

"You can't always trust the police," the woman said, with a sniff. "I don't know who he is."

Doreen pinched the bridge of her nose but nodded carefully. "Apparently. No, that's quite true. Maybe he did get his badge at a Halloween store." She tried to keep her words under her breath, but Mack caught them and glared at her. She shrugged. "Now that everything is okay, I'll let you handle this," she said, and she slowly called the animals to her and backed off.

"Wait," the old woman said. "I don't even know who

you are."

"I'm your neighbor," she said. "A few houses down. When you started screaming, I came running."

"I don't think I screamed that loudly," the woman said. "I'm sure I wouldn't have. That would be—" And she stopped, frowned. "It wouldn't be proper."

"When you are being proper, then you won't scream quite so loudly," she said. "But, this time, you were scared. Let's not forget you had an intruder in your house."

The woman nodded in relief. "Exactly," she said. "It was nice meeting you." She turned back to Mack. "Now you need to take him away."

It was all Doreen could do to keep the giggles at bay, as she heard Mack ask, "Take who away?"

"The intruder of course." The older woman raised her hands in the air. "Didn't you hear me?"

"Yes, I heard you, but nobody's in the living room."

"I told you exactly where he was."

Mack said, "You need to show me then. Maybe I just couldn't see him."

And he used such a properly humble tone that Doreen stopped in fascination, as she watched them walk back into the house. She desperately wanted to go inside and see whatever it was that they would be looking at. And, of course, with Mack there, Doreen really didn't have any right or any reason to barge inside.

Then Goliath tore off into the house.

Racing after her cat, knowing that was the last thing Mack needed, she called out, "Goliath, Goliath, don't! Stop! Come here, please!"

Just as she got inside, Mack stood at a doorway off the living room, where he'd come through, an odd look on his face.

Doreen raced up behind him. "What?"

He shook his head and motioned her away. "Go back." He spoke in such an authoritative tone that she knew it was serious. The old woman was standing here as well.

"See? I told you that he was there."

Doreen couldn't help herself, and she peered around the corner. This was like a den, more of a family room, but there was definitely a big TV and an open cabinet.

But also a man lying on the ground, blood pouring from his head.

Chapter 12

HOURS LATER MACK stomped through Doreen's kitchen. "How?" he asked, raising both hands in frustration. "How do you always get involved?"

"I didn't do anything," she said for the umpteenth time, as he paced back and forth. He'd been going through the kitchen into the living room, then back through the kitchen and out on the deck, before returning and retracing his steps. She knew he was frustrated and upset, but honestly it wasn't her fault.

"I don't know anything about it." She held her chin high. "This woman's scream just ripped through the neighborhood, and I went running. What was I supposed to do? Ignore it?" He stopped and glared at her. She frowned. "You're kidding, right?" But he didn't answer. "Fine! Next time some poor old woman screams for help, I'll just turn my back on her."

He rolled his eyes, walked to the kitchen counter, and proceeded to put on a pot of coffee.

"I think you've had enough caffeine," she said primly.

"There isn't enough caffeine in the world today," he countered right back.

She looked at the frustration on his face and realized he could be right. "So who killed him?"

He shook his head.

"Did Amie?"

He looked at her. "You tell me. You were the first on the scene."

Her jaw dropped, as she thought about it. "I guess I was."

"No doubt you were," he said. "That makes you a witness." And he gave her one of those hard grins. "That means lots of questions."

She shook her head. "No, no. No questions. I get to ask the questions."

"Not this time." He rubbed his hands together. "And that's exactly why you can't get any more involved because you're already involved."

"Right, so what's asking a few more questions then?"

"No way," he said. "Not happening."

She glared at him. "You're enjoying this."

"Oh, I absolutely am, now that you mention it," he said. "I might enjoy this case after all."

"An intruder was murdered in an old woman's house," she said. "What is to enjoy? It's probably a cut-and-dried, open-and-shut case. The old lady maybe came downstairs, saw somebody there, and banged him over the head with something, then ran outside and started screaming."

"Motive?"

"Fear," she said, "nothing else."

"You know what? That might just work."

"Of course it works. I mean, when you're terrified, you do all kinds of things you don't think about," she muttered. "So, a completely rational person, who has time to think about it, wouldn't have that reaction. Maybe they would just run outside, but anybody, depending on the circumstances in her life, might attack this guy and take off."

He stared at her. "We'll have to see what the coroner says."

"Yep, you do that." She stopped and stared. "When did he die anyway?"

"I don't have a time of death yet." He glared at her. "And you won't be the first person I tell."

"Of course not," she said. "I'd expect you to tell somebody else first. But I do want to be in the loop, so make me at least third or fourth."

He snorted. "As if."

She grinned at him. "There could be a bunch of other reasons too, you know. He just—I don't know. Maybe he got petrified when he saw her and tripped, hitting his head on the cupboard, killing himself."

"Maybe, but not likely."

"It depends. Was something sitting on the top of that cupboard? Maybe it came down and cracked him in the head. Some people have those really soft egg-shelly skulls," she said.

"Now you're conjecturing. We don't do that. Remember?"

"We do it a lot," she pointed out. "Every case, in fact." He sighed. "I know we're not supposed to, but that's a different story."

"Nothing is a different story with you." He groaned. "I still can't believe you're the one who was there."

"But I didn't see anything. She was standing outside already."

"Are you sure about that?"

She nodded. "Yes, she was outside on the deck, screaming and shaking in absolute terror."

"And you're sure?"

"I've told you over and over again. Yes, I'm sure."

"Could she have been faking it?"

At that, she stopped and looked at him, realizing that he had to consider other avenues, even hers, and she smiled. "She wasn't faking the shaking," she said. "If something else could have made her shake, then maybe, but she certainly wasn't faking that."

"What do you mean by that?"

"All I'm saying is, maybe she takes a drug or something, or maybe she has a condition that makes her shake, but she was definitely shaking."

He frowned. "I hadn't considered that either."

"Exactly, we're missing a lot of information," she said. "So, whenever you guys get to it, we could really use some more details."

He glared at her, then turned when he heard the pot *beep* to say the coffee was done and poured himself one. She cleared her throat, and he reached for her cup and poured her a second one.

"You're in a fine mood today, aren't you?" she said cheerfully.

"Yeah, because, once again, I find you right smack in the middle of a murder investigation." He turned, then glared at her. "*My* murder investigation."

"I don't think that you mean that you were murdered," she said, trying for clarification, "but that I'm involved in one of your cases."

He groaned and stormed outside again.

"I was just trying to make it clear, since what you said

was confusing."

He shook his head and continued down to the river's edge.

She followed him, frowning, realizing how upset he really was. "I didn't get hurt, you know?" she reminded him carefully. That didn't seem to help much. He sat down on the grass, holding the cup of coffee in his hand. "So, two things. First, I did see a man, all dressed in black, walk up the pathway a little bit earlier in the day."

He immediately turned and looked at her. "How early?"

"With my first cup of coffee," she said. "He reached up a hand in greeting, and I called out a good morning, and he carried on. He was gone really fast, it seemed."

"And how soon after you saw him did the woman scream?"

"Almost immediately," she said slowly. "Like, *five to ten minutes* immediately."

"Seriously? You saw him? That means you were probably the last one to see him alive."

"Except for the killer. And that's good, isn't it?"

"No," he said, "it's not good at all."

"Why not?" And this time she really was confused.

He groaned. "You're completely messing with my case."

"Well, I haven't done anything," she said, "so that's pretty unfair of you."

He glared at her. "Unfair of me?" His tone was ominous.

She snorted. "You act like I did this on purpose."

"If I thought for one minute you had done this on purpose," he said, "I'd be a heck of a lot angrier."

She frowned, as she realized he really was serious. "I didn't get hurt. I was just heeding a person's cry for help," she said, "and that's all I did."

"I know," he said. "That's why I'm not that angry. I'm more worried."

"Why?"

"Because what if that guy was still there? What if he wasn't dead? What if he came outside, prepared to run to get away from the screaming woman, or really wanted information from her or something that he couldn't find, and found you there?"

She looked at him. "I think that's a stretch."

He shook his head. "You're not even listening to me, are you?"

"Not a whole lot to listen to yet," she said. "So far, all we have is supposition." She warmed to her subject. "You know how well we do with that."

"There is no *we* in this," he said in a defeated tone.

"Of course there is." She gave him a bright smile. She leaned over, wrapped her arms around him. "It seems to me that what you really need is a hug."

He stilled for a moment and then nodded.

"You know I'm right," she said.

He pulled the coffee cup out of her hands and placed it beside his; then, taking her hands, he tugged her down to sit on the grass beside him, and he just held her.

Immediately she hugged him back. "I'm sorry." He was really bothered by the incident. "I didn't mean to scare you."

"You never mean to scare me," he said. "You never mean to get in the middle of trouble either, but somehow you always end up there."

"I should get points for having tried to help a neighbor," she said, trying for a reasonable tone. "And I should get points for listening to you as soon as you got there and for following your instructions. I should also get bonus marks," she said, "for calling you in the first place."

His eyebrow shot up. "You think this is some game, where we're ratcheting up points?"

"Of course not," she said. "Nothing about murder is a game. But, while you're sitting here, knocking me for all these things that I may have done or may have gotten involved in, you should realize just how many positive things balance out the negatives."

"Now, if only I could really truly believe that," he muttered. "The captain will have a field day with this."

"The captain doesn't have a problem with me, does he?"

"No. Not normally. Not until you start messing with our cases."

"I haven't done anything in a long time with any of your cases."

He snorted at that. "How about the last one, the one just last week, or the one the week before that?"

"Does he get a bigger budget for closing out these cases?"

"He is getting some positive support because we're closing so many cases," he muttered. "And that's probably the only reason he is okay having you around."

"I certainly hope it's more than that," she snapped. "I mean, I am legitimately trying to help."

"And often times you are helping," he said, "but that doesn't mean we aren't constantly using the entire police force, trying to catch up on all your cases and keeping you safe in the midst of it all."

"So, are you upset because I'm giving you overtime and all this extra work, or are you upset because the captain will be mad at you?"

"I am not upset because the captain will be mad at me," he roared. "How could you even say that?" He turned his back ever-so-slightly, dropping his arms from her and reaching for his coffee cup.

"Make sure you're drinking from your cup," she said quietly at his side. And that didn't even get a response. Finally she sighed. "What was I supposed to do?"

"I don't know," he said. "How about stay at home and call the cops?"

"Because a woman screamed?"

He nodded. "That would be what most people would do. Yes."

"Oh," she said. "See? I didn't even think about calling 9-1-1. I just called you."

"And I get that," he said, "and, believe me, it's a good thing you did. I'm really happy you did. That was the right thing to do."

"So, I'm in trouble for doing the right thing?"

He gave a very long slow exhale and then turned to her. "Are you being deliberately difficult?"

She quirked a smile at him. "Maybe a little," she said hopefully. "I was trying to ease the anger."

He let out another long slow deep breath.

"See? That's helping, isn't it?" She tried coaxing a smile out of him.

"Not enough," he said ominously.

She sighed. "Okay, well, keep doing a few more deep breaths then." He burst out laughing. And she grinned, with a refutable good humor. "See? I am good for you."

"I'm sure you are," he said. "At least sometimes."

"All the time," she said.

"No, I wouldn't go that far."

She frowned. "I really am coming from the heart."

"I get it," he said. "You've said that time and time again.

I get it."

"But you don't really believe it, do you?"

"I believe that you believe it," he said. "I just don't know that anybody else would listen to your methodology and agree."

"Oh dear," she said. "I guess it is what it is then. But do you want something else to make you smile?"

He looked at her, raised an eyebrow. "What?"

And she told him about what happened to Goliath. Mack glanced at her for a moment, then at the river, back at Thaddeus, who was even now sitting in front of them on the rock. "Are you kidding me?"

She was giggling so hard it was almost impossible to answer him, but she finally managed to say, "No, and poor Goliath raced all the way home, soaking wet. I am certain that Thaddeus targeted him intentionally."

At that, Mack started to laugh, really laugh, and she realized this was just the release he needed—from the stress of the day, finding her involvement in yet another death case, last night's strain from losing a friend, and everything else in between.

When he finally stopped, he was lying on the grass, wiping the tears from his eyes.

"See? I am good for you," she said. "I knew it."

He pulled her on top of his chest. "You absolutely are." And he kissed her.

Chapter 13

DOREEN LIFTED HERSELF off Mack's chest, completely surprised. With his eyes shaded, he studied her for a long moment. "Did that upset you?"

She shook her head, embarrassed, flustered, not sure what to say. "No, of course not." She brushed the grass off herself and shifted ever-so-slightly, then spied the coffee cups. Hers was sitting off to the one side, and she quickly snagged it up and used it to keep her hands occupied. Thaddeus, on the other hand, had seen what Mack had done, and let out a loud *caw-caw*. And another. And another.

She stared at him. "Where does he get these noises?

"That one, most anywhere." Mack had a big grin on his face.

She looked over at him and smiled. "His timing though …"

"Impeccable as always," he said, still laughing. "Not too many birds do what he does."

"Good," she said. "Can you imagine more than one Thaddeus?"

He groaned. "I can't imagine more of any of you. And

poor Goliath, he would be tormented all the time."

She smiled. "You know what? I still don't know if Thaddeus did it on purpose, but a part of me says he definitely did."

Mack chuckled. "So have you forgiven me?"

"For the kiss?" she asked, trying not to be too difficult about it.

"Yes, for the kiss."

She tossed her hair over her shoulder, studied him quietly. "I don't need to forgive you. You didn't see me resisting, did you?"

At that, a slow smile dawned across his face. "You really weren't, were you?"

"Nope, I really wasn't," she said, "but that doesn't mean that you have full license to do it again."

"Nah," he said, "at least not at the moment." And, with that, he sat up, grabbed his coffee, and took another big drink. But a quietly pleased look was on his face.

She knew they had turned a corner; she just wasn't exactly sure what corner it was. Well, she wouldn't fool herself though. She knew exactly where they were heading. She just wasn't sure she was ready for it. "You know I can't go down this pathway until I deal with my ex, right?"

"I know you think you can't," he said.

"I just …" She stopped because there really wasn't any logical explanation, except that it was important to her.

"Hey," he said, "no pressure. It's okay."

"Is it?" she asked, hating the fact that tears nearly clogged her throat.

He reached over, gently rubbed her shoulder. "Definitely, it is. It's fine."

She took a long slow breath and let it out, almost imitating his earlier actions. "If you say so," she said. "It just feels so wrong to have him back in my life at all."

"Has he contacted you again?"

She shook her head. "No. Not since my divorce lawyer's murder." She raised her hands in frustration. "That's not quite true. Not since I told you about him asking me about the divorce and saying he wasn't prepared to pay anything like that. And I have to admit I have been contacting your brother over and over again, almost incessantly, trying to see if there's any action. Nick called me last night, after I'd texted him again, surprised at my change in attitude."

"What was the change?"

"Because before I apparently sounded like I didn't even want to hear any updates. I just wanted it all to go away. But now, well, not only do I want updates," she admitted, "I want it all to go away, and I want to know what we can do to make it go away faster."

"That's a good thing," Mack murmured, gently studying her with those huge eyes of his.

She smiled and shrugged. "Maybe. I just … I'm not even sure what to say anymore. Everything is so dramatic and confused."

"That's only because we can't really do much about it," he said, "and we're stuck waiting for something to happen."

"Which is why I'm trying to keep busy in the meantime."

With an exasperated voice, yet clearly teasing, he said, "Could you possibly find something else besides my cases?"

She started to laugh. "I think I can do that." She gave him a big smile. "The thing is, when people scream, and I come running, it's not because it's your case," she said. "I didn't even know you had a case. I just thought someone needed help."

"And I think she did," he said quietly. "I don't understand what's going on there just yet, and I do have to head back to the office." At that, he turned, looked at his watch, and stood. "Like now."

"Of course you do," she said. She hopped to her feet, smiled. "Thank you for stopping by."

"Are you kidding? No way I wouldn't stop by and read you the riot act," he said. "No way were you getting out of that."

"You know something?" she said. "I think you like reading me the riot act, as some sort of stress relief."

He shook his head. "No, I don't think that has anything to do with it at all."

"Are you sure?"

"Positive," he said, "but it does give me the chance to tell you off for all the things that you keep getting into."

"Maybe," she said, "but I didn't deserve it today."

He stopped, looked at her, and then nodded. "Okay, so today I'll give you credit. What you did was try to help her, and that was a good thing. Calling me was also a good thing," he said. "The bad thing was coming back into the house, after you should have left, and seeing the man lying on the floor. That just complicated things."

"Not at all," she said. "Obviously I didn't do it on purpose."

He just looked at her hard.

She shrugged. "Fine, when Goliath raced inside," she said, "I had to come in after him. I didn't know where you guys were. I was chasing Goliath."

"Of course you were." He looked at the cat, who was off lying in the grass. "One for all and all for one with the four of you, isn't it?"

"Of course," she said. "We're a family."

He nodded. "A furry family."

"A furry, feathered family." She chuckled.

He nodded, turned. "I have to go back to work. You look after that family."

"I will." She smiled. "And remember. We always have room for more … in the family." At that, he stared at her. She shrugged. "Or there will be."

A slow smile dawned. "You better watch it," he said, "because, before you realize it, I'll already be here permanently and not just visiting."

As he strode off to the front of the house, she had to admit to herself that he already was.

Chapter 14

Monday Morning

THE NEXT MORNING she woke up, a smile on her face. She stretched in bed, yawned, rolled over, and opened her eyes to see sunshine streaming inside through her bedroom window.

"What a beautiful morning," she murmured. Mugs snuffled in the bedcovers beside her. She looked over, stretched out an arm, and scrubbed his exposed belly, all four legs pointing to the ceiling. She chuckled at him. "You do get into the oddest positions."

He didn't even hear her, or else he was ignoring her. On the other side of the bed, Goliath was curled up into a tight ball. Still wary of Thaddeus, the cat had chosen the place farthest away from the bird that roosted on the post at the end of the bed. Doreen looked up and saw Thaddeus studying her face. "Good morning, Thaddeus," she murmured.

Thaddeus ruffled his feathers, flapped his wings a couple times, and hopped down on the bed. He strode through the uneven bedcovers, where he dipped and swayed like a drunken sailor, before arriving at her leg. Then he hopped up and proceeded to move at a much faster rate toward her head. When he got there, he leaned forward, gently stroked her face. "Thaddeus loves Doreen."

Every time he said it, even though she knew he didn't know what it meant, or at least not the intent behind the words, it still melted her heart. She took a few minutes to love on him, to tell him how much she loved him too. And Mugs and Goliath. Where would she be without them—or Nan and Mack?

She took a shower, dressed, and then made her way to the kitchen. By the time she hit the bottom step, Mugs raced past her and barked at the rear kitchen door. She obliged by opening it for him.

"But you stay close," she warned. "And no chasing away people who are walking along the river. We're allowed to have other people enjoy the same river, you know. We don't own right up to the water." It was one of those things that she had never thought about, until she got here, but technically even the beachfront properties didn't own the beach. Other people were allowed to go across the beach in front of those houses.

Mugs went out with joy, bounding down the steps out to the grass. Afraid that he was taking off for the river, she watched as he went forward about ten steps and then got completely sidetracked by something in the grass. His nose went down, and he sniffed all around in a circle. "Probably just a squirrel from last night," she muttered to herself.

She watched for another few minutes, as he headed to the garden and back up and down, before he lifted a leg and relieved himself. After he scratched heavily on the grass, making her wonder how it was supposed to survive his onslaught, he raced back to the deck. Nodding, she headed inside and put on coffee. She studied the almost empty coffee tin in horror. "Surely I haven't gone through that much coffee," she muttered.

But, as she checked around further, it appeared that she had. Between Mack's multiple visits and her own coffee addiction, she was getting very low. "That's it. We're going shopping today," she announced.

Goliath was sprawled on top of her chair at the kitchen table, completely ignoring her, and Thaddeus cackled away on the table. She didn't know if he was agreeing with her or not. He was obviously happy that food was coming his way though. She immediately set to feeding the animals and then noted she was low on dog and cat food as well. Those were both big-ticket items. But then, who was she kidding? When it came to food, everything seemed to be a big-ticket item, and coffee topped the list. But none of those three items were negotiable—she had to have them.

Mack had paid her for the last time she'd worked in his mom's garden, but that wouldn't go very far, even though the forty dollars was something. She went to her purse, pulled out her wallet, and sorted through the bit of money she had there, before heading off to the cash bowl, where she pulled out another $60 to buy cat food and dog food. She had just enough to get a little bit of groceries too, but, if something didn't break soon, she would be up the creek again. She shook her head, wondering how she could have so many things in possible assets or in potential incoming money, yet have none of it available—or even sure to happen. At least none of it right now.

On that note, she sent Scott another email, asking whether she should be following up on the antique books and on the paintings individually, or were they all connected to him through Christie's. The response came back in a text message, saying they were all connected to him. It was followed almost immediately by a friendly *How are you doing?* email. She responded with a smile on her face because she had really connected with him. He had been kind and had really helped her to get an auction set up in the future, but she'd known there would be this extended time frame. She quickly replied, telling him that she was doing quite well, except for money being tight. He sent back a sympathetic note, writing, *We're working through the process as fast as we can. Money will be coming. Just hold on.*

Then she remembered Wendy's check that she'd put in the bank.

That had been at least $600, which she could turn around and put into groceries and bills. At that, she winced because bills were something she had been avoiding. She hadn't really sat down and done a proper accounting. She definitely needed to, and, since she had some money, this would be an excellent time. She picked up a cup of coffee, her bills stacked up on her desk to the side of the kitchen, a pad of paper and a pen, and sat down, making a compiled list of what she needed to pay.

By the time she was done with her list, by her math, her money was almost wiped out. The check from Wendy was helpful but just barely. Doreen had delayed paying a bunch of these bills because she didn't know where the money would come from, but that meant that she had a lot to pay now all at once. Although the first consignment check was in her bank account and would cover these bills, there wouldn't be much left over for groceries.

She sat here, looking down at the cash she'd pulled out of the bowl, feeling that old fear trickle through her once again. Without money, she had nothing. Even if she had the house, she still had to pay for all the utilities that went with it. And she didn't want to say anything to Nan because then she would insist on helping. And, while Doreen wasn't against accepting help, she didn't want to be a grifter and to freeload off her grandmother, who had done so much for her already.

After pouring another cup of coffee, gathering her laptop now, she sat down and went through the process of paying her bills online. It was unnerving, yet, at the same time, a relief because she didn't have to face some nameless person across a bank desk and ask them to pay the bills for her, which is what she'd been forced to do the first few times. But now, since they had set it all up online for her, she could surely sit here and work it out herself.

It took a bit, and she was very careful to make sure that she had enough to cover these bills, and, of course, Doreen had more money in her account than just the check she had gotten from Wendy. Doreen still had some of the money left over from what she had been paid for the pallet of car parts in Nan's garage. And yet to see the bank account balance drop like it did was a reality check Doreen hadn't been prepared for.

Feeling a little queasy and realizing that she still needed to take some of this money and get food for the animals—even if she changed her mind about her own food—she was determined to get that done today as well. She grabbed the money she had taken from her secret stash of Nan's cash—found in her clothes left behind in the house—and decided to leave the animals at home this time.

She walked out to the car, hopped in, and drove to the grocery store, and—with the ever-present bills that she just paid and the associated drop in her bank account fresh in her mind—she got the largest bags of pet food she could for the animals, to make sure they had enough to last a good while, and then, with that accounted for, she walked around the store, figuring out what she could get for food. She'd become a little too comfortable with some of Mack's meals, but it would be hard to continue those with her current lack of income.

She knew that she could still take some more cash out of the bowl, but surely there was a better way to keep her budget down, so she didn't feel this same sense of absolute despair every time she had to pay for something because—although she had paid those bills this month—they would just come back around again.

And all that sent her to the pasta aisle, which was cheap, thank heavens, plus bread and peanut butter. With those purchases in her cart, she calculated she had just enough left to get coffee. As she had done her planning, the animal food took priority over her own fruit and vegetables, but, when passing the produce section, she found a discount bag of apples. She snatched it up, checked the price, then added it to her list, and had about four dollars left. With that, she wondered what she could do with the rest.

She might get a pound of butter, maybe a bag of potatoes. She remembered that Mack had brought rice last time and had left a little bit behind. She knew rice was supposed to be cheap, but, if she didn't have anything to go with it, was that really an answer? It would fill her belly but wouldn't give her much in the way of nutrition. Pondering the vagaries of trying to live on nothing, she stood in front of the rice, while she calculated if she should take a little bit more money out of her bank account, writing a check this time instead of using her cash.

At that thought, she looked up to see the old guy from the orchid show, staring at her. *Stranden.* Immediately she smiled at him. "Hi," she said. "I'm surprised to see you here."

His eyebrows shot up. "Why?" he asked. "I live in town and need to eat. Looks like I'm buying more groceries than you are." He motioned at his cartful of meat and veggies and eggs.

She noted his purchases. "Oh, I forgot to get eggs." She immediately backed away from the rice. "I just needed to pick up a few things for the animals," she said.

Stranden nodded and watched, as she scurried off to get eggs.

She didn't know why she felt so bad because it was none of his business what she bought. She was cross with herself for even showing any reaction to seeing him. She grabbed the largest pack of eggs she could afford, and, after quickly checking out, she headed for her car.

Chapter 15

OUTSIDE IN THE parking lot, she quickly stowed away her few groceries. Just as she straightened up and closed the rear hatch of her car, she turned around to see the old man, standing beside her. "Hey," she said casually. "Something I can do for you?"

"Yeah, you sure can," he said. "You can call off your boyfriend."

She froze. "Boyfriend?"

He snorted. "Figured that you would question that, but that's not the actual gist of what I'm asking."

"I'm not sure what you are asking," she said. "Mack and I are definitely friends, but he's hardly my boyfriend."

"Whatever." He waved his gnarled hand. "You can call him off regardless."

"Call him off of what?" she asked succinctly.

"He's hassling me, but I didn't kill Gloria."

"Oh." She stared at him, although inside she was delighted that Mack had pursued this avenue a little further. "I thought she died of natural causes."

"So did I," he said, "but it's not stopping him from asking all kinds of ugly questions."

"If you cooperate and give him the answers," she said quietly, "then I'm sure he will disappear."

"Oh no, that's not how this works. The cops dig away at you, until they find something that suits them. It's not as if we have any chance to be innocent in any of this. We're basically guilty forever."

"No, that's not true at all," she said, "because I know he's just asking questions to get information. If you give him the information he wants, he'll go away."

"Then he'll just come back, looking for more."

She privately agreed with him, but saying that wouldn't make this guy leave her alone any sooner. "Why bring me into it?" she asked, looking at him straight. "If you want him to back off, tell him so yourself."

He glared at her. "I did, and it just seemed to make him angry."

"Well, like you, I don't think he likes being told what to do."

At that, Stranden gave a half-broken laugh. "Isn't that the truth?" he said. "I don't think any of us do." He shook his head, and, for the first time, she saw him differently, maybe for what he really was, but it was such a shock that she didn't really know. At this moment, he just looked like a broken old man.

She looked at the groceries he had in his grocery cart. "You better get those groceries home before something spoils."

He said, "Nothing here will make a difference for a few minutes." He frowned. "But at least I was buying more than just pet food."

"My animals happen to be pretty important to me."

He nodded. "And that's a good thing," he said. "You can

always tell what somebody is like by the way they care for their animals. It used to be the way we could tell a good man from a bad one—by the way he looked after his horse. But nobody has horses anymore, and they all hide under these disguises that make you think they're good, but they're really not."

Not exactly sure where the conversation was going but interested in spite of herself, she said, "Sounds like the voice of experience."

"You don't get to be my age and to live through the times that I have"—his voice was hard—"without coming across a few wolves in sheep's clothing."

"Ah, and I don't suppose Gloria's son was one of them, was he?"

"He was bad," he said, "plain bad, but nobody would ever listen to me."

"And why is that?"

"Because they didn't deal with him, so they didn't see him the way I did. They didn't have business dealings where he cheated them," he muttered, then shook his head. "I should never have gotten involved. I was just looking to stay close to Gloria."

And that confirmed something she had personally picked up on right away, but she knew other people wouldn't. "You were sweet on Gloria, weren't you?"

His eyes turned rheumy, and he reached up, as if to wipe a speck of dust from them, but she could see the moisture there. Somebody else was mourning Gloria, and it would probably surprise most of the world. "We were always sweet together," he said. "We had something for a very long time. But then that son of hers did everything he could to break us up."

"Why is that?"

"Because he didn't want to share his mother with anybody. I didn't understand why somebody would interfere, if two people were happy."

Now, if this Stranden guy had been abusing Gloria, that's a different story. However, as Doreen looked at him, he seemed to be more broken up over her death by the moment. "Hey," she said gently, "I know it's hard to say goodbye to somebody you cared for."

"I didn't get a chance to say goodbye, did I?" he said bitterly. "The family has kept me away all these years."

"Did you not see her or talk to her at all?"

"Sure, I did. When she found out I was putting an orchid in the contest, she contacted me and told me to forget it, that no way my orchid would be any good."

"Oh," she said, "that's not very nice."

"No, sometimes she could be a bitch," he said fondly. "But she was a heck of a good woman."

Those two statements together made no sense to Doreen, but she could see how in his mind it did. "I'm sorry for your loss," she said gently. "I only met her for a few minutes, but she seemed like a really nice person."

"She was, and she meant the world to me. Once she lost her son, I knew there would never be any chance of getting back together again. Her son was nothing but poison, so he pretty well made sure that my name was mud with her."

"Maybe not," she said. "And what about the niece?"

He shook his head. "I don't know her all that well," he muttered. "And all she knew about me was what Gloria told her, so none of that's any good."

"You don't know that though," she said. "We have to give her the benefit of the doubt."

He looked at her. "Wow, you really do have that whole innocent attitude, don't you?"

She frowned at him. "Hey, I've been through some tough times myself," she muttered, "so it doesn't have a whole lot to do with a Pollyanna attitude."

He motioned at the groceries. "You're broke, aren't you?" Her face flushed bright red and then faded just as quickly when he nodded. "Been there myself," he said. "I recognize the symptoms."

"Well," she said, pride making her back stiffen and her chin go up, "thankfully it's temporary."

"Yeah," he said, "it's always temporary. I've been in those temporary situations a couple times."

"Yet, look where you live," she said.

"I don't know about your situation," he said, "but, when you've got a place, you do everything you can to keep it because, once you lose that, the only thing left is the street, and that's a pretty hard place to live. I've been there too." With that, he turned and pushed his laden cart to his car. He popped open the trunk and slowly moved everything in.

She noted just how much pain he was in as he winced when he lifted his things.

Telling herself to leave it alone, she still couldn't stop her feet from going over there and quickly unloading the groceries into his car for him.

"Why'd you do that for?" he asked roughly.

"Because I could see it was hurting you," she said quietly. "The world might be a tough place sometimes, but that doesn't mean it has to be a tough place all the time." She turned and headed back to her car.

He called out, "Can I pay you?"

"For what?" she asked, as she turned toward him.

"For being a good person?"

"No," she said, with a smile. "That comes free of charge." She hopped into her car and headed home. But his words hovered on the edge of her mind for the rest of the day.

She was proud of the fact that she had paid all her bills and had managed to get as much food purchased as she had, but she still needed a serious plan before she ended up homeless. She didn't know how it worked if she couldn't pay the utility bills again, and this thing called property taxes was looming. In fact, she thought those payments were quite late, and she didn't know how that worked. What if she didn't pay them?

She grabbed her laptop, pulled up Google, and searched about what happened if she didn't pay her property taxes, and, of course, it was pretty terrifying when she looked at the results. She wondered if Nan would know. She frowned because Nan was still dealing with her own feelings over the loss of Gloria. Would this be a good distraction or would it make her worry about Doreen even more? Finally deciding to take the chance, she picked up the phone and called her grandmother.

Nan sounded a bit sad and even a little teary when she answered.

"I'm sorry," Doreen said. "I know you're still hurting over Gloria."

"Of course I am," she said, her voice a little more robust. "But I can't do anything to help her, and she's gone to a place that I'll be headed to sometime soon."

At that, Doreen gasped, because the last thing she wanted was any reminder that her grandmother could be going soon. "I certainly hope not," she said into the phone. "Please tell me that you don't mean that."

"It'll happen one day, child," she said. "Now, what did you call about?"

"Well, first I wanted to see if you were okay."

"I'm fine," Nan replied, "and you're a good child for asking."

"I don't feel like it sometimes," she said. "It seems like all you've ever done is help me, and I haven't done a whole lot for you."

At that, Nan started to laugh and laugh. "You make me smile every day," she said. "That's worth so much. You come and see me willingly because you care, not because you want something."

Doreen winced, wondering if she should even ask her about the taxes or not.

"So why else did you call?"

"I met the old guy in the grocery store—the orchid grower Stranden, who was in competition with Gloria," she said, changing the subject from what she'd planned on saying.

"Did he throw something at you?" she said. "He's got quite a temper and tends to be a cranky puss."

"He was cranky, but, at the same time, I think he's just a lonely old man."

"Oh, don't you go there," Nan said in alarm. "He has lots of things in life going for him and a lot of things not. But you don't want to get involved with the likes of him."

"Maybe not, that could be quite true," Doreen said. "But I also don't know that he's somebody I should actively avoid either."

"*Hmm.*" Nan seemed a little distracted, as she thought about that. "Maybe not."

"Oh, and can you explain to me about something called property taxes?" she began, then hesitated.

"Yes, go on," Nan said, but her attention seemed elsewhere.

"I'm not really sure what they are or how it works. I just heard that they were due, and now I can't find the paperwork about it, and I'm worried because I didn't pay it."

"Ah, that's right," she said. "You didn't pay it. I did."

Doreen stopped and gasped. "What do you mean, you paid it?"

"Well, one day when I was over there, I saw the notice in the mail. You hadn't opened the envelope and didn't even seem to know what it was, so I just brought it home, and I paid it. After all, it's the least I could do."

"What are you talking about?" Doreen said. "I don't have a clue how much it was or when it was due or what we're even paying for."

"Don't worry. You and most of the world have the same questions on that," she said, with a snort. "Property taxes are one of those things that we know we're supposed to pay in order to contribute to all the roads and maintenance and hospitals and all that good stuff that we all need, but, when tax time comes around, it can be really difficult."

"I thought that was income tax," Doreen said. "I didn't know about property tax too."

"Well, now you do. But this year, I took care of it," she said. "I lived there forever, so it only made sense that I pay it this time."

Doreen was not at all sure that was the way it was supposed to work, but she was grateful nonetheless. "I need to know how much it was, so that I can plan ahead for next year," she said, "because I'll have to pay for it sometime."

"Oh, yeah." Nan laughed. "You'll love this. It was over fifteen hundred dollars."

Doreen's heart almost stopped. "You're kidding. Fifteen hundred? Dollars?"

"Yep," Nan said cheerfully. "Goes up every year too."

"Oh," she said. "Wow." She didn't even know what else to say. What could she say except that would have completely decimated her bank account? "So is it always due at the same time every year? And is it only once?"

"It is," she said, "but I think you can set it up so you can pay installments, if that's easier."

That would not be any easier to pay the property taxes. Not at all. That's just not the way money in her world worked these days. "Interesting," she said quietly. "I had no idea it would be quite so much."

"Exactly. Which is why I wasn't too bothered about making you pay it." Nan added, "You're good for a year now at least."

Doreen sat back and swallowed hard. "So I'm not in arrears or anything?"

"No, I paid it on time," she said. "I just forgot to mention it to you. We've all been a little busy."

"Yes, that is very true." Then she took a deep breath. "Thank you, Nan. Really. That was very sweet of you." She tried her hardest to be sincere because she really was, but she also didn't want Nan to realize just how desperate she'd been, when she remembered she probably owed these taxes.

"You're welcome, child."

Such love filled Nan's voice that Doreen's tears came anyway. "Did you know I couldn't pay it?"

"Of course," she said. "it's all you can do to put food on the table. But what you don't see is that you're doing so much for all these other people, and, of course, nobody can pay you for the work you're doing, but that doesn't mean you shouldn't spend your time doing it. So those of us who can support that effort should help."

It took Doreen a minute or two to follow her grandmother's train of thought, and, when she realized that Nan truly meant every word, Doreen was overcome yet again.

"And don't you dare start crying," Nan said, her own voice getting teary, "or you'll set me off again too."

"I'm sorry," Doreen blustered. "But you're just such a good person."

Nan laughed. "No," she said, "I'm really not, but I'm learning to be. Ever since you came into my life, I've seen how much better I could be if I tried, and I'm working on it."

"Wow," Doreen said quietly. "That's one of the nicest things you've ever said to me."

"And that's a shame too," Nan said. "I've had a good life. I've lived hard, partied hard, played hard, and I've loved hard. You've missed so much in life, and I really want you to enjoy and to rejoice in some of what I had. And, for that to happen, you need to relax a little."

"A little hard to relax when putting food on the table is a major challenge at the moment."

"I know, which is why I paid the taxes," she said. "Are you still doing Millicent's garden?"

"Yes," she said, "and that's really all the income I have. I did get that first check from Wendy and caught up on the bills, but it didn't leave much. I was able to get enough food for the animals to last quite a while."

At that, Nan smiled. "Hopefully the lawyers can get your divorce all settled up pretty fast."

"Maybe," she said, "but you know my ex won't be very cooperative about it."

"No, that's not part of his makeup, is it?"

"No, it's really not," she said quietly. "Mathew's very unhappy."

"Of course he is. He wants to make sure that he gets to keep all the money from the marriage and that you get nothing."

"That's the gist of it, yes," she muttered.

"And what about your lawyer? Did all that get settled up?"

"You mean Nick?"

"No, Robin or whoever she was, the one who took your husband."

"I don't know that she took him, though he was available for the taking," she said, "because he wasn't mine anymore at that point."

"Good, that's one of the best things I've heard out of your mouth in a long time," Nan said. "You need to keep that up. Keep that attitude going and realize that so much more than Mathew is out there."

"I know," she said. "And there is definitely a better man out there."

"Ha. Like Mack?"

Such a note of hope filled Nan's voice that Doreen had to smile. "Yes, exactly like Mack."

"At last," she said. "Now you've put a smile on this old lady's face. You know I only want the best for you, and Mack, well, he's just a darn good man."

"I think he is too," she said, "and I know you don't agree with me on this, but I need to clear off the old before I start something new."

"Oh, I understand all right. I just think you're a fool if you don't realize that you've started something already," she said.

"Oh, I think I realize it." In a rush she blurted out, "He kissed me." Suddenly she felt like a schoolgirl, made all the worse when Nan squealed in absolute delight. Doreen had to laugh. "Okay, wait. It wasn't a really, you know, like one of those kisses."

"It doesn't matter," Nan said. "It was a kiss."

And, still flushed, from both the memory and from telling Nan, plus hearing her grandmother's reaction, Doreen quickly hung up, promising to come visit later in the day.

Chapter 16

QUITE A FEW hours later, Doreen had finished the laundry, cleaned up the kitchen, vacuumed, and generally taken care of the house that was sure to be hers for at least another year, when she turned to the animals. "Do you want to go visit Nan?"

Whether it was Nan's name, the word *go*, or something else—like her tone of voice or body language—Mugs immediately started barking and racing around, looking for his leash. Goliath even appeared interested, as he sauntered toward her. Thaddeus hopped onto the kitchen table and started in with, "Thaddeus loves Nan. Thaddeus loves Nan."

She smiled. "You and me both, buddy. You and me both."

Then she gathered up all the animals, looked around the house bequeathed to her by Nan, and decided she should take Nan something. But she hadn't bought anything, hadn't made anything, and didn't really know how to make anything, so that was pretty well the extent of what she could do right now. Shrugging, she headed out to the creek by way of her backyard garden, then stopped. She did have a dahlia with a beautiful bloom, so maybe she could make up a small floral bundle.

She raced back into the house, returned with garden scissors, and snipped off an open bloom and an almost-ready-to-open bloom. Then she grabbed some leafy greens from one of her other plants, just a few leaves to go around the edge. Back inside, she wrapped them up with a bit of ribbon. With any luck they wouldn't look quite as homemade to Nan as they did to Doreen. With flowers in hand, she headed to Nan's place.

At the corner she passed several people watching the river. Doreen smiled. "Good afternoon." They waved and smiled back.

One woman said, "Oh, those flowers are just lovely."

Doreen grinned. "Thank you. They are for my grandmother."

"Lucky grandmother," the woman said enviously. "That's a truly beautiful bloom."

"It's a dahlia," she said, "one from my garden."

"Wow," she said. "You must be quite a gardener if you can grow flowers like that."

Doreen looked at the dahlia critically. As a dinner plate dahlia, it was huge, and it had a really strong stalk, so, in that sense, it was doing very well. "I did put a bit of work in the garden," she said, knowing it was a load of crock because she hadn't yet done a fraction of what she needed to do, but she was getting there.

"It's truly beautiful." The woman hesitated. "Listen. I know you said that you're taking that to someone, but do you have any more that you could do up in a different bundle for them?"

Doreen looked at her in surprise. "Why do you ask?"

"Because I'm going to visit a friend, who just lost somebody very dear, and I haven't yet picked up flowers," she explained. "As I look at what you've got there in your hand, I think they're the prettiest thing I've ever seen."

Doreen immediately felt bad, wondering how could she give away the flowers she'd picked for her own grandmother, yet, at the same time, if anyone would understand, it would be Nan. And honestly Doreen did have more flowers in the garden. Impulsively she handed hers over. "Here. Please take these to your friend."

The woman looked at her, dazed. "Seriously?" she asked joyfully, her hand automatically reaching for the bouquet.

"Sure," Doreen said. "Why not?"

"Let me pay you for it at least."

Doreen shook her head. "Oh no, that's fine."

But the woman wouldn't listen. "No," she argued. "I was fully prepared to pay for a nice arrangement, and this is so much nicer than anything I've seen in the stores." Pulling out her wallet, she looked at the bouquet and back at Doreen. "Do you think fifty would be okay?"

Doreen's jaw dropped. She stared from the flowers to the woman holding them. "I think that's way too much." Yet Doreen could sure use the money.

At that, the woman immediately stuffed the money into Doreen's hand. "You have no idea how beautiful these flowers truly are or how much I appreciate the fact that I can get them right now and take them to my friend." And, with that, she raced to her car, parked nearby.

Doreen looked at her animals. "Now what do we do?" She wanted to return home to pick more for Nan, but, at the same time, she knew that would put her that much later getting to Nan's. "So what do you say we bring her some flowers next time then?"

She automatically started walking toward Nan's place, but she clutched the $50 as if it were a lifeline. It was more than Mack paid her for the gardening at his mother's place that sometimes took hours, and it required a lot of physical work, but here this stranger had paid Doreen more, just for putting a little bouquet together. She looked down at Mugs. "Do we have a business opportunity here?"

He barked at her but was more concerned about chasing his tail at the moment. Goliath was at her side, completely disinterested. Of course they were, as was Thaddeus, who had perched on her shoulder and remained quiet the whole time. She looked over at him. "What do you think, Thaddeus? Can we do bouquets for people?"

He just cackled in her ear, "*He-he-he.*"

And she wondered if that meant that she had somehow manipulated this woman out of $50 or if she was truly happy to pay it. She certainly seemed happy. Doreen remembered just how much cut flowers and bouquets cost in the grocery stores—even more in the florist shops—and she realized that $50 really was a decent price, especially considering how unusual the flowers were.

Pondering that thought on the walk to Nan's house, it seemed like no time before she stepped across the flagstones, leading to Nan's patio. Nan sat there, a pensive look on her face, until she saw Doreen.

She hopped to her feet and ran over and gave Doreen a big hug. Nan asked, "What's the matter?"

"Actually," Doreen said, "I'm feeling really guilty, but I'm also feeling excited. Something weird happened on the way over, and I feel terrible because I sold your gift." Nan frowned, and then Doreen explained what had happened.

Instead of being upset, Nan clapped her hands in joy.

"Oh my, that's marvelous," she said. "And what a perfect thing for you to do. You're so talented. That's so wonderful."

"The thing is, they were your flowers," Doreen confessed. "I was bringing them to you because I know how upset you are about Gloria."

At that, Nan grabbed Doreen's hand. "Sweetheart, you can come with flowers, or without, as long as you come," she said, "because the joy of having you close is knowing that you care enough to come at all."

Doreen smiled, leaned over, and kissed Nan on the cheek. "That won't change," she said. "It's just that I wanted to bring you something special. And I don't cook well, and I don't have money to buy you gifts, so I was walking outside in the backyard, and I saw the dahlias and thought of you."

"I'm delighted that you did. And, even more than that," she said, "I'm delighted that you sold them. I know how much you need the money, and this could be the perfect way for you to make a little bit of extra cash to tide you over until you get paid for the antiques. I had no idea all that Christie's would do before having an auction."

"Me neither." Doreen nodded. "I was wondering if selling flowers could be a business opportunity for me."

Nan's face lit up. "Oh my," she said, "you could do custom floral arrangements."

"I don't have any talent for that." Doreen frowned.

"I don't know about that," Nan replied. "You used to do them when you were with your ex, didn't you?"

At that, Doreen nodded. "Sure, I put them together in the kitchen all the time."

"Exactly," Nan said, "so I wouldn't worry about whether you have a talent for it or not. Obviously you do, if whatever you created today was pretty enough that a perfect stranger stopped you, wanting to buy it."

"Well, that's true," she said, "but maybe she was just desperate."

Nan chuckled. "There you go again, knocking yourself down because you think nobody could possibly ever want what you have."

"You have to admit it's an odd thing, bringing flowers for you and selling them to a stranger. I tried to just give them to her. Selling them made me feel like I was, I don't know, greedy."

"I couldn't care less," Nan said, "but I love flowers. So can you bring me more next time?"

"Of course," she said.

"Will you sell the next bundle?"

"I don't know, but I hope so." And she stared at Nan in delight.

Nan chuckled at the joke. "You have to consider every possibility in your situation, and what you have created right now could be a whole new doorway. Now it's up to you if you want to go through it or not."

Chapter 17

Monday Evening into Tuesday Morning

NAN'S WORDS RESONATED deep in Doreen's brain as she returned home again, and the words kept resonating through to the next morning, when she woke up, wondering … she got dressed and took a look at her garden, determined to take something to Nan today. Something to make up for the flowers that she had sold yesterday. She couldn't believe how guilty she felt; yet she firmly believed that Nan was happy with Doreen's decision to take the money.

And, even now, she gazed at the extra $50 in the cash bowl with absolute delight. If she could find a steady way to do that, it would be a whole different story for her because then she truly would make a little bit more. Even if she could sell one bouquet a week, it would supplement the $40 she made on gardening. And that was barely enough to keep her in tea and coffee. But, hey, she was doing something to pay her bills.

Outside, with a cup of tea in one hand and her garden scissors in the other, she wandered the garden, looking at what she had to make up future bouquets. She had quite a few different plants and flowers coming along, from green to ready to start opening soon. Dwarf sunflowers, more dahlias, a little bit of everything—even a very late tulip. She wandered over and stared at it. "What are you doing still trying to bloom?" she asked. "Your time has generally come and gone." The tulip didn't seem to care, but it valiantly struggled.

"So should we immortalize you?" she muttered. "Should we take you to Nan, so that she can enjoy you for a little bit?"

It was just starting to open, so a perfect time to pick it for a fresh bouquet. She cut the tulip, then wandered around her garden and picked several dahlias. She even had painted dahlias, which had bright pink petals. She also had some crazy daisies that always made her laugh because they grew in every direction but the normal one. She could use them to wrap around the base of the lone tulip and the pink dahlias.

All in all, by the time she had a little bouquet picked, she found some green tissue paper and a ribbon, bundled up the bottom of the stems, trimmed them up nicely, and put the ribbon around it. With that, she called the animals to her. "Let's go, guys." They raced to her, and she headed to Nan's again. As she walked across the grass toward Nan's apartment, Doreen heard a commotion. She called out, "Nan, are you there? Is everything okay?"

But, with all the yelling going on, nobody appeared to hear. Doreen walked through Nan's apartment from the patio and opened the front door to the hallway, leading to one of the common rooms. There, she found Richie and a few other people, including Nan, having a heated argument over something. Mugs woofed at the unusual noise. Goliath retreated slightly. Doreen stopped and stared. "Nan, are you okay?" she asked, moving to her grandmother's side.

Nan threw on a big smile. Then she saw the flowers, and her expression softened. "Oh my," she said. "Those are lovely."

In fact, the conversation died completely. One of the other women looked at the bouquet. "Oh my goodness," she said. "Where did you get that from?"

Doreen shrugged a little self-consciously. "I picked them from my garden and brought them for Nan."

And, just like that, the whole heated conversation, whatever it had been about, had completely switched over to talk of Doreen's garden and the flowers.

"They are really beautiful," the woman said.

"Right," Nan said. "Doreen wondered if she could go into business selling these bouquets, and I told her that she was doing a beautiful job with them."

"Well," Doreen said, "it doesn't seem quite right."

At that, Ritchie looked at her in surprise. "What's this?" he asked. "You'll start a business as a florist?"

"No, no, no," she said immediately instinctively stepping back slightly, forcing Mugs to shift around her legs. "It just crossed my mind that I might make a little bit of money selling some bouquets. But, hey, it's just an off-the-cuff idea."

"But it's a good one," one of the other Rosemoor ladies said. "All you really need is a website, listing what you have fresh for the day."

"Maybe," she said, "but can you imagine if somebody doesn't come and pick them up? I mean, I'd be pretty upset at the waste."

"You could find somebody else to sell them, or," one of the women said, "go to some of the local markets and sell them. Or, even better, go to some of the smaller grocery stores, the ones that buy all local and sell them daily. At the end of the day, whatever hasn't sold, you could pick up."

"Or the next day—or the day after that," Doreen said. "When they're fresh like this, they'll last for several days."

"There you go."

And, just like that, as if there hadn't been yelling of any kind, everybody added their thoughts and ideas to the plan of setting Doreen up with a business.

She stopped and stared. "Of course I do have to remember that it would be a secondary business."

Several of them stopped, looked at her. "What do you mean?"

"Obviously I'll still work on my cold cases," she said.

Big fat grins circled around the large common room immediately.

"Of course you do," one of them said. "Do you have a new case right now?"

She nodded. "Maybe, it depends on a local death."

"Oh, *Gloria*," said one of the women. "We're all just heartbroken."

"Yet really," Doreen said in a gentle tone, "it was her time, wasn't it?"

"You could say that for all of us." Richie laughed. "It's all of our times. Most of us here are pretty pragmatic about it," he said. "We face the possibility on a daily basis."

"Maybe," she said, "but Gloria had also lived a good long life and hopefully enjoyed a lot of it."

Richie nodded. "She did, until her son died anyway."

"Right," Doreen said, "and that is one cold case I was wondering about."

Immediately they stopped, stared at her, and everybody

agreed. Richie added, "That would be a lovely thing to do to honor Gloria."

"I'm sure she would have preferred to have the answers before she died," Doreen corrected him.

"But we can't always get what we want," Richie said gently. "But what we do want is not to be forgotten."

"Knowing that you would still look into her son's case, even though she's gone, would be sure to make her smile."

Doreen wasn't altogether certain that she was up for doing something just because an older lady had died a natural death. In Doreen's mind, it was more because of the niece still living, who might want answers. She turned to Nan. "Shall I put these in a vase for you, Nan?"

"Or," one of the other women in the room interrupted, "you could sell them to me. I'm heading to Gloria's right now."

For the second time in a row, Doreen found her flowers sold to somebody who was not the intended recipient. She turned to look at Nan with an open mouth. Yet Nan took the flowers from her hands and passed them to the other woman. At that point, Doreen didn't know what to say.

Nan just shook her head, a twinkle in her eye. "This is so much fun," she said. "I am absolutely loving it."

"Maybe you are," Doreen replied, "but I put a lot of time and attention in making that for you."

"And I thoroughly appreciate it." Nan gave her a beaming smile. "And now Gloria's niece will appreciate it too."

There wasn't a whole lot Doreen could say to that. And the bouquet was more or less Nan's to do with as she wanted, but, when the woman returned almost immediately with $60 and handed it off to Nan, who immediately turned and gave it to Doreen, she stared down at the money in shock, then groaned in wonder.

"It's beautiful," the other woman said to Doreen. "Thank you so much." The woman leaned over, kissed Nan on the cheek, and, with the flowers firmly in hand, she quickly disappeared.

Chapter 18

"MOST OF US have known Gloria all of our lives. … At least those who have been here that long," Richie noted, "and we're all sad to see her go."

"And yet," Doreen said ever-so-gently, "as you said, it's a natural progression, isn't it?"

He nodded. "It is. And I know my day will come." He paused. "Sometimes I even wish it would come faster." With that, he turned and slowly shuffled out of the common area, where everybody else stood around.

Doreen watched as he headed to his room, before turning to Nan. "Tough day here for everyone, isn't it?"

"For everyone," Nan said, trying to sniffle back tears as she bent down to cuddle Mugs. "Your arrival was a godsend."

"It sounded more like I was needed as a referee," she said, with half a smile.

"You could be right about that. But we get over this stuff."

"You do fight a lot here."

"Sometimes," Nan said. "When you get to be our age, it's too much effort to fight for very long. So we go at it, and then, all of a sudden, it's over because nobody can continue. Most can't even remember what started the fight in the first place."

Doreen smiled and nodded. "Still, it would be nice if you didn't do any fighting."

"But that's not reality," Nan said comfortably. "Come on. Let's head back to my room."

"I wondered if anybody here knew the old guy who had the orchid like Gloria's on display. He apparently was an old friend but now may be more like a 'frenemy' of Gloria's."

Nan turned to her. "Are you talking about Stranden?"

"Yes," she said. "He lives on Abbott Street, but he had an absolutely stunning orchid, when we went to see him for the flower show."

One of the other women involved in all the discussions and the ongoing fights stopped by them. "Yes, that'll be Stranden. He and Gloria were an item for a very long time. The son broke them up."

"Ah, I did get the impression that Stranden wasn't very happy about the son," Doreen said.

The woman shook her head. "It was more like the son wasn't happy about him. I think the son thought Stranden was after Gloria's money or something."

Nan nodded in understanding. "Christina's right."

"The trouble is," Christina explained, "when we get to be our age, we don't really care anymore. We just don't want to be alone, and we are happy to take any friends we can get."

"Still, you don't want to lose your life savings or be unsafe with your friends," Doreen said.

"There wasn't anything harmful about Stranden," Christina added. "He's a bit of a character, and, once they broke up, nobody else was in his world. He was smitten in a big way."

"He seemed to be quite struck with her, when we talked to him Saturday night."

"Oh, he was," she murmured.

"And yet the son has been gone for a long time."

"Yes," Christina continued, "but Lionel did a good job convincing her that Stranden was no good in the meantime, and Gloria wouldn't have anything to do with him afterward."

"Was that justified, do you think?" Doreen asked the woman.

"No, I don't think so," Christina said. "I've known Stranden a long time too. He's a bit rough around the edges, but he came from the heart with her."

"That's always a good thing," Doreen said quietly. "The world would be a better place if more people did that."

The older woman chuckled. "Oh, so very true," she said. "Yet it doesn't happen all that often."

When they reached the front door to Nan's apartment, Christina remained with them. Nan looked at Doreen and said, "You know what? If you solved the case of the son's murder, it might put Stranden to rest too."

"How is that?"

"Because everybody suspected he did it, which is why Gloria wouldn't have anything to do with him," Nan explained.

"Oh, wow." That's not what Doreen expected to hear. Yet she should have. "I'm sorry for Stranden then. Living under a cloud of suspicion isn't easy."

"You can never really clear your name when that seed of doubt is planted," Nan explained, "in the absence of another suspect. No, Stranden never had a chance, and Gloria wouldn't talk to him about it ever after."

Almost immediately Doreen felt sorry for Stranden because that had to be rough. "I'll see," she said, "but no promises."

"Ah," Christina said, "when you get to be our age, promises don't mean much either."

"That's not true." Nan looked at her in horror. "Promises are even more important."

"Sure, but old people get promises all the time from people who never intend to keep them," the other woman said, with a shrug. "They do it just so that you get off their back or so you stay quiet or so they feel good for the moment. But as soon as they're gone, they forget about you and anything else they may have said to you."

And, with that, she turned and headed down a different hallway, probably toward her own room. Doreen looked at Nan. "It sounds like she's not had an easy time of it either."

"Many of us here have been through a lot of family wars," she said quietly. "And sometimes the results are much less than joyful."

As they entered Nan's small suite, Mugs raced to the middle of the room and started to roll. Goliath jumped on the small table and stared at them both with disdain. Thaddeus, not to be outdone hopped up beside him and started strutting. "Thaddeus is here. Thaddeus is here. Thaddeus is here.

Watching the animals relax, Doreen asked Nan, "Did you know Stranden very well?"

"Of course," she said. "I knew him before he hooked up with Gloria, though."

"Ah," she said. "Was that an issue for you?"

Nan looked at her sideways, a light of laughter in her gaze, and she shook her head. "Absolutely not," she said. "As far as I was concerned, life was too short for just one man, and, once he met Gloria, he was a one-woman man anyway. That rendered him completely useless for me."

Doreen chuckled. "I think you want me to believe that you had a wild and woolly life," she said, "but I'm not sure it was all that risqué."

"You'll never know for sure," Nan said with a smirk, "but no point in living unless you'll make good of it. It's one of the reasons I was so worried about you, when you were with that ex of yours. You weren't living. You were merely existing."

Anxious to get off that topic, Doreen said, "Nan, did you ever hear any rumors about Stranden killing Gloria's son?"

"For a while that's all there was for rumors," she said, "until the next thing happened, and people had something else to talk about. You've got to remember that—whether in a small town, like Kelowna, or in a place, like Rosemoor—there isn't much to do but gossip. Well, outside of having sex of course."

Doreen winced at that. The last thing she wanted to think about was Nan having sex.

Nan started to laugh. "Oh, my dear, if you could only see the look on your face right now."

"It's a little hard to think about my grandmother having sex."

"So, don't think about it." Nan gave an airy wave of her hand. "But I have no intention of being lonely anymore."

"And that's fair enough," she said, with a brilliant smile. "Just be safe about it."

"Of course. And you too." She wagged her finger at her. "I know Mack will take good care of you either way but—"

Doreen felt her cheeks flushing again. "We're not to that stage," she said briskly.

"And whose fault is that?" Nan rolled her eyes at her.

She flushed. "Okay, enough of that."

"*Huh*. So it's okay to talk about my sex life but not yours?"

"That's because I don't have one," Doreen said in a wry tone.

Nan burst out laughing, long and hard. "Oh my, you are good for my soul."

"I'm glad to hear that," she said, flushing slightly, "but now, back to this guy and the murder."

"At the time, the thinking was that the motive was all the trouble the son was causing between Stranden and Gloria, plus the fact that Stranden was stupid in love with her," she murmured. "And people in love will do all kinds of things."

"I know that," Doreen said. "I'm just not exactly sure how this all fits together."

"But you'll figure it out," Nan said. "We all have faith in you." Suddenly she grinned. "You know what? That is exactly what we need around here."

"What's that?" Doreen asked, her mind wandering.

"I'll set up a little betting pool on how long it takes you."

At that, it finally slammed into her brain what Nan was talking about. "Wait, whoa. Nan, no. No, you can't do that."

Nan frowned at her, an odd look on her face. "Of course I can."

"No," she said, "you can't. Remember? We're not doing that anymore."

"Dear," she said, "that was your conclusion, not mine. I am perfectly capable of setting up and running a pool. Mack might have a problem with it, but that's because he's a bit of a stick in the mud." She looked at her granddaughter and added, "So are you, for that matter."

She groaned. "No, no betting pools, Nan."

"Says you. I'm perfectly happy to live life the way I am," she said, "and, of course, I don't want to be lonely. I have good friends here, but it's a very different lifestyle. And you need to be ready for it."

"I'm not sure I'll ever be ready for this place," Doreen said. "You guys can be a little over-the-top. Oh, and that reminds me." She stopped, staring at Nan. And then she told her about the neighbor woman. "She said she had heard absolute horror stories about this place."

Nan looked at her in surprise. "Oh my," she said. "Are you talking about that woman who is about"—she motioned with her hands—"this high, reed thin, with a really high forehead?"

Doreen thought about it. "Yes, something like that."

"And she lives about … four houses from you on the other side of the cul-de-sac?"

"Yes," Doreen said, "that's her."

Nan said, "A pitiful woman."

"What do you mean, *pitiful*?" Doreen cried out.

"Oh, you should hear that woman complain."

And that's when Doreen got it. "Oh no," she said. "You're the one who told her all those lies about Rosemoor, aren't you?"

Nan looked at her in all innocence. "What lies, dear?"

"About how horrible this place is and how they lock you up and keep you prisoner."

She started to snicker. "Is that really what she said?"

"Yes, that's absolutely what she said."

"Oh, that's funny."

"I don't think anything is funny about it. Now did you say something like that to her?"

"Yes, I did. I didn't want that woman here. She's a nightmare. But anything that son of hers does is totally perfect. We all got so sick of her."

"What do you mean, *sick of her*? Did she ever live here?"

"No, she came down for a couple, you know, welcome party get-togethers, and we all decided that she wouldn't fit in."

"I thought management made those decisions."

Nan gave her a completely naïve look that wouldn't have fooled anyone. "Of course they do."

Doreen groaned. "But really they don't do that."

"My dear, management likes to think they do everything, but, in reality, the less they know about what really goes on here, the better." She gave her granddaughter a look. "You won't tell them, will you?"

"Nope, I sure won't." She shook her head. "But I don't think they're quite as stupid as you'd like to think."

"Oh, yes, they definitely are," she said, pointing at her now. "You should listen to the stupid decisions they make. It's just amazing."

"They're probably doing it for very different reasons than you think."

"Doesn't matter what the reasons are," Nan muttered. "They're still stupid decisions. You can't get around that."

She groaned. "Nan, you're supposed to stay out of trouble here."

"I know, and I'm doing everything I'm supposed to do. And more." She nodded her head.

"You're not supposed to be gambling."

"I'm not gambling." She looked at her granddaughter in shock.

Thaddeus immediately started snickering. "Hehehe…"

Nan shot him a dirty look.

"Betting pools are gambling."

"Oh, that's hardly gambling," Nan protested, "not even a judge would get mad at me for that."

"Mack will."

"But you'll save me from Mack," she said. "Not that I need you to because Richie can handle Darren, and I'm sure that I can handle Mack just fine."

The trouble was, Doreen figured Nan could do it too. But wouldn't it be nice if they didn't have to? Doreen sighed. "If you find out any information, let me know."

"You're talking about Stranden now?"

"Yes, Stranden and whatever the son's name was."

"Lionel. An odious man," she said.

"Odious?" she asked. "Was he that bad?"

"Oh, he was beyond difficult." Nan shuddered. "A terrible person."

"Yet Gloria loved him?"

"Well, yes, she did. He was her son. And love knows no bounds when it comes to family."

That gave Doreen something to think about, as she kept on wondering, because, if the son was a problem in general, plus he was causing all kinds of nightmares in Stranden's world, then it made sense that Stranden wanted to off him. But it obviously had the opposite effect because, as soon as the son was dead, Stranden lost the love of his life. So, if he did do it, it wasn't exactly a good decision on his part.

Chapter 19

Wednesday Morning

THE NEXT MORNING, with the animals all tucked up safely at home, Doreen raced to the library. She just couldn't stop herself from trying to get some history on this son, ever since Nan had opened Doreen's eyes to his negative personality and to the problems that the family had experienced. Doreen had to wonder just how much all of this was connected. She also didn't know if there was even a remote chance that Gloria had been murdered. Given her age, it would be very easy to let that death slide and assume it was from natural causes. And maybe that's all it was. No real way to know otherwise, unless the coroner came back with something definitive. And that could take days, if not weeks, depending on any tox screen run, if Gloria took medications.

But the son? Now that son fascinated Doreen. An unloved man hurting his mother's chances of having a happy life supposedly. Maybe he hated Stranden for other reasons. And who knows what the reason was. Maybe Lionel was jealous. Maybe he and his mom always had a close connection, and he couldn't handle losing that to somebody else. He apparently didn't have a wife and children of his own, and he and his mother's relationship seemed pretty intense. Doreen frowned at that, wondering if that was even healthy. If the son had something to do with getting Stranden out of his mother's life, for no good reason other than loving his mother, then it didn't sound normal to Doreen.

But then again, who knew what Stranden really was like? He was an old codger right now, and that personality wouldn't encourage somebody to be nice to him. But then he was also grieving and going through a rough patch.

Some library time might help Doreen sort this out.

She'd already searched for what she could online at home, but not very much information was out there, especially from this long ago. And that was a little disconcerting as well. Just because she wanted information didn't mean that it was always readily available, and that was the constant battle she was up against with these investigations of hers, and it just drove her crazy.

Mack wasn't likely to give her too much information. She might very well get access to the case files, but only if she came up with something that would make Mack feel like she needed to delve into it. He could no longer argue that she hadn't been helpful in some of the cold cases, but he was even more protective of her now than usual, and that made it harder to get details from him because he was always afraid she would get hurt. And he had a valid reason for that to a degree. She didn't like admitting it, but she had to give him credit when he was right.

Getting into the library wasn't a problem, but avoiding the eagle-eyed librarian—whether Martha or Linda—now that was something else. Doreen didn't want to hide from them, but it felt like they were always watching her to see what she was up to when she came into the library. Thankfully nobody was at the reception desk, as Doreen walked in, and she quickly skirted into one of the aisles of books, rather than going farther down where the librarian might have been.

A door to the other side was where either they kept books to reshelve or they had a lunchroom or something, and, if the librarian exited that room right now, then she would pin Doreen in place; she just knew it. So she'd do a lot to avoid that complication.

Down the aisle of books, she quickly swept through the back and along to the far side, where all the microfiche machines were located. She signed into one, thankful that they just had a book for signing in, allowing her to get by with making her signature legible but just barely.

She started researching the family first, trying to get an overall view.

Gloria was married a long time ago. Doreen almost whistled out loud when she saw the age that Gloria was when she got married—only seventeen. That marriage lasted ten years, and she had one son toward the end of that period. Her husband died in an automobile accident, and she raised the young boy on her own. This would help to explain the close relationship, assuming they were super dependent on each other. No other marriages were recorded for Gloria. There had just been the two of them for a very long time, and Doreen imagined the son wouldn't have taken it lightly if his mom moved on to someone else.

Further information confirmed that Lionel had been born the same year as his father had died. So Lionel would have been seventy-one now, if he had lived. Seems he died when he was forty-six, some twenty-five years earlier. Although he should have moved on with his own life by that time, his address at the time of his death remained at Gloria's home. Doreen frowned at that and wrote down a few notes, but not a whole lot was here.

She started researching the family over the years, looking at any articles she could find. Doreen found nothing on the husband, other than his obituary. Gloria was involved in various charities. She'd been in various garden fair activities; she was on the PTA, when her son was in school. She supported various food banks and assistance groups as well. She was just a generally well-rounded person, who believed in aiding those in her community, and had stepped up to help out whenever the need was there.

Nothing negative or critical was mentioned about her in any of the articles. That always made Doreen feel good, but it also made her a little suspicious, because nobody was that good all the time. And, of course, that was her own critical nature saying that. But she was happy that Gloria seemed to have lived such a fulfilling life.

Her niece, Elle, on the other hand, was the daughter of Gloria's sister, who'd had multiple marriages, and Elle was from the third one. Apparently Gloria's sister had passed away a long time before her son had died. So there were several deaths in the family, but, considering that Gloria had been in her late nineties, that certainly wasn't out of the ordinary.

And neither did Doreen find anything of concern or which would make her eyebrows go up regarding these deaths in the family. It was pretty standard, given the day and age too. Gloria, her son, and her niece had all been close, mostly because there was a shortage of other family members. So that also made sense. Doreen kept looking but was getting a little discouraged, as absolutely nothing suspicious seemed to come up.

When she sensed somebody watching her, she spun around to see the librarian, staring at her, her arms crossed over her chest. Doreen gave her a bright smile. "Good morning. I didn't see you when I first walked in," she said brightly.

The librarian's frown deepened. "I was only gone for a split second," she said suspiciously.

"Oh, that must have been when I came through," she guessed. "Hopefully all is well in your world?"

"It's fine," she said, but it didn't waylay the suspicion in her voice.

Doreen continued to smile at her. "Good. Always happy to hear that."

"What are you doing here?" the woman asked, and there was that same suspicion again.

"I'm researching Gloria's family."

At that, the woman gasped. "Why?" she cried out.

Doreen grasped for an idea. "It's for the, uh, celebration of life." Doreen loved the one that she landed with.

The librarian immediately calmed down. "Gloria has certainly had a life to celebrate."

"She's also had a lot of trials and tribulations," Doreen noted. "I feel sorry for her. First her husband, her sister, and then, of course, her son."

The librarian's face immediately turned somber. "Definitely," she said, "but she's been an unbelievably staunch strong woman, who made all kinds of things happen in her life. And she wouldn't have managed it without being one of those people who were very gracious and giving."

"Absolutely." Doreen nodded. "I'm also not seeing much in the way of other family here, and, of course, being new in town, I don't really want to ask too many questions, so I was trying to research it myself."

"It's probably a good idea if you don't ask a lot of questions," the librarian said, "because people love her dearly."

"And I'm good with that," Doreen said, with a bright smile. "I did meet her but just briefly over the orchids."

"Oh, did you go to the orchid showings?"

"Yes, I did."

"That's right. You like gardening, don't you?" Once again, her suspicions were obvious again.

But Doreen chose to ignore it. "I do love gardening," she said, "but I'm an amateur at best, with an awful lot to learn. But it's always inspiring to see other people excel."

The woman relaxed once again. "That would be very much the case here," she said. "Gloria excelled at everything she touched."

Doreen wasn't sure if that was just empty praise or if it was a case of somebody who truly believed what she was spouting.

"The son was fine," the librarian said quickly, almost too quickly, something also off in her tone.

"Fine?" She looked at her and realized that quite possibly Lionel and the librarian were of a similar age. "Did you know him?"

"Well, of course," she said. "In my job I get to know a lot of people."

"But you *knew him,* knew him, didn't you?" She tried to keep the curiosity and that interrogation tone out of her voice. According to Mack, because she was not the police, she turned people off with it.

The other woman flushed, confirming her suspicions.

"It must have been difficult for you," Doreen murmured, "when he was killed."

"That's not quite the word I would have chosen," she said quietly. "I know a lot of people didn't like him, but he was a good man at heart."

"And very close to his mother, I understand?"

"Too close to his mother. It's the one reason we didn't get any further in our relationship."

"The mother?"

"Yes. She did everything she could to break us up."

At that, Doreen sat back. "Wow, that's the first I've heard about that."

"Nobody will talk about it," she said. "And, unless you were in a relationship with her son, you wouldn't really recognize it."

"You think it was deliberate?"

"Oh, I know it was deliberate," she said. "But I loved Gloria anyway, and I understood it was part of the dependency the two of them had, but it sure was frustrating."

"Of course it would have been," Doreen said. "I'm so sorry. That would have been very difficult."

"Yes, but I was angrier at him than at Gloria because Lionel needed to grow up and to make his own decisions, apart from his mother."

Doreen nodded. "That makes sense too."

"But he never would, and that was just beyond what he was comfortable doing."

"I'm sorry for that. I heard a couple people say that he broke up her relationship with Stranden."

At that, the other woman shrugged. "I don't know anything about that, but, in a way, it seems fair to me." And, with that, she turned and marched on.

It was an interesting conversation, and Doreen wished

she could get the librarian to talk some more, but she'd probably gotten all she would get out of her for now. Doreen might squeeze a little more from her later, depending on if she could find the right way to reopen their conversation. She didn't have anything against this woman by any means, and she had been helpful more times than not.

Right now the librarian was more emotionally disturbed and was prepared to leave Doreen alone to get out of the conversation. And that was fine with her. She quickly wrote her notes about the relationship, about how Gloria had separated them. Of course that would be a big red flag for most people, but it also brought up a lot of interesting possibilities too. Maybe Gloria had done that with other people; maybe Gloria and her son were playing a game back and forth—a sick game, mind you—but still a parent-child relationship based on the premise *If I can't have you, nobody can.*

That brought back horrible thoughts that Doreen immediately clamped down on because she had absolutely no reason to believe or no way to find out that Gloria had anything to do with her son's death. As a matter of fact, it would be stupid to even consider such a thing. After all, Gloria and her son were very close, had been for decades. Gloria had no other family but Elle.

But, of course, once Doreen's mind had glommed on to this line of thinking, she had to wonder. But, no, that theory didn't make any sense either, and there had to be a better motive where the pieces fit together and made sense. Yet, with Gloria gone, Doreen had no way to prove anything, and that would just make life a little more difficult for everyone to have all these unanswered questions.

Doreen had another thought of who else would know

about past relationships in the son's world. She sent Nan a text, asking if she knew, stating that Doreen had just found out the librarian had been in a relationship with the son many years ago. When Doreen didn't get an immediate response, she figured that either Nan didn't have an answer or she was off doing something. She was frequently busy these days, between lawn bowling, flirting, and running her betting pools. All in all, Nan was a very social person.

Doreen finished off her research but couldn't find anything else of interest. A small mention in the son's obituary stated his death was in Vancouver, but no further details were given. Frustrated with that, she sent Mack a text. **I need the details on the murder of Gloria's son.**

Instead of sending a text back, he called her. "Where are you?" he asked, as a preamble.

"At the library." Still frustrated, she grumbled, "There's no information to be had."

"No," he said, "but, when you get to that level of things, it's pretty hard to get anywhere."

"So I need you to help," she said bluntly.

"I don't know about that."

"It doesn't matter if you do or not," she said. "I need to try and solve this."

"Why?"

"Well, for one thing, everybody seems to think it's a good idea. For two, I'm curious, and, for three, none of it adds up."

"What do you mean, nothing adds up?"

"It doesn't add up. I was just talking to the librarian here, and she made a hasty exit from the conversation." Gathering up her things, she tossed a quick smile at the nervous librarian, as Doreen whipped past the front desk.

"Okay, now I'm outside the library."

"Why the panic?"

"Because I just found out that the librarian went out with the son many years ago, and she blames Gloria for breaking them up."

"Really?" Mack sounded more than surprised but also a little distracted. "Why would Gloria do that?"

"I'm thinking we have a dysfunctional codependent relationship here, where one didn't want to lose the other because they had no one else."

"Sure, but people are supposed to move on," he said, doubt in his voice. "I can't see that Gloria would hold her son back over something like that."

"Maybe not hold her son back but maybe disapprove just enough to make her son rethink things. Just enough to make the girlfriend believe she'd be playing second fiddle to his mother forever and that, when push came to shove on issues small or large, he would never stand up for the girlfriend in opposition to his mother."

"Maybe," he said, "but so what if she did? I mean, it's not like she'll get punished for something like that now."

"No, of course not, but maybe that's also why the son did what he did, to keep her away from Stranden."

"Ah," he said, "I see where you're going."

"I'm just testing out the theory."

"You're one of the few people who sounds like you're defending Stranden."

"I'm not so sure I'm defending Stranden," she said, "but definitely something was very sad about him."

"And again, most people wouldn't agree with you there."

"Of course not," she said. "Gloria was beloved by the community, but I'm not coming from the same perspective that everybody else is."

"And, if you don't," he warned, "people won't take your meddling kindly."

"I know," she said. "I got that. At the same time, I don't know what I'm looking at. The pieces don't fit together yet."

"Maybe they're not meant to," he said quietly.

"Isn't it a cold case?" She was surprised by his attitude. "I know you were close to her, but still you would never let that impair your judgment."

He sighed. "Was that a dig at me?"

"Did it feel like a dig at you?" she asked curiously.

"Oh no, no, you don't," he said. "No psychology, thanks."

"Okay," she said. "I'm totally okay not to get into the psychology of that. But you know what I mean."

"I know what you mean, and obviously I won't let my feelings stop me from doing my job. But we don't really have anything here to investigate."

"And yet, if you gave me the cold case information," she said, "I could take a good look at it and could potentially find some information."

"And is this where I get to say that we're already overwhelmed and buried in a backlog of work because of you?"

"Is this where I get to remind you of how many cases you've managed to close and how many families you've brought closure to?"

"Low blow," he said. "I'll talk to the captain." And, with that, he hung up.

She smiled, as she stood on the steps of the library, then looked over and saw a couple people staring at her curiously. She tossed off a casual nod of her head in greeting, pocketed her phone, and headed to her car. She knew that a lot of people would be on Gloria's side. But that was where the trouble came in. Doreen didn't think she was on anybody's side, and she didn't know how they had gotten to the point of even having sides in this.

All she was trying to do was deal with the fact that Gloria herself had never gotten closure for a case that had obviously impacted her terribly. And now another family member was grieving with her own problems. Surely Elle, Gloria's niece, would want closure. And then again maybe she didn't care. Maybe the death of Lionel was just such a long time ago—twenty-five years—and now that her aunt was gone too, it didn't matter anymore to anybody else. People were funny; Doreen had no way to know for sure how people would react.

Although she got an inkling a little bit later, when she drove home to find the niece standing on Doreen's front step.

Doreen hopped out of her vehicle and rushed to the woman's side. "Oh hi," she said, "and I'm so sorry. I heard the news, and it was just so devastating."

The woman nodded absentmindedly. "Thank you," she said. "I mean, even though we were expecting it any day, it's still quite a hardship when it happens."

"Of course it is," she said, with full understanding.

"So, when we were talking the other night, we talked about you working with the police."

"Oh, well sort of," she said. "I'm told I get in their way a lot."

The woman looked briefly startled, and a smile cracked her face, before it quickly disappeared.

"What can I help you with?" Doreen asked.

"Well, there are all these rumors that my aunt was murdered," she said. "I don't know how to stop them."

"Ah," she said, "I'm not sure that one can ever stop a rumor. They tend to be quite poisonous. Plus they tend to linger around and to show up to cause all kinds of hardship."

"Ah," Elle said, "you do understand."

"Oh, yes, I've been on the receiving end of quite a few in my time," she said. "Unfortunately there really isn't an easy answer."

"No, of course not. I was just hoping that maybe, if you could say something, then people would stop thinking that something was wrong."

"Why would me saying something matter?" she asked curiously.

The woman looked at her. "Because you have influence in this town."

Doreen slowly shook her head, quite surprised at this turn of conversation. "I don't have any influence in this town. I'm just a newcomer here."

"Well, that may be," she said, with a smile, "but you have certainly turned the town upside down, at least according to the people I spoke to."

"Ouch," she said. "Obviously it's not the same people I speak to."

"No, but you've been involved in lots of cold cases."

"That's quite true," she said, "and honestly I have been asked to look into the murder of Gloria's son."

The woman gaped at her in shock. "Oh my, why would you do that?"

"Because it bothered Gloria all her life."

"Good idea, any time you have a murder of somebody like that," she said, "but you know people like to forget in death that not everybody was a good person."

"Meaning that your cousin, Lionel, wasn't a good person?"

"No. He wasn't. He was mean and vindictive, and I didn't like him at all."

"Interesting,' she murmured.

"That doesn't mean I killed him." The woman looked at Doreen askance.

"No, of course not," Doreen said, "but you don't always hear the truth from people, until somebody has died, and then their real feelings come out."

"That's because we kept everything peaceful and quiet for Aunt Gloria's sake," she said. "But honestly I don't know why we bothered. She knew perfectly well what he was like."

"Did she?" Doreen was surprised to hear that.

"Oh yes, there wasn't any surprising my aunt."

"That's interesting," she said. "I assumed that perhaps she was a mother blinded by love and not really sure exactly what went on."

"Nope, not at all. Gloria wasn't a fool, and she knew what her son was like. She also did her best to break up a couple relationships of his that she thought were poisonous and were destined to take her son down the wrong pathway. But, other than that, she sat back and watched in dismay, as he broke a lot of hearts in town here."

That completely lined up with what the librarian had said, although she hadn't suggested that there were an abundance of broken hearts. "I hadn't realized he had that many relationships."

"He was well loved by the ladies," she said, with a sniff. "Too well loved. Because he was never the person to stick around."

She nodded. "And then we'll hear rumors to that end as

well, I suppose?"

"Of course. Somebody's always disgruntled. I know a couple ladies in town, who thought that he would do right by them," she said, "but they didn't realize that he had no intention from the very beginning."

"So he was a playboy, was he?"

"You could say that," she said, shaking her head. "And my aunt knew she couldn't do a whole lot about it. There wasn't a whole lot she cared to do about it really, and, as long as he didn't have somebody special in his life, their lives trucked along exactly the same."

"What about Stranden?" she asked.

"I don't know about that," she said. "Aunt Gloria never talked about him. I met him a couple times, and he seemed pretty angry and not her type, but there were rumors that they were together for quite a while. That was before I moved to town. So I don't know what might have changed, whether he improved or got worse." She shrugged. "I guess it doesn't really matter. She's gone, and he's still here, but I don't imagine he's changed very much for the better."

"Was his behavior really ugly?"

"Oh, yeah, he was very ugly. And he made all kinds of accusations about Lionel."

"Of course he did." Doreen nodded. "Unhappy people tend to do that."

The woman smiled. "Sounds like you do recognize what people are like."

"That I do," she said.

"So could you possibly do what you can to quell any of the rumors?" She added, "The last thing I want is to deal with people saying that she was murdered."

"That is a police matter of course, and I don't know that

they have any particular suspicions at this point in time," she said. "However, because it was an unattended death, they do have to look into it."

"Sure, but she had a heart condition and all kinds of things going wrong in her world."

"That is bound to be a part of their findings, but I certainly won't step into an active investigation and start sharing information. It's not my place."

"I understand that," she said, with spirit, "but could you at least try to stop the rumors?"

"I can do that, if it comes to a point in time where I hear something that I know to be incorrect and released for public information," she said, "but what I won't do is lie."

The woman looked at her, startled for a moment. "Oh dear, I hadn't considered that."

"Hadn't considered what?"

"That you might be the do-gooder person who won't lie to save the peace."

"Interesting take on that." Doreen cautiously looked at the older woman. "I certainly wouldn't want anything to happen to disrupt Gloria's end-of-life celebration or anything along that line," she said, "but, if something about the rumor should come out with any evidence, you have to know that Gloria's life will be examined in great detail."

"And I would really like to avoid that," she said. "My aunt was a good person. She doesn't deserve to have her life torn apart."

"And hopefully there'll be no need," Doreen said gently. "The police will only do that if they see a problem."

"I hope so." Elle started down the steps. "I thought you always had animals with you?"

"I usually do," she said. "They're all inside. I just came

back from the library."

At that, she stopped, shook her head. "Hopefully you didn't talk to the librarian there. That woman has had a hate for Aunt Gloria for years."

"Why is that?"

"Because of her son again. Like I said, he was a player, and she was one of his affairs."

"She did mention that she had gone out with him for some time," she murmured.

"Ah, so she did speak of him." Elle shook her head. "Everybody tries to grab on to a relationship now," she said, "even ones that weren't real."

"So, how long did they go out?"

"I have no idea," she said. "As far as my aunt was concerned, that was just a pie-in-the-sky relationship on the librarian's part and had zero meaning to anyone."

That was an odd thing to say, but Doreen kept quiet, as the other woman started down the porch steps again.

"Anyway," Elle said, "I don't know that there's any point in talking to you anymore about this. I just would like to preserve my aunt's memory."

"We have a lot of friends in common who want the same," she said.

At that, she stopped, looked back at Doreen. "Well, there is that, isn't there? Maybe they can be persuaded to help out too."

And Elle walked down the steps, over to and down the driveway, without another word.

Chapter 20

Thursday Morning

THE NEXT MORNING Doreen contacted Mack. "Any news?"

"I haven't had a chance to talk to the captain yet."

"Ah," she said, "well, you need to know that Gloria's niece, whether their relationship was good or bad, came to ask me to help shut down the rumors of Gloria being murdered."

"Wow," he said. "I wonder why she'd do that. We certainly haven't brought such a thing up."

"Neither have I," she said, "so I'm not sure where that's coming from. But it's suspicious in itself."

"Whoa, whoa, whoa," he said. "That's not true."

"No," she said, "but you know what it's like."

"I do, but we've got lots going on, and we haven't heard back from the autopsy yet."

"I'm surprised an autopsy was done."

"I know, but I think, because of the murder of her son, the captain wanted to make sure that everything was free and clear."

"Which is interesting in itself. I presume he knew her as

well."

"Everybody did," he said gently, "which is one of the reasons why we did it. Plus, her friend had power of attorney, and she agreed."

"A friend with power of attorney?" she repeated. "Not her niece? Now that brings up a whole different load of possibilities."

"No, it doesn't," he said, "not at all."

"Says you."

"Yes, says me," he said, "so don't you get involved."

"I'm already involved."

"Nothing's here," he said, "and you can't do anything about it."

"Somebody knows something about Lionel's death."

"That doesn't mean that a murder committed down on the coast has anything to do with anybody here."

"No, but it doesn't mean that it doesn't either."

He said, "I've got to go," and he quickly hung up.

Just then Nan called, in response to Doreen's earlier text. "The son had lots of relationships," Nan said. "He was well-known for playing the field. He was the guy you didn't want to get caught up with because he wouldn't be around a long time."

"Right, so he left a field of broken hearts."

"There was also talk about some abuse."

"Meaning?"

"He liked to knock around the occasional person," Nan said. "Definitely not my kind of man."

"Not anybody's kind really," Doreen said. "I don't understand why that wouldn't have been more public knowledge. Because if he was an abuser—"

"Nobody would go against him."

"Ah, that makes sense because, I presume, he would just become more abusive to pay them back. But surely the women would get fed up with that eventually, right?"

"I don't know," Nan said. "I couldn't get any information about it. And the one woman I could talk to, whose daughter did hang out with him a lot, is having a procedure done in the hospital today, so I can't talk to her until she's back home. Even then, it depends on what kind of shape she's in." Nan sounded a bit distracted too.

"Are you okay, Nan?"

"Sure," she said, "but all these discussions about Gloria are upsetting."

"Of course. However, if we're trying to solve her son's murder, we need a better idea of who Lionel was."

"I didn't know about this," she said. "I remembered hearing some stories, but I thought they were just ugly rumors, passed around by jilted paramours."

"Maybe they were," Doreen said quietly. "Ugly rumors can start from nothing and can become quite damaging."

"That's very true." Nan sounded a bit more relieved. "I think you need to sort this out." And, with that, she hung up.

"Really?" Doreen glared at the phone. "And how do you expect me to do that?"

Sometimes she found that, on a case like this, where somebody local was involved, it took time, and she suspected that maybe because Gloria was gone now, somebody's tongue might finally loosen. But, other than that, Doreen couldn't be sure. After her phone call with Nan, Doreen grabbed a cup of tea and her notes and sat outside. She didn't know what to do next. If she didn't get any additional information from Mack, not much else she could do.

As she sat here, Mugs started barking like crazy. She looked over to see him racing down the trail to the river again. She immediately bolted to her feet. "Mugs, Mugs! Come back here."

But he wasn't having it, and he raced to the water's edge. She got there just to see him stop at the boundary of the property. For that she was grateful, but he continued to bark at somebody around the corner and out of sight. She stepped forward to see who was there and was surprised to see the little neighbor lady Doreen had gone to help earlier this week, when she'd been screaming.

Amie stopped and gazed at her. "So this is where you live?"

"Yes." Doreen's eyebrows went up. "I'm just a few houses away from you."

The older woman nodded slowly. "I wasn't sure if you were telling the truth or not."

Flabbergasted, she could only stare at her. "I don't have any reason to lie," she said gently. "And I was just coming to help you."

"Maybe," she said, "but the police have deserted me."

She shook her head. "I don't believe that," she said. "Are they still working at your place?"

"No, of course not," she said crossly, "but they left a mess."

Now that she could believe. "I'm sorry. Apparently that's fairly common, after a crime scene, like they found at your house. I thought you would have moved in with your son for a few days."

Amie sniffed. "That won't happen," she said. "My son is a very important person."

"Too important for his mother to move in when she's in

trouble?"

"You don't know anything about it," she said. "I'm sorry I came down here." And she immediately turned and tried to head back.

Doreen impulsively reached out. "I'm sorry. I didn't mean to upset you."

The woman jerked her arm free. "Well, you did. I will not talk to anybody who speaks against my son."

"No, of course not," Doreen said. "Why would anybody do that?"

Amie stopped. "Isn't that what you were saying?"

"No." Doreen tried to come up with a reason for back-tracking. "I'm just glad that he's there for you."

"So am I," Amie said. "It'd be terrible if he wasn't."

Doreen nodded. "Did you get some help to clean up your house?"

Amie shook her head. "Of course not," she said. "My son certainly couldn't come and help, so it's up to me to do it." She shook her head. "I don't understand how the police get away with that."

"I don't think the police have any jurisdiction in your home."

"They made the mess. They're supposed to clean it up."

Doreen winced because, in theory, it would be nice, but she didn't think it would hold up or that Mack would even acknowledge that as being an option. "I think they would say that whoever broke into your house was the one responsible."

"Well, he's dead," she said, "so that won't do any good, will it?"

And again Amie had that odd look, causing Doreen to wonder if she was even all there or not. "Would you like me to walk you home? I was just about to walk with the animals."

"Why?"

"I need to get out for a little bit of fresh air anyway. It's good for me and for my animals."

Amie nodded immediately. "Fresh air is very good for you, and you should be outside every day," she said, scolding her. "Especially with the animals."

"I try," she said, "and we do get out a lot." At that, Mugs and Goliath fell into line, and she stopped to see Thaddeus running behind them. She waited until he caught up, picked him up, and put him on her shoulder.

Amie gawked at her. "You have a bird?" she asked, as if that were the worst thing ever.

Doreen gently tried to get a line on how to even talk to this woman, without setting her off. But maybe it didn't matter. Maybe Doreen should just be ignoring Amie. But it did seem like something was going on here that Doreen didn't understand, and, if it came to humanity, she did want to understand it. "Any reason not to have a bird?"

Amie shook her head. "You do know that they poop everywhere, right?"

"He's pretty well trained," she said. "We occasionally have the odd accident, but no more than we do with my dog."

Amie looked at the dog, shuddered. "You should have one of those show dogs. Those are the only ones that are any good."

"Ouch." Doreen patted Mugs. "I don't think he would take very kindly to that kind of disparagement." Amie once again looked at her, nonplussed. Doreen gave her a gentle smile. "Come on. Let's get you home again."

Amie didn't argue with that, but she almost seemed happier to get away from Doreen than to get home. As soon as they made it to her lawn, Amie turned. "I'll be fine from here. Thank you." Her tone was stiff, and she turned to run away.

"Did they ever find out who the intruder was?"

Amie shook her head. "No."

Doreen nodded and watched as Amie raced up her driveway and didn't even hesitate to go into the house. On Doreen's way back home, she called Mack.

"Now what?" he said in a clipped tone. "I still haven't had a chance to talk to the captain."

"I get that," she said, "but remember my neighbor? The one screaming? Where we found the dead body? Do you have any idea what was going on at her place?"

"Amie?" he said. "What about her?"

"She was just here, walking by the river. Though I don't really understand why because it seemed like she couldn't wait to get away from me, as soon as we got near her place."

"I think a lot of people have that experience." A note of humor was in his voice.

She groaned. "All joking aside, Mack, she sounded very strange. I'm not sure she's all there."

"We're not sure she is either," he said, "but we did get all the forensic evidence, and we're still trying to identify the man found in her house."

"Do you think she killed him?"

At first, silence came on the other end. "Do you think she did?"

"I think she's capable of it because again, I'm not exactly sure she's all there."

"Right," he said, "and that would be a very sad case, but

not the first time we've heard of anything like it."

"Right." Still upset and mystified by it all, she hung up, wondering if there was any way to find out anything.

When talking to Nan a little bit later, Doreen asked her grandmother if she knew anything about Amie's family.

"No, I don't," she said. "I don't think so anyway."

Doreen frowned. "I think she's kind of, you know, not all there."

"You think?" Nan said sarcastically.

Doreen sighed. "I wonder if, at any point in time, somebody stepped in to give her some help."

"Most people avoid stepping into things like that," Nan said. "The medical community would have to do something about it."

"Right now I don't think that's even an option for her. What if she can't contact her son? Or what if her son is not there to look after her? Surely somebody needs to."

"If you're really concerned about it," Nan said, "I think maybe you can contact a social worker or somebody."

"Yeah, I mentioned that to Mack."

"There you go. He'd know exactly who to contact."

"I don't think he was too worried about her mental health."

"At the time he may have been more worried about identifying the man who died in her house," Nan quipped.

"Exactly," Doreen said. "We still haven't found any other information on Gloria's son either. I've asked for the cold case file, but I haven't gotten anywhere there so far."

"So we're at a dead end there too. Let's just get Gloria buried and get everybody celebrating her life, instead of worrying about her son's death."

Very practical advice, just like that, was exactly like Nan.

Doreen knew she could get on board with that to some degree, but it still felt very wrong in some ways. And she could see that nobody else really wanted to do too much to upset the apple cart.

Saturday

TWO DAYS LATER, Doreen showed up in the morning at Gloria's house for a celebration of life. She'd picked up Nan, and Mack would be here as well. Two days she had spent doing a pile of gardening to keep herself busy, with an occasional search on the internet, where she found nothing more on Amie's family or Gloria's. Doreen had never felt like more of a fraud or a failure than she did right now.

As she stepped forward, Mack placed a hand on her shoulder. She looked up and smiled at him. "Hey, I didn't realize you'd already arrived."

"I can't stay either," he said quietly.

She nodded. "Well, at least this should go off okay, and everybody will have a chance to grieve," she murmured.

"That's the hope anyway." He looked around. "And I do need to talk to you."

"About what?" And then she glanced around. "This?"

He shook his head. "No. About your neighbor."

"Oh," she said. "You want to do it now?"

He hesitated. "No, I'll stop by later this afternoon."

"You're cooking dinner then too?" she asked, her voice hopeful.

"Not likely tonight. Maybe later." He looked at her. "Don't tell me that you've resorted to eating cheese and crackers?"

"Cheese, crackers, peanut butter, and bread," she said, with a nod. "The groceries didn't go all that far."

"And here I heard rumors that you sold several flower bouquets."

"I did," she said, "but it's not like anybody is lining up to get more."

"Have you put out a sign or built even a static website, saying you could do more?"

"I'm not sure how much more I can do," she said in surprise. "It's not like my garden is in full bloom, and I don't have access to tons of other flowers."

He nodded. "So I guess it's something that you have to plan for a little more, isn't it?"

"Absolutely," she said. "And it is something that I'm wondering about. In fact, I've been looking at costs of websites and how hard it would be to run something like that. But, even if business was generated just by word of mouth, it would be something though."

"Exactly," he said, with a note of encouragement. "It's too bad Gloria is gone. She would have been the ideal person to talk to about something like that."

She looked at him, as he walked away. She didn't know why he thought Gloria would have been a good contact, but obviously she had had a lot of local connections, living here so long, so maybe that was it. It seemed silly to keep worrying about Gloria, when she was now firmly out of the picture.

As far as the niece went, Elle was teary-eyed and thankful during Gloria's celebration of life, giving everybody hugs and motioning them out the door when leaving. She even surprised Doreen by giving Nan a big hug and whispering, "Thank you for coming."

Nan gave her a hug back and whispered, "She was one of my best friends."

Elle nodded. "She had a great many friends."

Something was dismissive about that statement, as if Nan was just one of many and how Elle wanted Nan to know it. The odd exchange caught Doreen's ear. She looked at Nan, as they left. "Did that sound strange to you?"

Nan looked at her. "What?"

Doreen shrugged. "What she just said, … it sounded *off.*"

"You're looking for trouble where there isn't any. Don't do it here, please."

At that, Doreen immediately shut up because Nan was more than a little upset over the whole thing. Doreen dropped her grandmother off at Rosemoor, but Doreen didn't go inside. Instead she went straight home to the animals. She hadn't been there very long, after doing more weeding, then just sitting with a cup of tea, taking a break, when Mack's truck pulled up. She recognized the sound of it from her garden, but she could also recognize the greeting Mugs always gave Mack, as he started barking like crazy. When Mack came around to the backyard, he sat down on the deck with a hard sigh. "So," he said, "what do you think of the old lady?"

"Which one?" she asked, "I appear to be completely overwhelmed by them lately."

He stared at her for a moment, then started to laugh. "Isn't that the truth." With a warm smile, he said, "In this case, I'm talking about your neighbor."

"Ah, the one who I went to rescue?"

He nodded. "Yes, that one."

She shrugged. "I don't know. Something's off with her.

It's like talking to somebody completely different, to someone who is having a conversation completely different from the one I'm having. But it's not the first time I've had things like that happen, so I don't know what to say. Maybe we're just not on the same wavelength."

"Wavelength, yeah, that's a good way to put it," he said. "I'm not sure she's on anybody's wavelength though."

Doreen sighed. "That bad?"

"I'm not sure yet," he said, "but we'll have to take a look at that."

"Did you ever identify who it was in her house?"

Before he could answer, a cheery voice came from the river again. Doreen turned in that direction. "Speak of the devil."

He looked up to see the same neighbor, walking up the pathway.

Amie looked at Doreen. "I hope I'm not too late for tea."

Doreen shook her head slowly. "No, not at all. Mack just stopped by. I'll put on the teakettle."

Amie gave Mack an odd look, and he said, "Sorry, I didn't mean to interrupt."

Doreen whispered under her voice, "I had no idea she was coming. We definitely didn't arrange this."

He looked at her, startled, as she nodded and quickly raced inside to get some hot water going. When she came back out, Amie was talking to Mack and telling him about her son.

He nodded slowly. "We've had some trouble contacting your son," he murmured.

She waved a hand. "He's very busy."

"Of course he is," Mack said.

With that, Amie looked at Doreen, sharing a vague smile. "Thank you so much for tea." Then she turned and walked away.

"But I haven't served her yet." Doreen shook her head, sat back down at the patio table, and exhaled. "So what the heck was that?"

"I was just about to ask you the same thing," he said.

They waited until the older lady disappeared around the corner. "I presume we need to get some mental health care for her?"

"Maybe more than that." He picked up a tissue that Amie had left behind. "I'll take this, if you don't mind."

"Sure, but why?"

He looked at her. "I don't want you to say anything, and I certainly don't ..." Then he stopped. "No. Let me talk to the coroner first." And, with that, he got up and dashed off to his truck.

She stared after him, and even Mugs looked completely upset that he had taken off so abruptly.

"I don't know what's going on." She thought about Amie. Doreen went back inside, grabbed her laptop, and searched for pictures online of the old lady and her family. Sure enough, she found one of her son. He was tall and worked as a plumber half the time, known for doing lots of odd jobs at other times. Doreen didn't quite understand what connection he had to any of this, except being Amie's son and that Mack couldn't get a hold of him. That was a little disturbing but not terrible.

Chapter 21

ON IMPULSE, DOREEN searched for the son's address and found that it was not very far away, just down on the other side of Rosemoor, where Nan lived. Deciding that a walk would be better than doing anything else right now, Doreen gathered the animals and headed down the river. She didn't know if she should stop in and say hi to Nan, when it had been such a rotten day for her. A hug might make her better, but, on the other hand, it might make it worse. She walked past Rosemoor, confusing the animals completely, as they tried to head for Nan's, where they knew they were well loved. But Doreen pulled them forward and farther down the road.

"We'll stop on the way back," she promised them. And again she wasn't exactly sure that was the right thing to promise because the animals were usually good for Nan's spirits, but right now Nan may not want the distraction. We all grieve in our own manner.

When somebody was sincerely trying to honor the life of someone else, maybe it was better to stay away. Doreen just didn't know; she didn't have any experience with death at this level. Unfortunately she was beginning to feel like her grandmother had far too much experience with death, and that had to be wearing.

Still, Doreen headed around the corner and kept walking. She talked to the animals. "Look at this," she said. "We haven't been in this direction at all." Realizing they were heading off on a new adventure, all the animals perked up, and even Thaddeus came out from under the fall of her hair and searched the area. He crowed and settled in, his head up and his eyes bright.

She chuckled. "See? We're all ready for this—just a chance to get out and to be by ourselves a little bit."

And they kept walking and walking. Doreen came across another interesting little spot, where she stopped with the animals to rest a bit, to just walk around, and to enjoy themselves. After a few minutes, she got back on the road and walked up to the street where the son's house was.

She passed several homes and came to a small house in good shape but older looking. She stopped and stared at it. A For Sale sign was in the front yard. One of the neighbors joined her. "Are you interested in the house?"

She shrugged. "I was looking for the owner."

"Yeah, the police were here the other day—and this morning." He frowned. "He's almost never here. If he's not here, he's generally looking after his mother."

"What does he look like?" she asked curiously.

He laughed and walked closer, pulling out his phone. "This is him. We were doing a bunch of fencing over the previous weekend. He's always walking up and down the river here."

She thought about it. "I've only seen one guy recently."

"That'll be him."

She stopped and stared. "Does he wear black a lot?"

He nodded. "Always." He selected another photo similar to one she'd seen earlier, but this time it showed him all dressed in black.

Her heart sank. "Okay," she said. "Thank you."

With that, she immediately hustled the animals back in the direction they came. As soon as the neighbor was out of sight and out of hearing distance, she phoned Mack.

"I don't have time."

"You need to make time," she snapped.

After a moment of silence, he said, "What?"

"You need to check the dead man in the old lady's house."

"Yes, we're working on it. What about it?"

"You need to make sure it isn't her son."

He spluttered to a stop. "You know that we are law enforcement, right? That we do this all the time? We've not yet confirmed his identity, but we think we know who it is."

And she told him what she just found out from the neighbor.

"You think that her own son was in the house and was killed? But that means we're looking for a third person."

"We were always looking for someone," she said, "but I'm afraid we're looking for nobody. I think we may already have all the players."

He said, "Okay, hang on a minute. Either you're not making any sense or I'm not understanding what you're trying to tell me."

"Given Amie's mental state," Doreen said sadly, "I'm afraid that her son went there to fix something. She came in, mistook him for an intruder, and hit him over the head with something."

Mack groaned at the other side. "Lord almighty," he

said. "That's not something I even want to consider."

"Me either but you better double-check to make sure."

"We normally would contact the mother to make the son's positive identification."

"Exactly, but his neighbor knows him, so that might be another person you could use."

"Only if it's the son."

"But there's no other way to know at this point that is fast."

"No, that's quite true. I'll get on it." He added, "But don't you say anything to anybody."

"No, of course not," she said. "This is way too sad. But you saw her mental state."

"Yes, I did." He paused. "And I was just talking to the captain about getting her some help."

"Now you'll have to pick her up and get some questions answered first."

"No, that's quite—never mind," he said. "First things first. I'll deal with it." Obviously disturbed, he rang off.

Doreen was plenty disturbed herself. As she headed back in the direction of Nan's place, she wondered at a woman who would kill her own son. In this case it was likely more a case of killing somebody she didn't recognize, and, given her mental state, Amie possibly didn't even know she had killed anyone.

But what about Gloria's son? He was supposedly stabbed in Vancouver. And, at that, Doreen wondered what really happened. She thought about everything she'd read about it and how he was found, already dead by a good five or six hours, and that just brought up another horrible thought.

She groaned, knew that Mack would not like anything about her second hypothesis either. When she called him back, there was no answer. "Good for you, Mack," she said. "At least I don't have to talk to you about this one. Yet."

As she headed to Nan's, Doreen kept talking to herself, muttering her way through it.

A sharp whistle came from her side.

She turned to see Richie standing there, Nan with him, both of them staring at her.

"You're talking to yourself," Richie said. "You better watch that, or you'll end up here with us."

Doreen smiled and headed toward them. "I didn't want to disturb you guys today," she said, "because I know what an important day it is."

"We lost a friend." He nodded. "Unfortunately it seems to be something that we're dealing with on a nearly daily basis sometimes."

"Right, and I'm so sorry about that," she said. "It's got to be tough."

"Very, but we're old hands at it now."

"Still," she said, "I was just around the corner, so I thought I'd stop in and see how you guys were doing."

"We're doing fine," Nan said warmly, "and it's lovely that you care so much."

"Of course I do," she said.

"Well then, come in and have a cup of tea."

She nodded. "So, Richie, can I ask you a couple questions?"

"Of course," he said instantly. "We're always interested in whatever cases you're working on."

"I'm taking a look at Gloria's son's case," she said quietly, "but I don't want to stir up bad memories."

"Oh, well, pretty much anything to do with him is a bad memory." He shook his head. "That boy could get into trouble like nothing else."

"Do you know any of the details on his mugging case?"

"Gloria called me at the time. He'd headed down to Vancouver, and he hadn't called her when he arrived, so she was pretty upset."

"I'm sure," she murmured. "Did he go alone?"

He looked at her in surprise. "You know what? I don't remember. I think he went down alone though, or maybe he went with his cousin. Not very many members left in the family."

"No," she said quietly.

"No, Gloria mentioned it a couple times," Nan interrupted. "But I don't remember hearing that level of detail. But I guess we should have asked that question, shouldn't we?"

Doreen turned to Richie. "If he was murdered in Vancouver, and he drove down there with somebody, it'd be nice to know if his vehicle was brought back home again."

"Oh," Richie said, "that's a really good point. Why didn't we think of that?" He frowned at Nan.

"We probably did back then," Nan said, "but, if we did have any answers, we couldn't have done anything with it."

"Yeah, so it's easy to forget just how far we came on some of this."

"Exactly." Doreen gave him a bright smile. "I'm not saying anybody missed anything," she said. "It's just hard to know what to even think."

"You're right," he said, "absolutely right. But we should be doing something about it now."

"I know the police followed up with all of us," Nan said. "Remember? The local cops were asked to check out a few things for the Vancouver police, but they put it down to a random mugging because he was found in his vehicle."

"And do you know what Gloria did with that vehicle?"

"No, I don't," Nan said.

Doreen nodded at that. "Okay, I'll ask the niece."

"You do that," Nan said. "And, if you find out anything, let me know."

"Will do." After a few minutes more she gathered up the animals and carried on, walking home.

Once she got there, she picked up her phone and called the niece. When Elle answered the phone, her tone was subdued. "I know it's not a good day to talk to you," Doreen said, "because of, well, you've had a big day, with the celebration of life and all."

"There's not likely to be a good day for a long time," she said tiredly.

"I just wondered, when your cousin was killed, what happened to his vehicle?"

"The police impounded it," she said, "but I don't know what happened to it afterward. Why?"

"I just wondered who went down to Vancouver with him at the time."

There was a moment's hesitation. "I did. Why?"

"Where were you when he was killed?" she asked, completely blown away by this newfound fact.

"Yeah, that's one of those questions that I keep answering," she said. "Lionel had dropped me off at my friend's place for the night. And I was supposed to meet up with him that morning for breakfast. So I was in the café, getting breakfast to go, and I came outside to wait for him, thinking I'd call to remind him. Then I realized Lionel's truck was out there. I'm the one who found him, you know."

"Oh dear, I'm so sorry," she said. "That must have been

terrible."

"It was very terrible, and, of course, it's not something that ever leaves you. I didn't need to find Gloria myself either."

"Ouch," Doreen said, "no, that would have been even more dramatic and brought up all kinds of bad things, I'm sure."

"Exactly," she said, "so, if you don't mind, I'd just as soon not answer any more questions."

"Of course not," she murmured. "I understand. How did you get home, by the way?"

"Gloria sent for me," she said. "There was just the two of us at that point in time, and she was beside herself."

"Right," she said, "and did you call her?"

"Yes, of course. What else do you think I did?" And Elle laughed. "I'm sorry. I'm not trying to be harsh, but it's been a crazy day."

"Of course. I'm just trying to figure out exactly what happened."

"How can you?" she asked. "It's been so long ago that you're better off just to leave it."

"Yeah, I don't leave things all that easily," she said, "sadly enough."

"Sometimes you just have to," Elle said, her voice blunt. "Because no good will come of bringing this back up again."

"But sometimes we don't have any choice," she murmured.

"What do you mean by that?"

"It just seems odd that it was never solved."

"Do you have any idea how many cold cases are down the coast? That place is just a nightmare of murders."

"I don't think it's quite that bad," Doreen said.

"They didn't solve it, so not anything that anybody could do about it."

"No, of course not," Doreen said. "Sorry to have disturbed you." She went to hang up. "Oh, just one other question."

"What?" Elle cried out. "What could you possibly want to know now?"

"You said that she sent for you. So how did you get home again?"

"Gloria drove me," she said. "I told you that she came down and got me."

"You told me that she sent for you. You didn't tell me that she came down and got you."

"She was looking for her son," she said. "She woke up in the middle of the night, with the most horrible feeling, and drove to Vancouver. And she was down there when I found Lionel."

"Oh, so she had a cell phone?"

"Yes, she was always quick to adopt technology, and it's not like we didn't have cell phones twenty-five years ago," she said in a waspish tone.

"No, of course not," she said. "And so you just came home in her vehicle?"

"Yes, that's what I said."

"Okay, sorry." And she hung up, still wondering.

When Mack called her back, almost two hours later, she was sitting down to a sandwich. "Oh, good timing," she said. "I'm just having a sandwich."

"A sandwich versus real food?"

"I was hoping you would stop by to cook one of these nights, but that didn't happen."

"No, it was on the agenda though, wasn't it?" he said.

"I'm sorry. My job does interfere a lot."

"I don't think that's an issue, as far as we're concerned," she said. "I will always understand if you have a case to go to."

He paused for a moment and said, "You know something? You're probably one of the few women who would. That's been one of the reasons I've broken off from other relationships. Nobody ever truly understood."

"Very short-term thinking on their part," she said, with a chuckle. "But we'll always bond over murder."

"And that makes us a very strange family," he muttered.

"And sometimes that's just what it is," she said. "It's only strange to people on the outside. I don't think it's strange to us at all. Anyway …" And she stopped.

"What's the matter? Losing your train of thought already?"

"Sometimes I wonder," she said, with a heavy sigh. "Just so many things are going on. Did you ever contact anybody about that body at Amie's house?"

"We do know how to do our jobs, you know?" he murmured.

"Which means you did … and?"

He sighed. "You were right. It's the son."

"Oh," she said, with a sad tone. "And are we thinking Mom did it?"

"It's sure looking that way, but we're not likely to get to the truth. We picked her up to ask her a few questions today, and she's basically lost all sense of reality. She's being cared for at the hospital right now, while she undergoes a bunch of tests."

"It was probably the final straw that sent her over," she said. "I was thinking she got up late and disoriented, came downstairs, saw him working in the house, and, without giving him a chance to turn around and to say anything, she popped him one."

"It certainly could have happened like that, but it's sure sad to think of."

"It may be sad, but I think, in this case, that's what you may be looking at."

"I do too unfortunately, and I know that everybody will be pretty upset about it."

"It's not how you want to see the end of your life, when you go help somebody out at home."

"Not at all. Particularly not when it's your own mother."

"Exactly," she said. "So I have another question for you."

"*Great*," he said. "Will it be just as depressing?"

"Maybe," she said. "Did you know that Elle, the niece, went on the trip with her cousin Lionel and was down there in Vancouver when he was murdered?"

"No, I didn't know that," he said. "Are you serious?"

She said, "Yeah, Elle told me. You need to pull the case file."

"I have pulled it." The fatigue in his voice made her wince. "I just haven't had a chance to look at it yet."

"And I'm sorry because I keep adding to it."

"You sure do. Particularly since you're bringing something up right now," he said, "and you know it'll stir up a lot of other memories."

"I know, and, for that, I'm sorry too," she said, "because I do think that this one may be fairly easy to solve."

"I don't want to think of that," he said. "I just know that, back then, they didn't have too much information to go by, but I do have an arresting officer on the case."

"Well, give him a phone call because the bottom line is,

the niece says she was there with Lionel. Apparently it was prearranged that he would pick her up. She was inside the café, getting food, and noticed his vehicle already sitting there, waiting for her. When she got the food, she went outside and found him dead in his truck. And supposedly he'd been dead for a few hours."

"Right," Mack said. "I remember something about the coroner estimating Lionel sat there for a while."

"Whatever *a while* means, yes," she said sadly.

"So what are you thinking happened?"

She sighed. "Is there any way to know where a cell phone is geographically when a call is placed?"

"Sure, but I don't know about how far back the records go though."

"Elle also said that her aunt Gloria was already down on the coast, when Elle phoned Gloria to let her know of the mugging."

"Gloria?"

"Yes, she'd apparently woken up with a horrible feeling and couldn't get ahold of her son, so she hopped in her vehicle and headed down there."

"That sounds like Gloria."

"Maybe," Doreen said. "But was she trying to save her son, to save her niece, or to save somebody else?"

"Uh-oh," he said. "Are you thinking the niece is guilty?"

"I'm not sure," she said. "I'm really not sure. Did you ever get any autopsy results back on Gloria?"

"The niece was trying to stop the autopsy. She didn't realize it was happening in the first place, so now she has a lawyer involved."

"Yeah," Doreen said. "Not only that, I think you need to take a look at the son's case file. I don't know if any tissue samples from Lionel were left from way back when, but maybe run it for whatever you find in Gloria."

"No, no, no. Now you're talking about the niece having murdered both people," he said, "and that's not fair. Again this is largely just conjecture."

"No, you're quite right," she said sadly. "However, I have an alternate theory, as I also see another trend here."

"What's that?"

"A family trend," she said, "but I won't give you my further reasoning, until you get back to me." And, with that, she hung up.

Chapter 22

Sunday Morning

DOREEN SAT OUTSIDE the next morning and looked up to see Amie, the older lady who Doreen had thought was safe and sound at the hospital, coming toward her, a determined look on Amie's face.

Amie looked down at Doreen, still seated. "You are an interfering busybody."

Doreen jumped to her feet, looked at her, and called Mugs back, who was getting aggressive. "In what way?" she asked quietly.

"You told the cops that intruder was my son."

"No, I did not," she said, flat-out. "I simply asked them to double-check to see if it was your son."

"And, of course, it's not my son," Amie yelled. "I told you where my son lives."

"Yes, you did," Doreen agreed. "Oddly enough, the cops checked his house, and it was empty. So they ran his blood and confirmed it is your son."

"No, of course it's not my son. How dare you keep saying that?" she said. "With all these lies, they'll never find the truth."

"The truth is often a very confusing and nebulous thing."

"No, it's not," she argued. "It's very clear. You just have to look for it."

"I can't argue that point," she muttered, as she studied the older woman. "What are you doing here?"

"I had to get a friend to get me out of the hospital," she said, with disdain. "All because of you."

She sounded so rational that now Doreen didn't have a clue what to think. But she also suspected that these rational moments came and went. "I'm sorry," she said. "You seem to be having a hard time right now."

"Of course I am. I can't find my son."

"At least you're at home now, where he can reach you."

Amie looked at her in surprise. "Well, of course, except that I'm here talking to you."

"So, what if your son was trying to reach you now?"

"I have a cell phone," she said. "It's not like in the olden days when we didn't have them."

"No, of course not." Doreen smiled. "And what about Gloria? Did you know her at all?"

"Of course. Everybody knew Gloria. Poor woman."

"Why do you say that?"

"Because of her son, Lionel, of course. He was murdered."

"Yes," Doreen said, "I heard that."

"But I don't really think he was murdered so much as Gloria took some things into her own hands."

"And what was it that she did?"

"I think she killed him herself, after he tried to destroy her relationship with the man she wanted to marry. They were engaged, you know?" she said in a conspiratorial whisper.

"Were they? Why would she have killed her own son?" Doreen asked.

"Because he was bad news, and he just wanted her money. Not to mention he thought that, if she got married, he would lose out and wouldn't be part of things anymore."

Doreen nodded. "That would make sense."

"Of course it makes sense. It always makes sense," Amie said, "but you young people, you just don't want to think about things anymore."

"Sorry. Maybe we're just missing out on all your experience."

"Maybe," she said, "but you have to watch old people too. They're very conniving."

Doreen looked at her, smiled. "Now that is very true. Because you killed your son too, didn't you?"

At that moment, a gleam of sanity filled her gaze. "Of course not," she replied. "I killed an intruder." Her tone was very clear, her diction very clean. "It's not my fault that I didn't know who that intruder was, is it?"

As Doreen gaped at the old woman, a thought crossed Doreen's mind. "He saw the signs, didn't he? The first signs that you're losing your faculties. He would have put you in Rosemoor, and you'd already heard how bad the place was, and you decided to stop it."

"I certainly wouldn't go to Rosemoor, would I?" she said indignantly. "How dare he say that."

"This son who has done so much for you," Doreen said, with a sad smile, fervently wishing Nan hadn't told the old girl those terrible stories about Rosemoor.

"He loved me. I know he did."

"Absolutely he did." Doreen recognized that the woman

was now using past tense. "And, if you keep it up, you might have a chance at that insanity defense."

Amie frowned at her. "I have no clue what you're talking about." She fretted then, looked at her watch, and said, "But you're right. I need to go home. I must get my phone so my son can call me." She faced Doreen, gave her a bright flashing smile. "I'll talk to you later."

And, with that, she turned and hastened away.

Chapter 23

DOREEN WISHED SHE could get into Gloria's house. She didn't have any reason for it, except an inkling that she would find something icky, probably not appropriate at all, but something that she might need to see for herself in order to believe. On impulse, she contacted the niece and offered to come over and bring her some tea or lunch or something.

The niece chuckled. "I'm fine," she said, "but you're welcome to come by. I know you were here during the tour but didn't get much of a chance to see much on your visit."

"No, I didn't," she said. "If you wouldn't mind, I'd love to see that orchid again."

"Yeah, I don't even know what to do about it," she said, "although I've already been asked if I'm interested in selling it."

"Oh my." Doreen slowly sank back into her chair. "Is that something you would consider?"

"Of course," she said. "I certainly can't keep it in any healthy condition. The only two people who cared about that orchid are dead and gone."

"Do you think the orchid had anything to do with your

cousin's death?"

"The orchid? I don't know. We often thought it did, but I'm not so sure."

"*Hmm.* Okay, I'll pop by soon."

After hanging up, she quickly loaded the animals in her car and raced to Gloria's house. As she walked up to the front door, it opened and there, she saw the niece. Mugs raced forward to greet her enthusiastically.

The older woman laughed, as she rubbed Mug's ears. "It's nice to see you again. Come on in, and take a look at the orchid, if you like."

They wandered through the lower part of the house, just talking casually, as Doreen's gaze took in the huge living room and the pictures on the walls and what looked like a family Bible on the coffee table. The animals strolled alongside them. "Do you live here?" Doreen asked.

"I moved in a few months ago," she said, "just to help keep an eye on Gloria. She aged so much this last year."

"I'm sure," she murmured. "And that's got to be difficult too."

"Oh, it's been deadly," she said. "It's one thing to know that somebody is in their twilight years, but another thing entirely to see it for yourself."

Nothing but sincerity seemed to be in the woman's tone. Doreen stopped in the hallway and looked at the photos here. "Oh my," she said, "look at this." Every photo was of Gloria with Lionel. "It was always just the two of them, wasn't it?"

The niece looked at her, then nodded. "I felt left out sometimes. And now I'm the only one left." She shrugged.

"You don't have any children?"

She shook her head. "No, I couldn't have any."

"Oh, I'm so sorry," she gasped.

The woman smiled a tight smile. "It was a sore point for a long time. But, when you get older, you have to make peace with those things. Otherwise you can't move on."

Doreen observed the sad note in her voice. She nodded. "It must have been hard not to have your own family and to watch everybody around you pass on."

Elle laughed. "It was, indeed. Though at the same time," she said, "it was an odd balancing of things both good and bad. When my own mother passed away—many years ago now—and my father as well, I was very grateful to have anybody to take me in at all."

Doreen glanced back at the photos on the wall, just of Gloria and her son. "They must have been very close."

"Too close," the niece said abruptly.

When Doreen looked at her inquiringly, Elle shook her head. "Just old feelings," she explained. "Come on. The orchid is this way."

With the animals at her side, Doreen followed the woman through the house, looking at the massive kitchen and realizing just how much value was in this property. Being the only family member left, Doreen wondered if it went to Elle or to charity, since Gloria was well-known for her philanthropic works. "I know it's an indelicate question," she said, "but will you inherit all this?"

Elle looked at her in surprise. "I was always told I would," she said, "but I haven't seen the paperwork."

"So you're not the executor of the estate?"

"No, that's her lawyer." Elle pensively looked around. "I would love to stay right here, but maybe it would be better to move on."

"Sometimes that's quite true," Doreen said agreeably, as

Thaddeus hopped onto the kitchen counter, then squawked to be let up on her shoulder. She stretched out her arm and waited until he was happily ensconced near her neck. He loved tucking into her hair. She looked around the incredible kitchen, adding, "On the other hand, it would be nice if you had the option to choose."

"Exactly," she said, "but it'll be whatever it is, so I won't waste energy worrying about it."

"That's good," Doreen murmured. "It is a truly beautiful place, and I think Gloria has had some blessings in her life to have had those years with her husband and her son."

"She has, indeed, although I know that she suffered through those losses, those rough times, but she certainly surmounted them all."

"Right, and, of course, that is what people will remember." Elle nodded, as they headed toward the huge greenhouse space. As they walked in, Goliath sprawled on the path, making himself at home. Doreen asked, "Do you have a green thumb at all?"

"No," she said, "much to my aunt's horror." And she laughed and laughed. "It was always quite a running joke between us."

"That must be hard too," Doreen noted.

"No, not really," she said. "I was happy being me."

"Good." Doreen nodded. "Learning to be you and to do you is a trick in itself."

"You sound like you know that from personal experience."

"Oh, yes," she said, "unhappily married for way too long."

Elle agreed. "I tried marriage too," she said, "but you know what? It seemed like our whole family was struck by bad luck."

"Oh dear, don't tell me that he died too."

She gave a one-arm shrug. "He died in a machinery accident in the first year of our marriage, and I never did remarry. I found out that I was just as happy to be alone at that point in time, though I know most people wouldn't understand."

"I understand," Doreen said impulsively. "I'm quite enjoying being alone right now." She motioned at the animals, with a laugh. "Except I do have them."

"Good for you," she said. "Everybody has an opinion of what you should do when you're single, and all opinions seem to revolve around having a partner."

"Exactly, and what if you don't want a partner?" Doreen said enthusiastically. "What if you're just happy enjoying life by yourself and not listening to anybody else or making decisions based on anybody else? It's just nice to be on your own."

"Exactly," Elle said.

The two women chuckled together, enjoying the camaraderie of their common experiences.

Chapter 24

As Doreen walked around the greenhouse, she sighed. "This is such a perfect property for this."

"I guess," Elle said. "I never really thought about it. I know the house didn't originally come with this greenhouse, so they did a ton of work over the years. Some of it was hard, backbreaking work, when she couldn't afford to bring in machinery."

"I can imagine, but, from what I've heard, she didn't know any other way to operate, did she?" She watched Mugs sniff the sides of the lower beds. She could only hope he didn't lift a leg in here. She looked around worriedly, as this was not a good place for that. She would have to watch him closely.

"Nope, not at all," Elle said, "and, of course, with her son always there to help, it made the burden a whole lot easier."

"Good for her. I'm so happy she had Lionel then because that solitary life could have been very hard for her otherwise." Doreen had said it without really thinking of Elle, then realized the implication was there that this niece wasn't helping Gloria, instead making Gloria's life harder.

"I'm sorry," she said. "I didn't mean that as a criticism of you."

"Oh, I've heard it all," she said. "You're not my age yet, but it won't take long before everybody has an opinion about what you should do. Then, all of a sudden, they give up and realize that it doesn't matter what they say because you'll *do you* anyway."

"So very true," she said. "I do get a lot of nudges in that direction, but, so far, nobody has been completely point-blank about it. But I'm still not quite divorced yet, so, in my case, there's lots of time for them to get in and to dig deep."

"They'll get around to bugging you about it all soon enough."

"Gosh, I hope not," she replied. "Like I said, I'm enjoying being single."

"Good. So what do you think about this orchid?"

"I think it's gorgeous," she said. "I just can't help but wonder if it's part of the reason why your cousin was killed."

"I don't know," she said. "It's hard to imagine that. But then I'm not into gardening, much less orchids."

"And you were down there in Vancouver with him," she said. "That must have been horrific."

"It was at the time," she said, "but, like everything else, you eventually become used to it. I forget what the correct term is for something like that. But you can't handle the thoughts, can't wrangle the thoughts, so you just block it out and keep on going. You put one foot in front of the other because you don't know what else to do."

"I'm not sure there's anything else anybody can do," Doreen said, with a smile, checking on Mugs again, but he just looked at her, with that mischievous grin.

"That seems like the best answer overall probably. Anyway, that's not exactly a conversation I'd like to remember."

"No, of course not. I'm so sorry." Doreen shrugged.

"All the conversations tend to veer one way or the other. It's either all about the glory of Gloria's life or about the horrors of it."

"Right," Doreen agreed. "I never thought of that, but I guess it tends to go positive or negative, doesn't it?"

"Always, and there's no real way to direct the conversation away from it. Everybody is fascinated with murder for some reason."

"I think they're fascinated with the mystery of it," she murmured, "not so much with the actual murder part."

"Maybe, but, for me, there's no fascination in any of it. And it's my family, so it just brings back so much pain."

"Of course it does." Doreen gently squeezed the other woman's arm. "And you have inherited a gorgeous orchid." She studied Elle's smile. "I wonder which came first though. This one or Stranden's?"

"Stranden's probably," she said. "That was definitely part of the problems between them."

"Do you really think that this was Stranden's original orchid?"

"Yeah. Lionel was nothing but a liar and a cheat."

"Ouch," she said. "In that case no wonder Stranden's so angry."

"He's angry because he lost his love. I think he probably gave her this, whether it was an anonymous gift or he left it in wait for her. The next thing he knew, Lionel had presented it as his own, saying he would develop it into the perfect orchid and grow a whole orchard full of them and make tons of money."

"Ah, so was he full of moneymaking schemes?"

She rolled her eyes. "Was he ever. He spent so much money just on his day-to-day living that it was impossible to keep track of. It's the only thing he and Gloria ever fought about. And I wasn't even around here all the time when they did fight about it, but I certainly noted the atmosphere here as it changed tremendously. If Gloria had spent a long time trying to get enough money to live, it must have been hard for her to watch somebody else squander it."

"Hard, indeed," she murmured.

"You have no idea." She laughed again.

"Did he spend a lot of money on the orchids?"

"He spent way too much money on the orchids," she said, smiling. "This orchid and a million others. He was constantly buying something new, so that he could have the very best."

"And Gloria never denied him, did she?"

"No, she loved him dearly."

"Well, there's love, and then there's love," she murmured.

"Exactly, it's funny how most people didn't see that, but you saw it immediately."

Doreen wasn't exactly sure what she noticed, but certainly something was going on. "I guess I just worry that it wasn't a healthy love."

"Nope, it certainly wasn't," Elle said cheerfully, "and again you couldn't talk to Gloria about it. You couldn't say anything against Lionel to her. He would always be the best thing in her life."

"And yet she wouldn't let him have a partner."

"Honestly, I don't think he wanted one. I think he liked the way things were. Something was very odd about him."

She nodded. "Let's hope that everybody's memories are

kind to her."

"Yeah, and I don't quite understand that either." Elle shook her head. "You can go two ways. You can completely forget about who they truly were and make them to be something that they weren't, so that everybody is happy, or you can finally come out with the truth, as to what they were really like."

"And that's what you would like to have happen, I presume?"

"I don't know. It sounds mean, doesn't it? But honestly, after a lifetime of keeping it all hidden inside, you wonder."

"Anything you'd care to share?" She motioned for Mugs to come to her side. He did so immediately and sprawled on the floor at her feet.

Elle laughed and shook her head. "Oh no," she said, "I'm so not ready for that."

"Okay," she said, "as long as it doesn't have anything to do with murder, then you're probably totally fine."

"Probably?" she asked, her head tilted. "Do you really think that I could change the outcome of any murder in my family?"

"Oh, absolutely," she said, "because I think you already know in your heart of hearts what happened."

"Ah." Elle looked at Doreen with a narrow gaze. "You're dangerous."

"No," she said, "I'm not dangerous at all. I'm just somebody who understands people."

"Well, that can make you very dangerous." Looking around, Elle added, "I'd really hate to lose all of this."

"No reason why you should. I'm sure Gloria is taking care of you."

"I don't know about that," she said. "As much as I'd

hate to lose it, I'm back to thinking it still would be a good thing if I did."

"Yeah, some of these life lessons can be very hard, but that doesn't mean that the outcome isn't what we should have had in the first place."

"Exactly, but getting through those life lessons is often painful."

Doreen chuckled. "I'm going through a few of those myself."

Elle nodded. "So, what do you think I could possibly know that would make a difference in any of these murders?"

"Well," she said, "how long was it from the time you called Gloria, before she showed up at the parking lot, where your cousin was killed?"

She looked at Doreen in amazement. "I don't know," she said. "Maybe an hour."

"And where was she coming from?"

"She couldn't have been very far away, if she arrived in about an hour," she said. "She told me that she'd gotten worried and came down after him but pulled off on the side of the road for a nap."

"And did you believe her?"

Elle nodded slowly, staring at Doreen in surprise. "You don't really think that Aunt Gloria had something to do with it, do you?"

"What did the police say about that?"

She looked at her, nonplussed. "I don't know," she said. "I don't think I ever heard any thoughts on that."

"Interesting," Doreen murmured, "because, if you think about it, all kinds of motives could be involved in something like this, but I highly suspect that it was very personal."

"He was stabbed about thirty times," Elle said. "Several

were around the face and the neck."

"*Very* personal." Doreen nodded. Thaddeus muttered ominously in her hair.

"Oh, I don't know. I don't see why or what her motive would be."

"Maybe he was planning on moving in with somebody and finally leaving her," Doreen murmured. "Maybe he found out something about Stranden, and he was determined to not let Gloria go off and have a happy life. I don't know either."

"See? That's the trouble. We can talk until we're blue in the face, but we'll never know."

"Not necessarily," she said. "The vehicle could be still in the impound lot here or in Vancouver."

"So what? It'll have her DNA anyway because she drove it a lot. It'll have the normal things that every vehicle has. And, yes, it's got Lionel's blood from his death. But big deal. They never did find any other DNA, as far as I know."

And that just accented what Doreen was considering. "And I guess that's partly why I'm wondering," she said, "because, when you think about it, when there is nothing else, what remains is the truth."

Elle stared at Doreen, walked over a few steps, and half sagged into a nearby chair, sitting beside one of the garden beds. "That would be a lousy thought," she murmured, "and a definitely lousy idea, leaving me with something like that to think about."

"But you've already thought about it, I'm sure," Doreen said.

"No," she said honestly, "I hadn't. You have to understand what their relationship was like. It was almost a love-hate thing."

"Of course, plus a dependency between them," Doreen said.

"Yes, but I think the dependency was because they cared too much," Elle replied.

"That would make sense too," Doreen murmured. "When you think about it, it's a hard thing to care, and, if you care too much, you don't want to lose somebody. But, at the same time, you know that it's a bad deal to care to that point, so you need to lose the relationship. Like what you were saying about losing this place."

"And that sounds lousy too."

Doreen shook her head, disturbing Thaddeus's cozy slump against her neck. "I think you're wrong." When she didn't get a response from Elle, Doreen added, "If you think about it and if anything pops into your mind, let me know."

"Okay," she said.

Doreen took one last look at the orchid, and then, as she went to leave, Goliath raced forward, as if he couldn't get out fast enough. Doreen turned back to Elle. "I understand that most orchids are named. What's the name of this one?"

She smiled. "Gloria named it My Deepest Love, which makes sense."

"Ah, now that's lovely," Doreen said, "especially if it is named after Stranden."

Elle shook her head. "It was always because of her son."

"Well, okay then. I guess that's lovely too." And, with that, she turned and walked out, tugging Mugs with her. He raced out to join Goliath on the grass.

Elle followed her to the front door. "There wasn't anything inappropriate about their relationship, if that's what you're thinking." She sounded almost defiant about it.

"I wasn't thinking that at all," Doreen replied, looking at

her. "Honestly, I just think the interdependency of the relationship was probably pretty rough on everybody."

Relief filled Elle's expression, as she studied Doreen. Then Elle smiled and nodded. "I just wouldn't want any of those kinds of rumors to go around."

"I have better things to do than spread rumors," she said. "Besides, you know that, once the police release their evidence, I'm sure things will get settled."

"Evidence?" Fear seeped through her voice.

"Oh, I don't mean that she's been murdered or anything, but I know that an autopsy was done."

"I tried to stop it," she said. "I couldn't understand why on earth they would want to have an autopsy, but they said that some concerns had been raised. And I didn't know what to do, so I just let them do it."

"It's probably for the best," Doreen said comfortably. "When you think about it, the police are a force unto themselves. So it's often much better if you just let them do what they need to do."

"Maybe," she said, "but it felt like a betrayal to me."

"I'm sorry," Doreen said. "I don't think they would have liked that either. I know Mack was a good friend of Gloria's. I'm sure he would have done everything he could have to avoid unnecessary pain. But he also would want to get to the truth."

"You really trust him, don't you?"

She turned and looked at her. "Mack? Oh, I definitely do."

Elle nodded. "I think what started to break down Gloria's relationship with Lionel was the lack of trust."

"In what way?"

"He started lying," she said, "and my aunt could never

pin him down. I know they had several big fights about it. He was lying about money, lying about the women, just lying about everything, and it was driving her nuts."

"Ouch," Doreen said. "You know what? I can understand why that would get her fired up."

"Me too, but I still don't think that she would have killed him."

"Maybe not," she said, "but, after his death, she didn't have anything to do with Stranden anymore, did she?"

"No, and I was pretty sure that was because she suspected him, so she couldn't ever be with him. But with what you're saying—" Then Elle stopped, shook her head. "No. I refuse to believe that my aunt killed him."

"No, it doesn't mean that she did it. It would be nice to know for sure, but, if we don't have the luxury of getting the truth, we may never know."

"What would you need for truth?" she asked.

"I still come back to the fact that Gloria was down there in Vancouver, when she wasn't supposed to be."

"And I explained that," she said patiently. "She had a terrible feeling."

"Yes, and did she ever say anything about it?"

"Only that it was the worst day of her life. But she was always very sorry that she never got there in time."

"She said that?"

"Yes, she did."

Doreen frowned. "Well then, maybe it's something completely innocent then."

"You could always ask Stranden," Elle said, "not that he'll tell you. But he's the only other person who would know. She contacted him almost right away, and they talked about it for a long time."

"Ah," Doreen said, "and that could be my next step then—if you really think it'll do any good."

"I don't know why he would talk to you though," Elle said.

"Because I think he misses Gloria terribly."

"Sure, but for how long? She's gone, and he's so old. I don't think he'll care either."

"Maybe not." Doreen smiled. "Thank you. I will go talk to him."

Elle shrugged. "Let me know what you find out, will you?"

"Of course I will," she said, and, with a wave, she headed out with the animals, happy to see Mugs taking care of business in the grass.

By the time she got into her vehicle and headed toward home, she decided to do a bypass and turned toward Stranden's. As she pulled into his driveway, he came out and glared at her. She hopped out of her car and smiled. "Hey," she said. "I'm just checking to see how you're doing."

"No, you're not," he said crossly. "You're checking for information because you're a nosy busybody."

Stunned at his very correct assumption, Doreen winced. "Wow, I must have come across really badly to you."

"I know people like you," he said. "You're just out to make trouble."

"What is trouble to you?" she asked. "Is finding the truth trouble?"

"Oh, don't go playing games," he said. "That's what everybody always does."

"Is that what Gloria did?"

He nodded. "Oh, she did, indeed. That was the thing she loved the most, games."

"With you?"

"With her son. That's what the two of them did all the time. It was just enough to drive you crazy."

"I have a question for you," she said, "and I would like the answer."

"Doesn't mean I'll give it to you," he said, "particularly if it involves Gloria. I don't want to see her name besmirched."

"No, but what about getting justice for your orchid?"

"That little bastard is already dead," he said calmly.

"And everybody thinks you did it."

He shrugged. "They can think it all they want. The police never came and never checked. The police don't give a crap."

"I think they do care, but they didn't have any proof, so they couldn't do anything about it."

"I didn't do it, so there is no proof of that," he said in a testy voice, "and, if that's all you're here for, you can leave anytime."

"Well," she said, "I believe you'll protect her, right?"

"Of course," he said. "Why wouldn't I?" And his eyes dared her to say it.

"Because I think you know the truth of what happened to Lionel, and I don't think you killed him."

He took a step back. "You're barking up the wrong tree. Some things are meant to be left alone."

"No," she said, "the truth still needs to come out."

"No, it doesn't," he yelled at her. "No way any of this needs to happen. She's dead, and no good will come of it."

"I'm assuming that's because you know that she's the one who killed her son."

He stared at her, the color draining from his face. "I

don't know any such thing," he said, his voice chilly, "and now you need to leave."

She nodded slowly. "And I get that," she said. "You protected her secret all these years—because you loved her."

Tears came to his eyes, as he shifted his gaze to somewhere behind her. "I don't know what trouble you've caused," he said, "but absolutely no good will come of it."

"No, of course not," she said, "but what about the woman left behind?"

He looked at her. "Her niece?"

"Yes, the woman who's never had a home of her own, the woman who's always been on the outside, the one who's never really had a family, except what others doled out to her."

He frowned at that. "She's a nice lady," he said, "and she was really good to Gloria."

"True, so don't you think she deserves some truth?"

He snorted. "You know what? The trouble with truth is that it doesn't always end up being what you expect it to be."

"So, does that mean you don't know what happened?"

"Oh, I know what happened," he said, "but it'll go to the grave with me."

And, with that, he turned, stormed back into his house, and slammed the door.

Chapter 25

DOREEN SAT IN her car outside Stranden's place, the animals restless beside her. Finally she pulled out her phone and called Mack.

"What?" he asked, his voice distracted.

"I just wonder what happened to the son's vehicle," she said. "I was talking to Stranden, and he definitely knows what happened back then, but he's not talking. Out of his love for Gloria."

"Right, and it's been long enough that Lionel's truck would have been released to the family a long time ago," he said, "and, of course, in Stranden's mind, he'll think it doesn't matter anymore after all these years."

"Of course not," she said, "but somehow it does seem to matter."

"Why is that?" he asked.

"Don't you like closing cold cases?"

"Sure," he said, "but not a whole lot of family left in that case."

"But the niece is still here," she said gently.

He sighed. "No, you're right. Even if it is a cold case, and everybody is gone, we still need to know the answers. I'll make a call." He hung up.

She quickly started her engine and slowly backed out of the driveway. As she got to the far side of Stranden's fence, she noted big garages off to the left. The property was huge, and she hadn't seen these buildings for the trees before, but the driveway split, one side going here, the other to the main house. On impulse, she parked up at the edge, and, moving the animals out with her, she walked down to the garages.

Now she was technically trespassing, since Stranden hadn't given her permission to be here, but somehow her instincts took her in that direction. And, if she needed anything else to confirm how interesting this was, Mugs himself was pulling on his leash, dragging her closer and closer to the garages. Thaddeus was on her shoulder, but Goliath was free to walk and run along as he pleased.

When she got there, she stopped and took a look. The buildings were old, but a good newish lock was on one of the doors, so it was safe from any unwanted visitors, like Doreen. Yet nothing appeared to be suspicious about any of it. Except … didn't Mack mention all the vehicles that Stranden had? What if Lionel's truck was here? He could be safekeeping it, all to protect Gloria. Maybe behind the door with the newish lock? But then what did she know and what could she prove?

Doreen shook her head. Apparently this case was a little bit convoluted. The fact was, Lionel's death wasn't even local, and that really bothered her. How was she supposed to talk to anybody if nobody was around there to talk to? Mack had the arresting officer on his radar, Doreen knew Mack would talk to him. It just didn't seem like anybody else was left on this case to get answers from because everybody could be dead and gone now, some twenty-five years later.

She really would like to go back to Gloria's house and take another look, a closer look, at those photos on the walls in the living room of Gloria's house. Doreen had only a long-distance glance at them, and she didn't understand the full relationship between Gloria and Lionel but knew something was going on. Maybe they each knew a dirty little secret about the other? Doreen knew that would be hard to decipher now. Sometimes a shared action joined two people together, like when people are in a drowning ship or in a burning house—or when committing a crime. Unfortunately, she might never find the truth.

Surely the relationship between Gloria and Lionel appeared odd to others as well. It must have been noticeable to others, and surely there would have been talk about it. Yet Gloria maintained a good reputation in town. Doreen had really enjoyed the little bit of time she had shared with Gloria. But that didn't mean anything other than the fact that the woman herself was quite nice.

Lionel had been gone twenty-five years now, and who knows what that might have changed in Gloria's world. It was a sad thing to even think about. But Doreen was still dying for answers and had to wonder if she was just looking because of curiosity, in which case, what right did she have to dig into all this? Or was there somebody who needed answers who could benefit from the truth? Doreen frowned, as she wondered if she had crossed some line here. She didn't want to think about it in that way. However, it was something she needed to consider.

Mugs yanked on his leash, bringing Doreen back to Lionel's truck.

As it was, she couldn't get into the garage she had found on Stranden's property but saw a window off to the side. She made her way through the bushes and the overgrowth, of which there was a lot. She moaned as she stepped into a pile of sharp-thorned bushes, just sticking out, ready to attack anybody. Mugs and Goliath were wise enough to avoid it. "If I ever needed a defense system, this would be a good one," she murmured.

She looked in through the window and could see a truck inside. As a matter of fact, there were four of them. A couple older ones, a couple newer ones. She again wondered if any of these were Lionel's. She wished she knew more about the make and model and the color of his truck. She needed that cold case folder from Mack. Shaking her head, she just wanted to go confirm how far Stranden would go to protect his beloved Gloria.

Except she more or less already knew.

Plus, people who had excess money always seemed to have more vehicles than they could possibly drive. Like her ex. With that thought, Doreen shook her head, stepped away, and winced when her foot landed on something that crackled and snapped loudly.

Mugs barked at her several times. She tried to shush him, but he wasn't having it. Realizing she and her animals should race back to her vehicle and get away before they were discovered by Stranden, she grabbed Mugs's leash and urged him to run. But, of course, just because she wanted to run didn't mean that Mugs or Goliath had any intention of running. She called him again.

However, Goliath just sauntered along slowly. "Come on, Goliath. Come on."

"What are you doing back here?" Stranden's tone was hard and unfriendly.

She turned to look at him. She threw up her hands, improvising quickly. "I'm sorry, but my cat got out and got off of his leash." She held it up. "I've been trying to get him back again."

He looked from her to the cat and back, frowning, as if figuring out whether she was telling the truth or not. "Why would you even have a cat on a leash?" he asked. "Of course the cat will not stay in it."

"I was trying," she said. "He's been really good, but he bolted at some noise or something over here, and I came after him. I'm so sorry. I'm really not trying to intrude."

He snorted at that. "Your kind always intrudes."

She winced. "Hey, I know I'm not welcome here," she said, "so if you can give me a hand ..."

"Or you could just leave them and the owls or the ospreys will grab them."

"Oh my." She looked at him in horror. "I thought you loved animals?"

"I do," he said, "just not so much the two-legged ones that come with them." And, with that, he glared at her. "Hurry up and get the cat."

She raced to Goliath's side, trembling slightly inside, worried that she'd misjudged the man and that he was more dangerous than she thought. As she tried to snag Goliath, the big cat took off again. Swearing under her breath, and, with Stranden still watching, she followed Goliath deeper and deeper into the brush, until finally Stranden called out, "Don't go in there."

She was at another entrance to another garage, it seemed. She grabbed Goliath, who even now, at the sound of the man's voice, had stopped, and she carried him gently back to where Stranden stood, still tugging on Mug's lead. "Is that building nothing but a bunch of garages?" she asked.

He glared at her and shrugged. "Obviously," he said. "Even you can't be that stupid."

She stiffened at that. "I'm hardly stupid."

"If you keep coming around here," he said, "anybody would say you're stupid."

"You don't scare me," she lied. She tossed her hair back. "Just because you've had a tough life—and you're mean and cranky because life didn't work out the way you wanted it to—doesn't mean you're a killer."

He looked at her in shock, his eyes widening. "Wow," he said, "most of this town would disagree with you."

"Oh, mostly this town is full of new people, young ones who don't even remember most of what happened way back when," she said.

He shook his head and gave her a harsh grin. "You never wondered where I was for all those years, huh?"

"What years?"

He snorted, shook his head. "Whatever. Just get going."

"I don't know what you mean."

"I disappeared for a while," he said. "It was better for me."

"How long ago?"

"A long time ago." His tone turned heavy and almost disgusted. "You're just pulling on and irritating the scabs," he said. "Stop it. Just let it go."

"I can't let it go," she said. "Injustices have occurred."

"So what?" he snapped. "That's life."

She stared at him. "I can't believe that you don't care about her."

"Of course I care about her," he yelled. "Why do you think I don't want to bring any of this up?" And, with that, he stopped, and, as if having said too much, he snapped his lips together, then pointed at her car. "Just go."

She nodded. "I will," she said, "but there's got to be a reason why you're keeping your silence."

"Just like you said. Because I love her. There is no other real reason."

"Unless she has something on you too." Her gaze narrowed.

At that, he stiffened and turned on her.

She immediately backed up. "Oh," she said, "she does. You two were entwined as much as she was with her son."

He shook his head at that. "That boy needed a bullet."

"She gave it to him," she said, "at least metaphorically."

"Not fast enough," he said. "He was poisonous, and he made her life miserable."

"And why was that? She loved him."

"Yeah, and he played her for it constantly. There was nothing she could do to make him happy, and she turned herself inside out trying to make it happen."

"I'm sorry," she said. "I'm sure she's not the only mother to have made that mistake."

"Probably not," he said, "but she deserved so much better. And he wouldn't let her have it."

"Is that why she killed him?"

He shrugged. "Probably doesn't matter anyway, not now," he said, "but more or less. They had a ripping fight. And I mean a *ripping* fight. She stabbed him, probably in self-defense to be honest, and then she called me."

"Oh my God." Doreen stared at him. "You helped her deal with the body."

"Somebody had to. Besides, like you said, she knew I would do anything for her." He leaned against a tree, crossed his arms over his chest, and looked so very old.

"I can understand that, just by the look on your face," she said, but something else was there too.

"That's the thing," he said. "You don't understand. I'd tell you, but you'd turn around and tell somebody else, and then they'd be coming around, asking questions, and of course I'd lie and say I didn't know anything about it. But, because it's you, people here are staring at me all over again."

"I did figure out that Gloria had killed her own son. Somewhere in Kelowna. Probably at or near their home. Not in Vancouver. But I hadn't considered that you had helped her deal with it—though, if the death happened here, I should have." She nodded. "That makes more sense than anything. You had her drive Lionel's truck down there, didn't you?"

He nodded. "And I came behind her and picked her up."

"Wow," she said, "if it was self-defense though, Gloria would have gotten away with it, and the police wouldn't have charged her."

"It was self-defense all right because that bastard beat on her whenever he didn't get what he wanted. Have you ever heard of elder abuse?"

"Of course I have." Her heart sank, as she thought about all the horrid things she'd heard about Lionel. "I'm sorry Gloria didn't have somebody she could call when it first happened."

"Who would she call? That friend of yours? Not likely. Mack was just a kid, back when Lionel died. Twenty-five years ago Gloria didn't really know Mack or his family or trust him any more than she trusted anybody else. Lionel had made it very clear that he would make her pay, if anything happened to him."

"So she just kept paying and paying, didn't she?"

He nodded. "She wanted to hook up with me, but Lionel wouldn't have that. He came to my place and made several threats. The little bastard was just lucky I didn't kill him then." He shook his head. "And I didn't because of her. I held my temper, but, when they got into it that last time, she lost her temper, and he lost his, and the fight was on. She was pretty banged up and beaten, but, of course, the niece didn't know about that because Gloria managed to keep all the bruises hidden."

"So, hang on a minute. Gloria drove the truck to Vancouver with Lionel in the front seat? That would have been lovely, sitting in his blood. And where was Elle?"

"Even though he had stopped bleeding for the most part, his blood was all over him, so plastic tarps helped to contain the rest of his blood, until we set the stage," he said. "We made it look like he was sleeping, like Elle was, and Gloria drove them all in Lionel's truck to Vancouver. I drove behind her with the flatbed, carrying her car. We drove through the night, parked his vehicle near the coffee shop, away from street cameras, then dropped off the niece at a friend's house, where we put her to bed.

"Luckily the friend was at work and had been told to leave the door open for Elle, so we just put Elle on the couch. She spent the morning with her friend, not really remembering how she got there, and that was fine because I had called earlier, pretending to be Lionel, spoke with her friend, setting up how Lionel would meet Elle at the café on a food run. That had been the plan anyway, and her friend dropped Elle off at the coffee shop to get coffee and breakfast, expecting Lionel to pick her up. When Elle looked outside and saw Lionel's truck there already, she headed over and found him. Dead."

"Wow," Doreen said, "and the friend didn't suspect anything?"

"No, they'd done that many times before, just left the door unlocked so Elle could get in whenever the timing worked out."

"Why was the son to be in Vancouver this time?"

"Supposedly he had a flower show to attend. However, he regularly visited various women there. He had women all over the place, you know? And he beat them up too."

Doreen nodded, remembering her talk with the librarian. "I talked to somebody who had been his girlfriend, but she never mentioned he was abusive."

"No, a couple he didn't beat up too much. He didn't care for any of them, or, if he did, it wasn't for long. He was worried about long-term impacts. He wanted somebody who wouldn't cause any trouble. So not everybody got the same treatment, which is why you'll see just enough women in town here singing his praises. He was a little bastard though. And he sure as hell didn't deserve to have a mother like her."

"No." Doreen could see how this possibly worked out. "So she kills him. But where?" She looked at Stranden. He remained silent. "Not in her house. Too messy. And not in her greenhouse. No way she could garden in there all the time with that memory. Oh." She looked at Stranden. "In her garage? Or the surrounding grounds?"

He gave her a one-arm shrug.

"The garage would have a concrete floor. She could have etched it with an acidic cleaner or poured another layer of concrete on top."

Stranden didn't confirm or deny.

"So the police see all that fresh blood in Lionel's truck in

Vancouver and figure it was several hours old anyway, which it was, because that's how long it took to drive down there."

Thinking about the timing to drive from Kelowna to Vancouver—at least four and a half hours—Doreen frowned. "You guys must have really booked it."

"During summer nights the roads are wide open," he said. "Absolutely no problem. We got there in no time. I know that highway like the back of my hand, and it's pretty darn easy to get where you want to go." He looked down to see Mugs staring up at him, having inched closer to Stranden. "Get your mutt away from me."

"I will." Moving cautiously forward, she crouched down. "Mugs, come here. Please, come on, baby. Come over here."

"All that baby talk," he said, "makes me sick."

She looked up at him, questioning his professed love of animals. "Sorry."

"What will you do with the information now?"

"There's probably no proof of any of it, like you said. Just your word."

"You can bet I'll never repeat any of that," he said, with a sneer.

She nodded. "And all because you don't want to ruin her memory? Why did she have nothing to do with you afterward, if that's what happened?"

"You know what? I never really understood that. But it was as if she couldn't face me and what she'd done. So she just built up this fantasy world and walked away. I was really thinking that it would bind us together, but it didn't."

Still, an odd note remained in his voice that she didn't quite understand. "Maybe," she said, "or maybe there was something else."

He stiffened, straightened up from where he leaned

against the tree, and glared at her. "Stop digging."

"No, I'm not so sure about that," she said. "How long have you known her?"

"Since forever."

She nodded slowly. "And you said that you had disappeared for a while, a long time ago."

"I didn't like it when she got married," he said.

And then it hit her. She gasped softly. "Did Gloria know?"

"Did she know what?"

"Did she know that you were responsible for the accident that killed her husband?"

Chapter 26

STRANDEN STIFFENED AND gaped at her. "How did you figure that out?"

"You just told me," she said.

"I did not tell you." He glared at her. "No way in hell I told you that."

"You just did," she said gently. "And that explains why you were gone for a while. You didn't know if she knew or not. You didn't want her to suspect you. As a matter of fact, you didn't want her to have any inclination that you could have been involved."

"She didn't know," he said, "and it *was* an accident."

"Of course it was," she murmured, "but a convenient one, wasn't it?"

"Not likely," he said. "I've lived in fear forever."

"Well, you did kill a man."

"Sure, but I mean there should be guys who are okay to kill and those who aren't."

"How do you figure that?" she asked. "Just because you loved her and because she loved somebody else? That's hardly fair."

He said, "You still don't understand, do you?"

"I'm not sure what I'm missing."

"You know the saying about how the sins of the fathers are passed down to the kids?"

She frowned, then gasped. "Oh," she said, "so what you're saying is that Gloria's husband beat her up too, and she accepted the abuse from her son simply because it's what she was used to?"

He looked at her and nodded slowly. "You do get it."

"Maybe," she said. "So, was it an accident, or did you do it on purpose?"

He shrugged. "You know, at the time, it was an accident," he said, "but, over the years, I've had to wonder if maybe I didn't have an ulterior motive."

"Of course you did," she said gently. "You loved her."

"I did, but she sure as hell didn't love me, and, even when we had a chance to make a life together, we couldn't."

"And most of that," she said, "was because of fear on her part."

He looked at her in surprise. "What do you mean?"

"Once you killed her husband, and she killed her son, she was too afraid that she'd end up being you. She'd look in the mirror every day and see what she'd done, and she couldn't live with it."

He growled. "But we were the same. We were absolutely the same. It would have been safe for her."

She smiled gently. "That's the thing though. She didn't want to be the same as you. And she loved Lionel, as despicable as he was. So, after killing him, she couldn't face what she'd done. She knew she needed to do it to get out of the abuse she was caught up in, but still she couldn't believe it. She couldn't accept what she had done, and she was probably going through all kinds of things to justify it."

"That makes no sense," he said. "I loved her."

"But I'm not sure she ever loved you," she said gently. "You were very convenient. You were the person who helped her out, and she knew that you would, which brings me back to the fact that she probably understood that her husband's accident was less of an accident and was more intentional than you thought it would be."

"I told her that it was an accident," he said, "and I don't think I did it on purpose. Sure, subconsciously maybe I wanted it to happen, but really I just wanted him to stop beating on her and to get out of her life."

"And that's what happened, isn't it?" she said gently.

He nodded. "But I didn't do it on purpose."

"She couldn't stand the fact that, when she looked at you, she also saw what she had done. Self-loathing, regrets, guilt, or whatever," she said, "it would have been even worse for her, if she had hooked up with you."

"Yet I would have loved her every day," he said passionately.

"You did love her every day," she murmured. "You just couldn't live with her."

"She wouldn't live with me," he said, his tone turning ugly. "But I wanted her to."

Doreen sighed. "I know, but you were off living in a prison of your own making, weren't you?"

He nodded slowly. "Because she wasn't happy," he said, "and I really wanted her to be happy."

"The sign of somebody who truly loves."

He looked at her. "So you don't think I killed her?"

"No, I don't think you killed her," she murmured. "No, I don't think so. But I do think she was murdered."

He gaped at her in shock. "Tell me who then," he said

fiercely. "I'll take him out. I'm so old nobody will charge me anyway."

"They *would* charge you," she said, staring at him in fascination. "So don't be so quick to jump into that fight."

"No," he said, "I really don't give a crap at this point. I'm done anyway. I'm old. I've got cancer. I couldn't care less," he said, "but I would like to take that bit of justice to the grave with me. She was my whole life."

"I'll let you know if anything comes of it," she said, "but that's all I'll do."

He stared at her, his anger growing, then stepped toward her.

Mugs immediately growled, placing himself firmly between the two of them.

Stranden looked down at the dog, then at her. "Do you really think I won't kick him to Timbuktu?"

She shrugged. "Bigger men than you have tried." She whistled to Mugs and coolly said, "Come on. Let's go back to the car." She turned to Stranden. "I know you're angry," she said, "so just think about what I said about revenge. I'll go talk to Mack."

"About me?"

"That car accident was already investigated and closed." She gave a wave of her hand. "The murder case on Lionel is a whole different story. I don't know if you have any way to prove that you didn't kill him, and that it was Gloria, but it would be nice to close the case."

"It's just paperwork," he said. "Who cares?"

"A lot of people spent a lot of time investigating all this," she said. "And an awful lot of people loved Gloria, maybe even some loved her son," she admitted. "He might have been a jerk to a lot of people, but that didn't mean he was a jerk to everyone."

Stranden shook his head. "I shouldn't have told you."

"Like you said, maybe it's time to clear the decks. At least that way, when it's your time to go, you can go with a clear heart."

He turned and headed back to his house. "I sure hope you're wrong about Gloria."

"I'm not," she said, "but I wish I was."

And then she gathered her animals and returned to her vehicle, but, instead of driving home, she drove back to Gloria's house. She texted Mack, saying she was heading there again.

Just as she pulled into the driveway, he called. "What are you going back for?"

"I've only just arrived, pulled into the driveway, and, well, you won't like the reason," she said, then filled him in on what Stranden had told her.

He started swearing at her halfway through.

By the time he was done, she said, "I know you think I'm nothing but an interfering busybody," she said, almost teary-eyed, "but why does everybody have to be into lies and cheating?"

"Hey, calm down," he said, taking a gentle tone.

"Me?" she said. "You're the one yelling and swearing at me."

"I'm not trying to," he said. "Just go home. I'll be there in a few minutes. Please go home."

"No, I can't do that yet."

"Why not?"

"I have to talk to Elle about something," she said sadly.

"No, no, no," he said in alarm, "just go home."

"This isn't official police business," she said. "I just need to let her know how very sorry I am."

"Please just leave it be," he said. "You're too emotionally overwrought."

She snorted at that. "It has been a rough day."

"I know, and that's just the way some days are," he said. "Please just let it go."

"No, Mack," she said. "I can't do that, but, if you want to come and join me here, that's fine."

And, with that, she hung up.

Chapter 27

DOREEN WALKED UP to the front door, her animals in tow. Mugs lifted a leg on one of the rose bushes in the front, and she didn't even stop him. When she reached the front door and knocked, there was no answer. She looked around, but the vehicle was here, so Elle had to be here somewhere. Just how to find her was the question. When a bark from Mugs caught her attention, she looked down at him, now pulling on the leash. She pulled back, but he jerked hard and snapped it out of her fingers. "Whoa, whoa, whoa," she said. "Come back here, Mugs."

She chased him down, but now Goliath was way ahead of her and running after Mugs too. Thaddeus was on her shoulder and yelled out, "Giddyup, giddyup."

She almost wanted to whack him one. "Don't you say that to me," she cried out. But he was stretched out with his head forward, as if in racing mode, still calling out to her, "Giddyup, giddyup."

All she could remember were the times he had been on the back of Goliath or Mugs, calling out for the cat or the dog to go faster and faster. "We'll be having a talk about this when we get home," she muttered.

"*He-he-he-he*" was all he would say.

She laughed, and, when she came around the side of the house, the greenhouse door was wide open, and Mugs ran inside. "I'm so sorry," she cried out to Elle, who stood there, looking at Doreen in shock. "Sorry to barge in. I parked out front, and Mugs just took off on me."

Elle looked at her, looked at Mugs. "Why are you even here?"

Doreen sighed. "I wanted to pop by again," she said. "I just came from talking with Stranden, and I told you that I'd fill you in."

A look of comprehension formed on the woman's face. She nodded. "Oh." But she acted as if she were not quite sure what was going on.

Doreen stepped forward and, reaching down, snatched Mugs's trailing leash. "Come back here, Mugs," He pulled hard, dragging her down a few more feet, and there she stopped. "Oh my." She turned to look all around her. "The orchids."

"Yes, the orchids," Elle said.

Doreen studied her and saw the knife in her hands. "What were you doing?" she asked.

"What does it look like I was doing?" Elle said in disgust.

And then Doreen got it. "You were destroying the orchids, weren't you?"

"Yes," she said, "just like they destroyed my life."

She stared at her. "Because they preferred the orchids to you?"

"Wow, you just had to put that right out there in black-and-white, didn't you?" she said, a sneer on her face. "That's just what you do though, isn't it? You poke and you prod, and you squeeze people, until they let out the pus of their lives."

"Most people would say that is a good thing."

"No, they wouldn't. Nobody who has pus inside wants to let it out. The process is too painful. And it comes with circumstances most people aren't ready to deal with."

"That's probably quite true," Doreen murmured. "But that doesn't mean it's not a process worth doing. If you get some help, I'm sure you can feel better about Gloria and the relationship you had with her."

She looked at her, smiled. "No, I really won't."

"You don't want to?"

"Of course not," she said.

Surprised at her response, Doreen looked around again to see that every one of the orchids was gone. Except for the star attraction. "Oh, you saved that one," she said. "I'm so happy to see it." And, with that, Elle lifted the knife and cut it off. Doreen stared in shock as the knife went slash, slash, slash a few more times, as she watched the fury on Elle's face. "Wow," she said, "you really hated Gloria, didn't you?"

"I despised her," Elle said. "She was weak. She was mean, and she was a terrible person. Everybody only saw the one side of her. But they never saw how she treated me."

"But you were blood."

"No, not close enough. Gloria didn't like my mother, her own sister," she said. "Only Gloria's direct bloodline mattered. Lionel was supposed to procreate and to give her grandchildren, but all he ended up doing was paying for abortions. And she couldn't handle it. She so desperately wanted to be a grandmother and to have his kids to carry on the family legacy, but he just couldn't handle the responsibility, didn't want long-term relationships. That was the reason for their last fight," she said. "Everybody thinks that I'm an idiot and that I don't know what happened, but, of course, I do."

"Ah," she said, "how is it that you know what happened?"

"Because they gave me sleeping pills to knock me out, but sleeping pills never really worked well with me," she said, "and I was already aware of what they'd done, that she'd killed him. Honestly, I couldn't believe that she finally had the balls to do something, and what does she do? She kills the one thing that she loves. Or supposedly loved," she said, shaking her head.

"So you knew."

"Sure, and I also knew they would have to hide it, so I watched and waited to see what they would do. It was pretty amazing to see all the things that they struggled to hide. Even getting me into my girlfriend's house. You can bet I just laid like dead weight for that. But, of course, I knew. Of course I saw it. Yet, as far as the police were concerned, I didn't know a thing." She smiled at Doreen. "But you figured it out."

She shook her head. "I'm not exactly sure how or why," Doreen said. "The thing that I keep coming back to is the fact that I talk to people and that people have this way of saying things they don't really mean."

"Well, whatever. It's all BS anyway," she said. "It's got nothing to do with me."

"Why are you so angry?"

"For the most basic reason of all," Elle said. "You were right. She didn't leave me anything in the will."

"Where's it all going?"

"Charity. To charity." She turned to look at Doreen. Tears were in her eyes. "After everything I did and all the time I spent with her, she's just handing it off to strangers, rather than to me."

"Maybe she thought you didn't need it."

"And I don't," she said. "At least not in theory. But I'm not sure anybody ever has enough in this life, and it was just something she could have done for me."

Right beside Doreen was the same book she had seen in the living room before. Not a family Bible. A diary. "You haven't talked to the lawyer yet, have you?"

"I did. I talked to him today. He was all apologetic."

"But you already knew, didn't you?"

"Knew what?" Elle looked up at her.

"You already knew that she wasn't leaving you anything."

"Why would you say that?"

"Because she put it in her diary, didn't she?" Doreen pointed at the book, guessing, having not opened it yet.

Elle stared at the diary, and a cold calmness came over her face.

"She absolutely did, and that was really not very smart of her," Elle murmured in a hard tone.

"You know that she would have died anyway and pretty darn soon," Doreen said.

"Yep, she would have, but she could have lasted another year or longer, and she might even have won the next orchid contest."

"I still don't understand what any of that has to do with this."

"If you thought about it, it has to do with Stranden winning this year's orchid contest. I guess something between them would never be healed, and she couldn't let him win. She had to preserve Lionel's memory, and she was mad at Stranden for even trying to take that away from her."

"Right, and, of course, Stranden didn't want her to do anything to honor her son because Lionel was such a bad man."

"Exactly." Elle smiled. "See? You do understand."

"I understand that people like to take from this world," she murmured. "You know that she killed her own son, and, promoting his orchid, putting it in this competition, was her way of giving back a little bit. I think she was hoping for forgiveness from him. Presuming he was on the other side, waiting for her."

"Is that why she stopped sleeping at night?"

"I'm sure it probably was," Doreen said gently.

"He was beating her up all the time." She nodded. "He liked to do that. He never touched me, at least not after the first time, when he realized that I wouldn't be the same pushover she was. But she kept taking it and taking it. Sometimes I helped her out, and other times I'd walk away. I mean, what do you do with somebody who just keeps letting themselves get beat up?"

"I'm sure the shrinks would have a field with that," Doreen murmured. "I don't know that I understand it."

"You should. It's not like you were well taken care of. You were a puppet, weren't you? I've heard the rumors. Your rich husband got your divorce lawyer into bed with him, so he could twist everything around to go the way he wanted. You're just as much of a pawn as Gloria was."

"Interesting take on it," Doreen said coolly. "And, I guess, for some people, that may be the way they look at it."

"It's not like you're fighting back, are you? You're just letting him have everything. It's the same as physical abuse. It's that slow, insidious decline of who you are, as you let them do it." She laughed. "Just like Gloria, it took me a lifetime to accept it, after having her shove it in my face all the time, about how I wasn't *her* family and how she missed Lionel so terribly. Even to the point where she totally changed the narrative, so she believed her own stories about it. If you'd have asked her, she wouldn't have had a clue who killed him because, at this point in her life, she had twisted the story so that she only knew what she wanted to believe."

"People who are guilty often do that," Doreen murmured. "When you think about it, it's the only way they can survive."

"Why should she survive like that and be so happy? She murdered her own son and never paid for it!"

"So what did you do?" Doreen asked. "What's in it for you?"

"Nothing," Elle said. "I'll bury her, when I get her body back, and that will be the end of it. I'm finally free. The whole freaking family is gone, and maybe that's better. That's why I never had any kids, you know? This family is all so messed up."

"Maybe," she said, "but I'm not exactly sure that, uh, all of that's genetic."

"Oh, I hear you," she said. "So you're wondering if I came by the same traits because I was raised in it?"

"To some extent, you could have made something out of your life and been someone completely different. Or you could have gone by the wayside, like they had, and done exactly what you wanted to do."

"I was happy—most of my life anyway," she said. "But it wasn't that great of a way to grow up."

"What about now? Will you find peace?"

"Oh, yes," she said. "I don't get the house, and that's

okay. I also don't get all the memories that come with it. And I'll get a clean break, like you."

Doreen nodded and stepped away, with a wave of her arm. "And the orchids?"

"They were Stranden's all along," Elle said. "He deserved to win. It'll be the only thing he ever actually won in his life. My aunt could have been so much happier with him. He loved her."

"I know," she said. "He really did, didn't he?"

"Yeah, but she wouldn't ever give him the time of day."

"She couldn't. She couldn't acknowledge who they were and what they'd done."

"That's the thing about being guilty. It eats away at you," she said.

"For some people."

At that, Elle stopped and glared at her. "Just what are you implying now?"

"Just that, well, you don't seem to be bothered."

"Why should I be?" she asked casually. "I put up with all kinds of hell from that woman. And, even now, she's trying to make my life difficult."

"So you killed her, even though she only had … what? Weeks left to live—or months perhaps?"

"Oh, she would have gone on for a few more years yet to spite me. Her own mother lived to be a hundred and four. She planned to be at least that old."

"And so, you took what? The last six years away from her?"

"Why not?" Elle casually tossed her hair. "Besides, it's not like you'll ever prove it."

Unbelievable. Elle had let all this dominate and rule her life, when she had many opportunities to move on and to live her life as she wanted. She could have done that at any time, but instead she'd hung around all these years, bitter and disillusioned enough to plan an ugly revenge. But Doreen had to keep her talking. "Interesting, isn't it? Everybody likes to talk, and nobody ever likes to say they're guilty."

"Of course not," Elle said. "Why should I spend the last few years of my life in jail? I will take pleasure in watching this place get sold, probably to some big fancy millionaire, who will level it all to build some modern concrete structure. Gloria would really hate that."

"It's too bad if she would, since she's the one who set it up that way. In order for a charity to get any value out of this," Doreen said, "they'd have to sell it."

"I don't think she thought that far ahead." The sneering woman laughed. "She was all about making sure I didn't get it."

"Right up to the end, huh? Did you tell her why?"

"I told her. She was horrified but couldn't wait to tell me that she had 'seen the seeds of evil in me right from the beginning,' or some such thing." Elle laughed at that. "I told her that I knew about her son, and I already knew about Stranden and her husband's car accident. I heard the talk. Everybody thinks you don't hear anything, but you know what? Those of us who get ignored hear the most. We have no value in their life, so they ignore us. But believe me. I heard everything."

"Interesting," she said. "Stranden swears it was an accident."

"It probably was but a convenient one for him."

"I thought so too," Doreen murmured.

Elle looked at her in surprise. "You already knew, didn't

you?"

"He told me." She smiled.

"Wow, you must have really charmed him to get that out of him."

"I don't know about that," she said. "I think he was finally looking to find peace."

"Why should he find peace?" Elle asked, clearly startled. "Why should anybody?" With bitterness she looked around at the orchids. "I'm glad this stage is over with. It was such a mockery, listening to her go on and on about her son. The son she killed." She shook her head. "Such malarkey."

"Maybe," Doreen murmured, "but it is what it is."

"That's a good way to look at it too." Elle laughed. "Now, what will I do about you?" She picked up the knife again and waved it around in her hand, as if brandishing it.

"You certainly won't kill me." Doreen quietly moved strategically backward.

Chapter 28

"WHY NOT?" ELLE asked Doreen.

"You don't have any reason to, for one thing."

"Really? You're not stupid," she said. "I mean, obviously if you're gone, I don't have to worry about anybody having heard me."

"Possibly"—again Doreen smiled—"but I'm also not the biggest reason that you must be concerned about. You just want to move on, right?"

"Yep, I do. I'll bury her—and not with a lot of pomp and ceremony either. I won't even give her a decent stone or anything," she said. "She can go to an unmarked grave for all I care. She's not exactly anybody I care to memorialize."

"No, I can see that, but it may not be your choice."

"It should be my choice," she said. "I'm the last of the family."

"Yes, but a lot of people see her as a local icon."

"Well, they won't for long," she said, "because I put it all in my book."

Doreen stared at the woman, in shock.

Elle started to laugh. "Now I've surprised you, haven't I?"

"Absolutely you have," she said. "I hadn't considered that."

"You should. It's all in there. I told her what I was doing too. She started swearing and cursing at me. She was already so mad about Stranden winning the orchid show. It was pretty funny at the end of the day."

"I'm not sure *funny* is quite the right word for it," Doreen said.

"No? I thought it was hilarious. When I told her what I was doing to her memory and that everybody would know what her son was truly like, she got agitated and really, really angry. I didn't have to do much of anything, besides protect myself from her, and that was enough. She died in my arms, hating me," Elle said. "That felt pretty damn good actually, and I told her that's exactly what it was like growing up here, hating them for always being on the inside and leaving me on the outside."

"Wow." Doreen stared at her.

And, without any warning, the woman lunged, as Mugs jumped. The sharp knife flicked out, catching Doreen's face, as Mugs knocked Doreen backward to the ground at the last second. Otherwise it would have been much worse. Doreen bounded to her feet, placing one of the garden benches between them. "You really think you'll kill me now?"

"Don't you see? My book," she said, "it will garner me a bunch of money. I've already stripped the house of anything of value that was easily looted over the last few years. I've built myself a nice little stockpile. I don't really care anymore," she said. "I didn't really kill her. Of course I might have helped at the end, but I certainly didn't have anything to do with it. It was all her. And I know that, even if it went to trial," she said, "it'll be one sad case, and all of the family's dirty laundry will come out. I don't really have a problem with that either."

"Wow, so much hate," Doreen murmured.

"Yeah, a lot of it. That's what happens when you treat people like dirt all their lives. All because of so many lies and so many secrets. But that's fine," Elle said. "It's all in her diary too, which I've handed a scanned copy over to the publisher. They're having a great time with it right now."

"Ah," Doreen said. "Maybe it won't get published after all."

"Well, it should," Elle said, "unless the estate knows about it and can stop it somehow, but I don't think they can stop anything at this point."

"You're just doing it for the money, so I'm not sure how that works. But you sure have to be harboring an awful lot of hate to want to upset so many people."

"The only ones I want to upset are Gloria and that mess of a son of hers."

"But they're both dead," she said, "so what does this get you now?"

"The last laugh." With that, she laughed and laughed and laughed.

Doreen stepped farther and farther back, until she came up against something. She spun to see Stranden standing there, glaring at Elle.

"You did it?" he said to Elle.

Elle stopped laughing and sneered at him. "You're hardly one to talk. You killed her husband and helped her cover up her crime of murdering her own son, and now you're standing there, blaming me?" She shook her head. "It's a surprise I didn't do it a long time ago."

Doreen privately agreed. Elle obviously had a lot of issues.

"If you think I didn't know exactly what happened to Lionel all those years ago," she said, "you're wrong. "Everybody thought that I was with my friend, but I know that you drugged me and dropped me off there. And I let you, so I had all the more power over Gloria and you." She smiled. "How does it feel to know that your secret's not safe anymore and that I'll make sure the world knows?"

He got angrier and angrier as she spoke. "You could have at least told me," he said. "You weren't any lightweight."

She smirked. "Yeah, and, when my friend woke me up the next morning, she asked me all about the trip, and I just lied and said it was great. In truth, I did sleep." She laughed. "But it wasn't hard to work out the details, once I heard the two of you discussing it. It's not like I was a child anymore, though that is how I was treated. I was already an older woman."

"You were certainly old enough," he said. "You could have helped us."

"Why would I do that?" she asked delicately. "I could have just turned you in to the cops."

"That's the part I don't understand." Doreen stared at her. "You could have, but why didn't you?"

Elle looked at her, smiled. "Because it always made me feel superior to know what Gloria had done and to know that she would always live in fear of being found out. That was worth a lot. Besides, it gave me a huge opportunity to start squirreling away money because I figured she wouldn't look after me in the end anyway."

"Maybe she knew." Stranden studied her. "Maybe she knew what you were really like."

"*What I'm really like*?" she said. "That's a funny thing

coming out of your mouth."

"The accident was just that," he said bitterly. "An accident. And I've paid time and time again for it. Then everybody accused me of murdering her son, and that wasn't easy to live with either."

"Maybe that was your punishment for having helped her cover it up." Elle sneered. "You also could have turned her in at any time."

"No, I couldn't have," he said. "I loved her."

"God, that's pathetic," Elle murmured. "Yeah, you did, so that's your loss." She looked at Doreen. "Now what will you do?"

"I'll go home and have a shower." She calmly wiped at the cut on her chin. "This conversation is enough to make anybody feel dirty."

Stranden looked at Doreen. "I didn't have anything to do with Gloria's death."

"Nope, I heard that." Doreen rubbed her arms, wishing that Mack were here. Where was he anyway?

Elle looked at the two of them. "It doesn't matter," she said. "The funeral is coming up, and then I'm leaving town."

Stranden looked at Doreen. "Is there anything you can do?"

"About what?" she asked, feeling the strain of the last few days. Weighed down somehow, just by the enormity of humanity. "Sometimes I think all humans should be completely wiped off the face of this earth," she said quietly. "We're a sad lot."

A man's hard voice came from the other side of the room. "Not all of us," he said, "but there will always be those few."

She looked over to see Mack standing there, two cops at

his side. She grinned at them. "Hey, Arnold, Chester. Nice to see you."

Arnold glared at her. "It'd be nice to see you too, if you weren't always in trouble."

"I'm not in trouble," she said.

And, with that, Elle sent Doreen's feet flying out from under her, as Elle came down on top of Doreen, holding a knife to her throat. "Back off," she said to the police. "I'm leaving town, and you guys are not stopping me." A note of desperation was in her voice.

Mack looked at Elle steadily. "Which part is it you wanted to get away with? Killing your aunt?"

"Whatever," she said. "Gloria was a bitch."

"Apparently," he said. "We all have secrets, and you've just now shared a whole pile of them."

"She's also apparently written a book," Doreen murmured. "With all the family skeletons exposed, including how Gloria killed her son." Mack looked at her in shock. Doreen nodded gingerly, acutely aware of the sharp blade at her throat. "I found that out earlier. Stranden here helped cover it up." Stranden turned on her angrily, and Doreen shrugged. "I think it's well past the time for secrets, isn't it?" she said tiredly.

The older woman looked down at her and poked at her throat a little bit harder. "You know that everybody else was killed in this family, at least as far as I could figure," she said. "But why the hell should you get away from all this? You just go around and cause disruption everywhere. It would be much better if you were dead too."

"Thanks for that," Doreen said. "Let me remind you that I didn't cause the deaths in your family."

"No, but you're the one who brought it all out in the

open," she said. "So we could just as easily lay the blame for all of it at your feet."

"Not convincingly." Doreen slowly turned her head, trying to figure out how to handle the situation, when she caught sight of Stranden, who glared down at Elle. "Stranden, don't," Doreen said tiredly.

He looked at her and frowned. "Why the hell not? Why should she get away with what she got away with?"

"Why should Gloria have gotten away with what she got away with?" Elle snapped. "Why did you help her?"

"I loved Gloria, even though she just took and took," he said. "I realized the relationship wasn't healthy, but I couldn't do anything about it."

And, for him, that's all there was to it; his love was all-encompassing and complete. So much so that it almost restored some faith in Doreen's heart in terms of what love really meant. Almost. Because there was a negative side to it as well. Doreen looked at him. "Leave Elle alone."

"I won't do anything," he said, hands up. But his gaze was hard on the woman holding a knife to Doreen's throat.

At that, Mugs growled. "Mugs, no. You don't want to do anything right now."

"No, he sure doesn't. Any little thing will make my hand push down, and I'll cut that artery right here," Elle said, poking a little bit deeper and cutting Doreen slightly.

Doreen winced. "That's nice," she said. "You know you won't survive this if you do that."

"I don't really care," she said. "Once that book comes out, I'll be vindicated. My life will be a whole lot easier."

"Why? Because everybody else will find out the truth about Gloria?"

"Exactly," she said, "and I won't have to cover up all

those lies. People will know the truth about that horrible woman and her horrid son." She looked up at Stranden, who still glared at her.

Doreen glanced at Mack. "You got a solution for this?"

"Not an easy one," he said.

Chapter 29

DOREEN SIGHED AND then said, "Thaddeus, Doreen loves you."

Immediately, out of her hair, and still on her shoulder, Thaddeus popped up. "Thaddeus loves Doreen. Thaddeus loves Doreen."

Elle reared back in shock, which quickly turned to disgust. "You have a filthy bird on your shoulder."

"He's not dirty," Doreen snapped. "Thaddeus is very clean."

"Oh, God," Elle said. "Spare me the atrocities. That thing is just nasty."

Thaddeus glared at her. "Thaddeus loves Doreen," he said in a firm voice.

"That's nice. Hopefully nobody will care if you love her or not." And Elle pushed down the knife, obviously enjoying the moment of being in the limelight and having control. Doreen could only imagine just how sad Elle's life had been prior to this. Thaddeus walked along Doreen's shoulder. "Thaddeus loves Doreen."

"I don't give a shit. Shut up!" Elle snapped at him.

But Thaddeus wouldn't be silenced. And Goliath was

doing a sneaky creep around to the side and was about to come up on Elle's back. Then Thaddeus flapped his wings into the woman's face, forcing her to scoot away from the beak, the claws, and the wings all moving closer to Elle.

She cried out when Thaddeus landed on her head, shifting, which also lifted the pressure of the knife off Doreen's neck. Doreen grabbed Elle's knife hand, then twisted her hold, pulling Elle to the ground, plunging the blade into the boards beside her. But Elle still screamed from the bird's attacks. "Thaddeus," Doreen said, "get off her. Come on. Get off."

Doreen hopped to her feet to find Goliath on the woman's back, his claws digging in, as he climbed and hung on back there. Elle shifted and screamed, trying to get away from him. Stranden just stared in shock. Mack raced forward and secured the knife, then snatched up Thaddeus and handed him to Doreen. With that, Elle continued screaming, trying to dislodge Goliath from her back. Mack snagged Goliath by the scruff of the neck, his claws leaving long red marks.

When Goliath turned on Mack, all his claws out, Mack gave him a hard stare. "Goliath! Enough."

Goliath, almost as if he understood exactly what was happening, relaxed, and he was handed off to Doreen too. She held him against her, then sat down on a bench, with Mugs at her feet. Thaddeus, not to be outdone, left her shoulder to walk up and down the bench.

"Thaddeus loves Doreen. Thaddeus loves Doreen. Thaddeus loves Doreen." His voice got harder and louder every time he said it.

"I got it," she murmured, gently trying to stroke his feathers and to calm him down. "You do love me."

He looked up at her, batted his eyes several times, and then cuddled close. She took several deep breaths, as Mack handled the situation. Stranden sat down beside her, looking shaky, and said, "That bird really is dangerous, isn't he?"

"He is and he isn't." She smiled. "He loves everybody, unless you don't love me."

He smiled, nodded. "It sounds like you've got a protector at least," he murmured, "and that's a good thing since apparently you keep getting into trouble."

"She does. Indeed." Mack groaned, as he stood Elle on her feet, now in handcuffs.

Elle glared at him. "I didn't do anything."

"Yes, you did," Stranden yelled. "You shortened Gloria's life."

"She attacked me," she said. "Then she had a heart attack and died. What did I do? I didn't even have to touch her. She was already dying."

"Well," Mack interrupted, "it'll be up to the DA to see what he wants to do about pressing charges."

Doreen pointed to the diary. "And that," she said, "is Gloria's diary. It most likely has all the information you need to settle up the cold case on her son's death."

Mack turned to Stranden and raised an eyebrow.

Stranden nodded slowly. "She did kill him. She didn't mean to. It was self-defense. Her son was definitely an abuser. He and I had come to blows about it several times," he said sadly. "But this time she fought back. She called me in a panic, and I helped her set up the mugging scenario. We drove his body down there to Vancouver and brought Elle here along. We knocked her out with sleeping pills, put her in the vehicle, and took her with us, so she'd be part of the alibi."

"Only I was awake for most of it anyway," Elle said, "so I never let Gloria forget it. It was the only way I could get money and possessions and any sense of control over her. My revenge for making me feel like an outsider my entire life."

But now, instead of an angry woman in control, Doreen just saw a tired old lady. After looking at her for a moment, Doreen said, "I'm sorry."

Elle looked back at Doreen, gave her a half smile. "You know what? I'm not. Right now, for the first time, I finally feel free." She faced Mack. "Let's go."

He looked at Elle. "And what is it you're confessing to?"

She shrugged. "I guess I might have helped Gloria along a little. But there were extenuating circumstances," she said, "so let me talk to a lawyer, and we'll see where we go from there."

He nodded, looked over at Stranden. "And you?"

"Yes, I did help her with Lionel's body, after the fact," he said steadily. "So, if I'll be charged for that, then so be it." He held out his hands, palms up, as if in surrender. "I would do it again."

Mack turned toward Doreen, who shrugged. "Stranden, you might want to know that, according to what Elle said, that was your orchid."

He looked at the remnants around the greenhouse, then nodded. "No way it couldn't be," he said. "But Gloria would never admit it. It was one of the things she held over my head. She just never would admit it."

Sadly, with his head down, he let himself be led away by the two officers.

Mack stood in front of Doreen. "Are you okay?"

She touched the cuts on her chin and neck. "I am," she said, "just a little sore."

"To be expected." He helped her to her feet and held her close. "Could you please just go home now?" Looking carefully at her chin, he said, "I don't think you need stitches or anything, but you'll need to clean those up."

"That sounds like a great idea," she said. "Home sounds perfect."

Epilogue

A Full Week Later, … Very Early August

SEVEN DAYS LATER Doreen tried once again—slowly—to stand up on the paddleboard and again promptly wiped out. As she splashed into the water, she heard Mack's laughter ringing beside her. She stood in the shallow water and glared at him, then flipped her hair off her face. "I thought this was supposed to be fun."

"It is fun," he said gently, "Just relax you're doing great. Besides we needed to get you out and away from all that chaos."

"You've got a point there," she muttered, "but I don't know about *this* kind of chaos."

He stood beside her on his board, with Mugs comfortably slouched on the front end of it. She, on the other hand, was spending more time in the water than atop it. Even Thaddeus was on Mack's shoulder to avoid getting dunked.

"This is unbelievable," she muttered. Goliath had elected to stay on the beach. She felt bad about leaving him there, but, until she could control her board, no point in even thinking that he should come out in the water with her. He'd looked at her in horror when she'd invited him and had promptly stalked off to the side, where he'd sprawled in the sand and had remained, tail twitching the whole time.

"Try again," Mack said. "Now remember. It's all about balance. You need to relax."

"Relax?" she murmured. "I'll relax you."

He grinned. "Keep up that fighting spirit. It's good to see."

She brushed her hair off her forehead and slowly clambered onto the paddleboard. The water was warm; the sky was blue. The sun was shining, and it was a gorgeous day. She managed to stand steady on the board and, with a triumphant turn, she spun to look at Mack. "I did it," she crowed. And immediately wiped out again.

When she came back up, sputtering this time, she just stood in the shallow water, her arms resting on the board. "I think it's coffee time."

He grinned. "In your world it's always coffee time."

"Always.

"That's fine," he said, "but you have to get back up on the board, so we can paddle you to the shore."

She turned to stare at the beach, her gaze easily picking up Goliath. He hadn't moved. "Ugh, you know that'll take an hour. So maybe only half that but still…"

"Don't be discouraged. Next time you'll do that much better. I promise," he said. "You will."

"I didn't realize I was so uncoordinated," she muttered.

"I don't even know that it's about coordination," he said. "Most of it's balance."

"And yet you seem to be doing fine. And you said you'd never done this before."

"I hadn't."

She glared. "You know that it's really not fair that you

should take to something like this so easily, while I'm an obvious failure."

"You're hardly a failure," he said. "And, speaking of which—"

She glared at him. "There is no topic where that is a suitable intro. Nobody wants to think of being a failure."

"I was just wondering," he said gently, "if you'd heard from my brother."

"Several times, but mostly because I'm the one hassling him."

He grinned. "I like the fact that you're pushing to have that divorce taken care of."

"I don't want anything to do with my ex, soon-to-be ex," she said, "and the sooner this is done, the less stress for me."

"Oh, I agree," he said. "I just wasn't sure how you felt about it."

"You were just afraid that I would go back to him," she teased as she attempted to get on her board. When there was a long silence, she glared up at him.

He shrugged, but she could see the color mounting high in his cheekbones. She stopped and stared. "And I told you very clearly that I wouldn't."

"I know you did." His lips quirked. "But, in my job, I've heard a lot of women say otherwise."

"No, they say the same thing, but then they change their mind. I get it," she said. "I'm not really into changing my mind right now."

"Good," he said. "So can we get moving?"

"I hope so." She managed to get back up on the board, and, kneeling, she slowly paddled her way back to the shore. "I can kneel just fine." She slid off on the other side at the beach.

Mack slowly paddled toward her, standing calm and graceful on his board. She looked at him in admiration. "I should really hate you for this," she said, "but you look just great up there."

"I mean it," she said. "It's a totally natural thing for you."

"And it will become that way for you as well."

She didn't want to say that she doubted it, but, well, she doubted it.

He shook his head. "Nope, none of that," he said. "Give it time."

"Time is something I do happen to have."

"Yeah, until you get a job anyway."

She winced. "Did you really have to go there?"

He chuckled. "Hey, you've had a couple callbacks at least."

"Yeah, but all they wanted to do was ask me questions," she wailed, "about all the different cases I've been involved in."

"Of course," he said, "that does make sense."

"Yet there are more cold cases. They matter too. How come there isn't more curiosity about those?"

"They do matter, but everyone wants juicy details," he said. "Remember, you're the one who went down this pathway even though I warned you. You wanted a quiet life out of the public eye. How did that work out for you?" At least his tone was cheeky, not arrogant.

Still she glared at him. "Of course I went down this pathway," she muttered. "Besides, I'm doing a lot of good."

"You are," he said, "and, even though I wasn't terribly happy to find out about Gloria's past, I still think we're all better off having it out in open."

"What about Elle?"

"That's a different story," he said. "The lawyers are still fussing over that one."

"Can we prove that she killed Gloria?"

"No, I don't think so. They'll probably end up with some plea deal."

"Whatever works," she said. "And is it true that she's not getting anything from Gloria's estate?"

"That is true," he said. "It'll all go to charity. Which means, sadly the place will get sold."

"Yes, and what about dingbat?" she asked, his name escaping her mind for a moment.

He looked at her. "You mean, Stranden?"

"Yes," she said, "Stranden."

"That's another problem. He was cleared over the car accident many years ago. But for aiding and abetting a murder? Well, that's another thing for the DA to sort out."

"It's been a lot of years."

"It has, indeed, but again it's a murder case."

"Right," she muttered. "No statute of limitations. No closing those."

"We want to close them," he corrected her. "They just stay open until they're solved."

"Right." She pushed the paddleboard to the sand and, at that point, watched as Goliath sauntered toward her. "Do you think he'd ever get used to being on a board?"

"I won't say never." Mack hopped down lightly beside the cat, with Thaddeus still sitting nicely on his shoulder, and Mugs now happily paddling around on the shoreline. "Goliath has done more than I would have ever thought possible for a cat."

"He has been pretty amenable to many things." She pulled the paddleboard up on the sand. "Now what?"

"We have a picnic. Remember?"

"Oh yes," she said. "Did you bring a thermos of coffee?"

"I did." He looked around the beach. "There's a spot over by the gardens." Mugs raced up shaking water everywhere.

"That sounds perfect."

She lifted her inflatable paddleboard, carried it off to the side, and put it down on the grass. Then she pulled out her towel from the bags that they brought, and Mack had kept on his board spread it out, and threw herself down. As soon as she was stretched out, she gave a big happy sigh.

"You doing okay?" he asked.

"I am," she said. "It's a beautiful day. Thank you for this."

"Hey, I borrowed the equipment, so all I really put together was the picnic," he said. "We both needed to get out for a bit."

"Absolutely," she said. "And this is lovely." As she relaxed, she added, "How come I'm the only one who's wet?"

"That's because you spent more time in the water than out." And so much laughter was in his voice that she rolled over and grinned at him. "It was fun though."

"Good," he said, with a big smile. "I'm glad to hear that. We'll do it again."

"Maybe I should try your board next time."

"You think my board is the magical answer?" he teased.

"Maybe," she said. "Mine certainly didn't work worth a darn."

"I don't think the board had anything to do with it."

She glared at him but no real heat was in her gaze. She

rolled over and took a look around. "Didn't you say there was coffee?"

"There is." He pulled out the thermos from the other bag and handed it to her. She sat up and filled the cap, looking around. "I wasn't really expecting so many beaches here."

"There are a lot of them," he said. "This is Sarsons Beach. It's got a nice little lawn. The beach itself is rocky though. Several of the others are sandy. But not this one."

She studied the footwear that he had told her to get for this venture. "And I guess it's a good thing I wore these. Otherwise it might be hard to walk."

"It can be, here."

"Still, it's good," she said, "and it's a perfect day." She pulled her legs up and sat cross-legged, sipping her coffee, as she stared out around her. It was one of the few times she had put on a bathing suit all year. As it was, she felt good. She'd gained a little bit more weight, so she didn't look quite so gaunt, and, although she was skinnier than she was used to, she still felt healthy and vibrant. And that was worth a lot.

She let out a heavy sigh, and he looked at her quizzically. She shrugged. "Just, uh, …decompressing."

He nodded. "Glad to hear that. You've been through a lot lately."

She nodded. "You don't even realize how much it all adds up, until it all adds up." Then she let out another heavy sigh, and they just kept coming after that. As if she really needed this. After her coffee was gone, when she laid down and nodded off, he let her.

When she rolled over not long afterward, she lifted her head to see Mugs stretched beside her, Goliath stretch along her side and Thaddeus was at her throat muttering softly. "Wow, I think I was out there for a bit."

He smiled. "You were tired."

"Yeah, I sure was." She blinked several times then yawned. A moment later, she said, "But I'm feeling better now."

"Good," he said. "Ready for some food?"

She laughed. "Have you ever known me *not* to be ready for food?" She slowly sat up. "I'll use the washroom first though." She hopped up, walked over to the public bathroom, and, when she was done, she returned, this time walking through the gardens. "They're really pretty."

Mack watched her as she strolled looking at the flowers. "You okay? You look a little out of sorts."

She shook her head. "I'm fine." But she wasn't. Not really. She needed an income and soon. Still it was a beautiful day and she didn't want to ruin it with depressing thoughts."

"Something will break for you soon," he said confidently as if reading her mind.

"Yeah." Maybe, but she wasn't holding out hope. How about the will? Any update on that?"

"For your lawyer?"

"Yes, Robin."

"Well, you know that it's good to go. But all that lawyerly stuff has to happen."

"Meaning I don't get anything until after probate?"

"Yes," he said, "so it'll be a few months yet. Well a lot of months. I think it's nine months."

She snorted. "You'd think they could give me something."

"Have you asked the estate lawyer?"

She frowned. "No, I didn't want to let him know how

broke I really was."

He chuckled. "In that case you might want to reconsider. Maybe he can give you an advance for expenses or something. I'm not sure how that works."

"He said it was all about the probate and due process and that he would let me know as soon as he could. Also he hasn't given me any figures, as the property needs to be sold, and there are outstanding bills to be paid by her estate first."

"It's still worth checking to see if he might give you something up front to help out."

She shrugged. "I mean, if I have to keep going without," she said, "it will be fine for a few more months, I guess."

"What about Wendy?"

"I have to wait another week, I think, to get the next consignment check," she said, "They are coming, although not as big as the first one. Still, hopefully they'll be enough to keep me going for a few more months." She shook her head. "After that, well, I don't know."

"Don't worry about it," he said, "because a lot can happen in those weeks."

"I know," she said. "It's just become more of a habit to worry than not."

"And I get it," he said, "but you're doing okay, honestly?"

"I guess so." She looked at the huge bunches of yellow and purple pansies nearby and walked closer. "These are really pretty." A big pile of dead ones was in the center though. She frowned. "Except for these guys. They need some care. Is this a city park?"

"Yes, so the city gardeners look after it. When they can…"

She nodded, then walked closer to where the dead plants

were and noted powdery stuff all around the base of it. "It looks like something was dumped here, something toxic—to the plants anyway."

"Don't touch the stuff then."

She stepped back, looked down at her feet, then winced. "I better go rinse off." She headed to the water, swooshed her feet around a little to clean them off, and then she came back out. "You know, Mack. If families come here, you might want to get that cleaned up."

He looked at the flowers. "Do you think it's bad news?"

She shrugged. "It killed the pansies. I know we haven't had any rain lately, but the rest of the flowers look okay. It's just that one spot. And it's not doing much for the plants. I'd hate to see a kid or some pets get into it. It gave me a tingly feeling on my toes."

At that, he frowned, then hopped up and walked over to take a closer look. "A partially buried box is in the sand here." He took a closer look at it and frowned. "Rat poison."

She looked up at him. "Why would somebody put that here?"

He shook his head. "It doesn't matter why they put it here. They shouldn't have. This is a public site." He made a quick phone call. "We should get this cleaned up in no time."

She nodded. "So please tell me there haven't been any current deaths by poisoning." He stared at her, so she shrugged. "I mean, if you ran here, and you had a murder weapon in your hand," she said, "what better place than to toss it into a garden, where nobody will see it?"

He looked at her, then at the flower bed. "Crap."

She stared at him. "What?"

"We've been keeping it under wraps," he said, "but two

days ago we had a man walk into the hospital, saying he'd been poisoned. He was in immediately, but he didn't make it."

She stared at Mack. "Poisoned … in the pansies?"

He squeezed his eyes shut, then glared at her. "No! And again it's not a cold case, so you stay out of it."

She frowned, but inside she was like, *Poisoned in the Pansies*. Perfect. And she grinned at him. "Of course I'll stay out of your case."

He glared at her, while she just beamed. "At least until I can't."

And then she burst out laughing.

This concludes Book 15 of Lovely Lethal Gardens:
Offed in the Orchids.

Read about Poison in the Pansies:
Lovely Lethal Gardens, Book 16

Lovely Lethal Gardens: Poison in the Pansies (Book #16)

A new cozy mystery series from *USA Today* best-selling author Dale Mayer. Follow gardener and amateur sleuth Doreen Montgomery—and her amusing and mostly lovable cat, dog, and parrot—as they catch murderers and solve crimes in lovely Kelowna, British Columbia.

Riches to rags … Chaos has calmed … At least while out on the lake … Until poison is found, blowing up the peace again …

Enjoying a beautiful day on the lake, while Doreen tries her hand at paddleboarding, ends up on an odd note after finding poison in a bed of pansies. She garners a tidbit of information out of her BFF, Corporal Mack Moreau, about a man who'd recently walked into the emergency room, complaining he'd been poisoned.

Only on a threat of good behavior (surely it doesn't count if given under duress), Doreen agrees to stay out of his case. But, as it happens, the mention of poison to her beloved Nan brings up another recent death and an old woman who'd been saying someone was poisoning her for months. Only no one listened. Now she is dead.

When Doreen's case and Mack's collide, she's delighted, and so is he. NOT. But, when Nan decides to join in the sleuthing, with her pal, Richie, it's Doreen's turn to worry—and with good reason!

Find Book 16 here!

To find out more visit Dale Mayer's website.

https://smarturl.it/DMSPoison

Get Your Free Book Now!

Have you met Charmin Marvin?

If you're ready for a new world to explore, and love ill-mannered cats, I have a series that might be your next binge read. It's called Broken Protocols, and it's a series that takes you through time-travel, mysteries, romance… and a talking cat named Charmin Marvin.

Go here and tell me where to send it!

http://smarturl.it/ArsenicBofB

Author's Note

Thank you for reading Offed in the Orchids: Lovely Lethal Gardens, Book 15! If you enjoyed the book, please take a moment and leave a short review.

Dear reader,

I love to hear from readers, and you can contact me at my website: www.dalemayer.com or at my Facebook author page. To be informed of new releases and special offers, sign up for my newsletter or follow me on BookBub. And if you are interested in joining Dale Mayer's Reader Group, here is the Facebook sign up page.
https://smarturl.it/DaleMayerFBGroup

Cheers,
Dale Mayer

About the Author

Dale Mayer is a *USA Today* best-selling author, best known for her SEALs military romances, her Psychic Visions series, and her Lovely Lethal Garden cozy series. Her contemporary romances are raw and full of passion and emotion (Broken But … Mending series). Her thrillers will keep you guessing (By Death series), and her romantic comedies will keep you giggling (*It's a Dog's Life*, a stand-alone novella; and the Broken Protocols series, starring Charming Marvin, the cat).

Dale honors the stories that come to her—and some of them are crazy and break all the rules and cross multiple genres!

To go with her fiction, she also writes nonfiction in many different fields, with books available on résumé writing, companion gardening, and the US mortgage system. She has recently published her Career Essentials series. All her books are available in print and ebook format.

Connect with Dale Mayer Online

Dale's Website – www.dalemayer.com

Twitter – @DaleMayer

Facebook – facebook.com/DaleMayer.author

BookBub – bookbub.com/authors/dale-mayer

Also by Dale Mayer

Published Adult Books:

Bullard's Battle

Ryland's Reach, Book 1
Cain's Cross, Book 2
Eton's Escape, Book 3
Garret's Gambit, Book 4
Kano's Keep, Book 5
Fallon's Flaw, Book 6
Quinn's Quest, Book 7
Bullard's Beauty, Book 8
Bullard's Best, Book 9

Terkel's Team

Damon's Deal, Book 1

Kate Morgan

Simon Says… Hide, Book 1
Simon Says… Jump, Book 2
Simon Says… Ride, Book 3
Simon Says… Scream, Book 4

Hathaway House

Aaron, Book 1
Brock, Book 2
Cole, Book 3

Denton, Book 4
Elliot, Book 5
Finn, Book 6
Gregory, Book 7
Heath, Book 8
Iain, Book 9
Jaden, Book 10
Keith, Book 11
Lance, Book 12
Melissa, Book 13
Nash, Book 14
Owen, Book 15
Percy, Book 16
Hathaway House, Books 1–3
Hathaway House, Books 4–6
Hathaway House, Books 7–9

The K9 Files

Ethan, Book 1
Pierce, Book 2
Zane, Book 3
Blaze, Book 4
Lucas, Book 5
Parker, Book 6
Carter, Book 7
Weston, Book 8
Greyson, Book 9
Rowan, Book 10
Caleb, Book 11
Kurt, Book 12
Tucker, Book 13
Harley, Book 14

Kyron, Book 15
The K9 Files, Books 1–2
The K9 Files, Books 3–4
The K9 Files, Books 5–6
The K9 Files, Books 7–8
The K9 Files, Books 9–10
The K9 Files, Books 11–12

Lovely Lethal Gardens

Arsenic in the Azaleas, Book 1
Bones in the Begonias, Book 2
Corpse in the Carnations, Book 3
Daggers in the Dahlias, Book 4
Evidence in the Echinacea, Book 5
Footprints in the Ferns, Book 6
Gun in the Gardenias, Book 7
Handcuffs in the Heather, Book 8
Ice Pick in the Ivy, Book 9
Jewels in the Juniper, Book 10
Killer in the Kiwis, Book 11
Lifeless in the Lilies, Book 12
Murder in the Marigolds, Book 13
Nabbed in the Nasturtiums, Book 14
Offed in the Orchids, Book 15
Poison in the Pansies, Book 16
Lovely Lethal Gardens, Books 1–2
Lovely Lethal Gardens, Books 3–4
Lovely Lethal Gardens, Books 5–6
Lovely Lethal Gardens, Books 7–8
Lovely Lethal Gardens, Books 9–10

Psychic Vision Series

Tuesday's Child
Hide 'n Go Seek
Maddy's Floor
Garden of Sorrow
Knock Knock…
Rare Find
Eyes to the Soul
Now You See Her
Shattered
Into the Abyss
Seeds of Malice
Eye of the Falcon
Itsy-Bitsy Spider
Unmasked
Deep Beneath
From the Ashes
Stroke of Death
Ice Maiden
Snap, Crackle…
What If…
Talking Bones
Psychic Visions Books 1–3
Psychic Visions Books 4–6
Psychic Visions Books 7–9

By Death Series

Touched by Death
Haunted by Death
Chilled by Death
By Death Books 1–3

Broken Protocols – Romantic Comedy Series

Cat's Meow

Cat's Pajamas

Cat's Cradle

Cat's Claus

Broken Protocols 1-4

Broken and... Mending

Skin

Scars

Scales (of Justice)

Broken but… Mending 1-3

Glory

Genesis

Tori

Celeste

Glory Trilogy

Biker Blues

Morgan: Biker Blues, Volume 1

Cash: Biker Blues, Volume 2

SEALs of Honor

Mason: SEALs of Honor, Book 1

Hawk: SEALs of Honor, Book 2

Dane: SEALs of Honor, Book 3

Swede: SEALs of Honor, Book 4

Shadow: SEALs of Honor, Book 5

Cooper: SEALs of Honor, Book 6

Markus: SEALs of Honor, Book 7

Evan: SEALs of Honor, Book 8

Mason's Wish: SEALs of Honor, Book 9
Chase: SEALs of Honor, Book 10
Brett: SEALs of Honor, Book 11
Devlin: SEALs of Honor, Book 12
Easton: SEALs of Honor, Book 13
Ryder: SEALs of Honor, Book 14
Macklin: SEALs of Honor, Book 15
Corey: SEALs of Honor, Book 16
Warrick: SEALs of Honor, Book 17
Tanner: SEALs of Honor, Book 18
Jackson: SEALs of Honor, Book 19
Kanen: SEALs of Honor, Book 20
Nelson: SEALs of Honor, Book 21
Taylor: SEALs of Honor, Book 22
Colton: SEALs of Honor, Book 23
Troy: SEALs of Honor, Book 24
Axel: SEALs of Honor, Book 25
Baylor: SEALs of Honor, Book 26
Hudson: SEALs of Honor, Book 27
Lachlan: SEALs of Honor, Book 28
SEALs of Honor, Books 1–3
SEALs of Honor, Books 4–6
SEALs of Honor, Books 7–10
SEALs of Honor, Books 11–13
SEALs of Honor, Books 14–16
SEALs of Honor, Books 17–19
SEALs of Honor, Books 20–22
SEALs of Honor, Books 23–25

Heroes for Hire

Levi's Legend: Heroes for Hire, Book 1
Stone's Surrender: Heroes for Hire, Book 2

Merk's Mistake: Heroes for Hire, Book 3
Rhodes's Reward: Heroes for Hire, Book 4
Flynn's Firecracker: Heroes for Hire, Book 5
Logan's Light: Heroes for Hire, Book 6
Harrison's Heart: Heroes for Hire, Book 7
Saul's Sweetheart: Heroes for Hire, Book 8
Dakota's Delight: Heroes for Hire, Book 9
Tyson's Treasure: Heroes for Hire, Book 10
Jace's Jewel: Heroes for Hire, Book 11
Rory's Rose: Heroes for Hire, Book 12
Brandon's Bliss: Heroes for Hire, Book 13
Liam's Lily: Heroes for Hire, Book 14
North's Nikki: Heroes for Hire, Book 15
Anders's Angel: Heroes for Hire, Book 16
Reyes's Raina: Heroes for Hire, Book 17
Dezi's Diamond: Heroes for Hire, Book 18
Vince's Vixen: Heroes for Hire, Book 19
Ice's Icing: Heroes for Hire, Book 20
Johan's Joy: Heroes for Hire, Book 21
Galen's Gemma: Heroes for Hire, Book 22
Zack's Zest: Heroes for Hire, Book 23
Bonaparte's Belle: Heroes for Hire, Book 24
Noah's Nemesis: Heroes for Hire, Book 25
Tomas's Trials: Heroes for Hire, Book 26
Heroes for Hire, Books 1–3
Heroes for Hire, Books 4–6
Heroes for Hire, Books 7–9
Heroes for Hire, Books 10–12
Heroes for Hire, Books 13–15
Heroes for Hire, Books 16–18
Heroes for Hire, Books 19–21
Heroes for Hire, Books 22–24

SEALs of Steel

Badger: SEALs of Steel, Book 1
Erick: SEALs of Steel, Book 2
Cade: SEALs of Steel, Book 3
Talon: SEALs of Steel, Book 4
Laszlo: SEALs of Steel, Book 5
Geir: SEALs of Steel, Book 6
Jager: SEALs of Steel, Book 7
The Final Reveal: SEALs of Steel, Book 8
SEALs of Steel, Books 1–4
SEALs of Steel, Books 5–8
SEALs of Steel, Books 1–8

The Mavericks

Kerrick, Book 1
Griffin, Book 2
Jax, Book 3
Beau, Book 4
Asher, Book 5
Ryker, Book 6
Miles, Book 7
Nico, Book 8
Keane, Book 9
Lennox, Book 10
Gavin, Book 11
Shane, Book 12
Diesel, Book 13
Jerricho, Book 14
Killian, Book 15
Hatch, Book 16
The Mavericks, Books 1–2
The Mavericks, Books 3–4

The Mavericks, Books 5–6
The Mavericks, Books 7–8
The Mavericks, Books 9–10
The Mavericks, Books 11–12

Collections

Dare to Be You…
Dare to Love…
Dare to be Strong…
RomanceX3

Standalone Novellas

It's a Dog's Life
Riana's Revenge
Second Chances

Published Young Adult Books:

Family Blood Ties Series

Vampire in Denial
Vampire in Distress
Vampire in Design
Vampire in Deceit
Vampire in Defiance
Vampire in Conflict
Vampire in Chaos
Vampire in Crisis
Vampire in Control
Vampire in Charge
Family Blood Ties Set 1–3
Family Blood Ties Set 1–5
Family Blood Ties Set 4–6

Family Blood Ties Set 7–9

Sian's Solution, A Family Blood Ties Series Prequel Novelette

Design series

Dangerous Designs

Deadly Designs

Darkest Designs

Design Series Trilogy

Standalone

In Cassie's Corner

Gem Stone (a Gemma Stone Mystery)

Time Thieves

Published Non-Fiction Books:

Career Essentials

Career Essentials: The Résumé

Career Essentials: The Cover Letter

Career Essentials: The Interview

Career Essentials: 3 in 1

Printed in Great Britain
by Amazon

71019192R10183